GW01605119

GOLDHAWK

Brian Hayles

NEW ENGLISH LIBRARY/TIMES MIRROR

A New English Library Original Publication, 1979

First NEL Paperback Edition July 1979

NEL Books are published by
New English Library from
Barnard's Inn, Holborn,
London EC1N 2JR
Made and printed in Great Britain by
C. Nicholls & Company Ltd
The Philips Park Press, Manchester

450042650

The bell to the warehouse cargo door rang twice, harsh and loud. Harry ignored it and went on stirring the brew for the 3 am tea-break.

'No bloody consideration, have they?' he sniffed. It was a standard moan among night workers at Heathrow's Cargo City; from the major airlines down to the smallest independent, people called to collect air freight at all hours. But two could play at that game, brooded Harry – let them wait. He sniffed again and pushed a steaming mug and the cracked bowl of sugar across to Clem, the gaffer. Without shifting his piercing Welsh Chapel stare from the glossy centrefold nude spread wide before him, the senior nightwatchman doled three large spoonfuls of sugar into his tea without spilling a single grain.

'Shameful, boyo.' His soft voice lilted in agreement with Harry but their minds were completely at cross purposes. 'Just look at those creases . . .' He pointed to the folds in the well-thumbed page. 'Ruined, she is.'

Harry smirked as the older man tried to smooth the naked body flat. 'I'd soon have her ironed out, don't worry, mate!'

The bell rang again, a long, insistent call. Clem flicked a casual glance at Alan, the burly but baby-faced 'lad' of the team.

'Do us a favour, boyo – see who it is, will you?'

Alan pouted as he put his tea down. It was too hot to drink anyway, but he resented being dogsbody to this randy, middle-aged Taff.

'Always bloody me,' he grumbled. 'It's my magazine, remember!'

'Give the gaffer a break, kid,' said Harry. 'You know how studying form makes him go weak at the knees.'

'It's the stuff you put in his tea, I reckon,' said Alan, and walked out of the stuffy warmth of the office into the chill of the echoing warehouse.

Before he had reached the heavy metal doors to the cargo area, the bell rang again. Alan slowed his pace, deliberately taking his time. Partly from routine, but largely out of sheer 'bloodymindedness', he made a point of peering through the small glass window set awkwardly high in the door panel. The protective wire mesh and months of rain and grime made visibility almost impossible, but the familiar shape of a security guard's helmet could just be seen. With a sullen grunt, Alan started to ease the heavy door ajar – and found himself staring into the twin barrels of a sawn-off shotgun.

'Inside!'

The rasped command jerked Alan out of that first frozen moment of fear, and the masked face behind the shotgun came into focus. Dry-mouthed and numb, he felt his body obey, but not fast enough. The shotgun was slammed across his chest, thrusting him back, turning him so that his spine hit the metal door with a wincing thud. The chill of the deadly muzzle pressed beneath his jaw, and Alan was sweating.

'Shut it, Bev!'

Four, maybe five more, shadowy figures had slipped inside, and the last to enter heaved the door shut. Number Two, eyes glinting through the holes cut into his Balaclava mask, had quickly slapped a broad strip of surgical tape over Alan's mouth and spinning him round, clammy face against cool metal, tied the nightwatchman's hands behind his back.

'Move!'

The intruders fanned out warily, but they knew where they were going. Number One pushed Alan ahead of him towards the brightly lit night-duty office. Clem came out to meet them. He didn't see the masks or shotguns until too late.

'Good God Almighty –' he muttered, but he barely had time to register the fear in Alan's eyes before the butt of Number One's shotgun hit him just below the heart, hard. Pain ripped through him and he slumped against the door-frame, retching and choking. Number One was already past him and standing over Harry as the remaining nightwatchman stretched across the table for the phone. The gun barrel slammed down on to his wrist, pinning it to the table and sending a shaft of agony searing up his arm from fingertips to shoulder. The same movement had knocked over one of the mugs, and Harry had a brief, ridiculous glimpse of a naked girl drowning in a puddle of hot tea. A second later he found himself hauled back into his chair, with the barrel of the shotgun tight against his windpipe.

'Keys to the strongrooms!' demanded the face behind the nylon mask. Harry was a realist; you don't argue with a nutter holding a gun. But it wasn't going to be easy. He indicated the tangled bunch of keys chained to his belt. For the first time, he realised that none of the villains were carrying tools, only weapons. If they couldn't cut the keys free, what would they do? Number One made the answer easy.

'Bring the berk over,' he growled.

While Number Two taped and tied Clem, and Bev stood guard by the main entrance to the cargo area, Harry was half dragged, half carried, over to the strongroom doors. First one door, then the other was opened, and he watched with growing amazement as the intruders raced through the vaults, ransacking the few goods there with casual venom. An Italian leather suitcase was ripped apart, then discarded, the fine clothes and jewellery inside handled like junk on a flea-market stall. A small crate was broken open to reveal what must have been a priceless porcelain; that too was tossed aside, miraculously without damage. The second strongroom held several crates of Scotch whisky; they weren't touched.

As the search stumbled into stalemate, it dawned on Harry that whatever these villains were after – bullion, gemstones or currency – wasn't there: and suddenly, he was afraid. These blokes were rough. If they didn't get what they'd come for, somebody was liable to get hurt. They were huddled together at the far end of the strongroom, a tight, frustrated knot of anger. Harry couldn't make out what they were saying so fiercely, until Number One broke away to make straight for him, his scrunched-up face pale with rage. As he came, he called back to the others: 'It's here! It has to be!'

He reached Harry and ripped the tape from his mouth. Harry gasped.

'There's another safe, isn't there?' Harry shook his head, but Number One persisted, his throaty rasp growing even more harsh. 'A combination safe – something special –' 'No, guv'nor!' blurted Harry. He could see tension growing behind the distorted eyes, and waited for the blow to come.

'Don't you bloody lie to me!'

'I swear it – honest – there's no other safe!'

The gun swung too fast for him to dodge. It struck home on the upper cheekbone, splitting the skin and hurling Harry to the ground, stunned and helpless. In a stride, Number One loomed over the sprawled nightwatchman, the gun in his hand ready to blast, and Harry knew he was closer to death than he'd ever been. Almost instinctively, a mutter of defiance broke past his gritted teeth.

'You've been conned, mate...'

It was as if someone had turned off the mains. Anger turned to ice, and Number One stepped back, the shotgun held loosely at his side.

'Sling this berk in with the other two,' he grunted. 'We're getting out of here.'

Monday was going to be one of those days. Already Mackay was nearly thirty minutes late, thanks to Joan. He pushed the image of her lazily demanding body from his mind. Blaming her did no good, it only reminded him of his own weakness; the small croon of triumph she gave as she drew him on to her still trembled in his ears. When at last he had left the house, chaos had gathered round him like a snowball. Those lost thirty minutes meant being caught up in the grinding stop-and-start of local traffic; the daily executive assault course had begun, and Mackay hated it. The advantages of an automatic gear-change didn't completely take away the irritability and even when he finally broke free of the neat tangle of suburban groves and closes, he met trouble.

Blocked by an articulated lorry straining to overtake a lumbering dust-cart, he was forced to crawl behind and fume, while later, a nervous learner driver became the infuriating stick-to-the-limit obstacle on a stretch of single carriageway. Trapped, he felt the Monday morning blues flood towards him, and for the moment, he gave in.

Sundays were when Mackay regularly saw his kids, eight-year-old Darren and Tina. They had taken their parents' separation with a cheerfulness that even now surprised Mackay, but Joan quickly put him right. While they were still living together, the kids had found him almost always uptight with work and the strain of getting the new firm on to its feet and making profits. The quarrels that Joan's pert nagging invariably started, spread to include the twins, turning them into pawns in the bitter game their parents played. When the break came, far from shattering the family it had drawn the poison, and a strange peace took over. Now, Mackay's visits were a source of pleasure, something to look forward to, a holiday event. It was Joan who almost smugly claimed the credit for the 'reasonableness' of the arrangement. She and the children still had their home, their school, and their friends; they were financially secure, and Mackay was now a well-loved if only occasional visitor, not a grey-faced, evenings-only tyrant. But Joan had put a price on the arrangement: if she could never be completely free, then neither would Mackay.

For three months or more, they had acted out their new, quarrel-free parental role; hostess and visitor, day trips when fine, indoor games with the kids when wet or wintry. At the end of the day, a kiss for the kids, a formal handshake and goodbye. But yesterday was different. For a start, after lunch Darren and Tina had announced that they were going out to a friend's birthday party. Dad hadn't been told, but they'd see him when they got back, wouldn't they? With the kids gone, Mackay was lost, uncertain, uncomfortable with this stranger who'd once been his wife. Still was, legally.

'I ought to go,' he said.

Joan looked at him and his mouth dried; they knew each other too well not to recognise the signs. He moved away from her, to the other side of the kitchen.

'Not yet.' Her reply was casual but firm. 'You haven't said goodbye to the kids. Not properly.'

He nodded, reluctantly. 'Cup of tea, then?'

Her answer was a quiet, amused challenge. She stood a full yard away, but he could feel her body as though it were pressed tight against him. He trembled.

'Before?' she queried lightly. 'Or afterwards – the way we used to?'

He swallowed hard. So that was it. The status quo, with bed as the carrot.

'I'm not coming back,' he said. 'Forget it.'

She shook her head, and the swing of her hair touched the half-smile on her parted lips.

'Not as Joan and Mike,' she said. 'They're married, and proper . . .' She gave a little nervous laugh, and memories surged through Mackay, making his heart pound. 'Let's be strangers,' Joan said, bright-eyed.

He made no reply, no denial; his throat felt too tight to speak. She moved closer and put her hand on him, working the old magic, and he loved and hated her for it. He gasped, and she smiled against his face as his hands came to her body, but still his mind resisted. Not for long.

'I need a lover, Mike.' She moved against him, slowly, making silent promises. 'Don't you?'

He bowed his head, his mouth against her neck; he tensed in one last effort to deny his hunger for her body, but he knew it was useless.

'It'll be so good,' she whispered. Their mouths found each other, and he was lost.

He had stayed the night, and Joan had kept her promise They had pleasured each other as new-found lovers, playing Joan's fantasy that she was Mike's whore, his mistress, anyone but his wife. She had teased him that he'd never get such service from his secretary, and laughing, he had agreed.

For a few hours they forget their separate loneliness, and later slept like young animals, loose-limbed and replete. But at dawn Mackay woke suddenly, alarmed at where he found himself, trying, half-conscious, to figure what it meant. Then Joan awoke, and there was no escape. Their final coupling before Joan left the bed to make the morning tea only confirmed his growing dread: he was tied to Joan as tightly as he ever had been. She had won.

Mackay's mind snapped back into the present as the chance came to overtake three cars and the learner driver with one sharp burst of angry acceleration. He made the manoeuvre with space to spare, but the oncoming car blared its horn at him as it passed, making his anger flare again. He remembered Joan's face staring at him over the rim of her cup; the kids had left for school, surprised and pleased at having their dad with them for breakfast. He had looked into Joan's placid eyes and seen no affection there, only a need, and that need satisfied. When he stood to go, not knowing what to say, she had kissed him brightly on the cheek and moved away from his half-hearted, fondling hand.

'No strings, remember,' she said coolly. 'I like having you as my fancy man.' Then she laughed, coarsely. 'You can come again any time!' This had been their own personal bedroom joke years ago, and deliberate or not, it stung. He had left the house without another word, but Joan had stood in the open doorway, waving. She knew he'd be back.

The worst part of the journey was over. Turning on to the Southern Perimeter Road that bounded the cargo terminal buildings of Heathrow, Mackay felt close to familiar ground and his tension began to slip away. Looming on his left, the first block of massive freight sheds wore their airline emblems like jaunty car stickers – Air Lingus, Air Canada, Air France and eventually Alitalia. Mackay knew them by heart, but still glanced across, instinctively. Around one of them, he noticed an unusual cluster of police vehicles, banded fluorescent red – trouble for someone, he thought – and in that same moment, only his alert reflexes prevented a minor collision. A dirty van had pulled out into his path from the adjacent slip road without looking or signalling, and then shot away with a whine of over-revved gears and a billow of blue smoke. Mackay swore under his breath. The jinx was on, even here; it *was* going to be one of those days!

He wasn't wrong. Peeling off from the main road, he made a tight left turn on to the service road that would take him to the agents building. Almost immediately, he was forced to bring the car to a halt. Two police cars, one a panda, were so positioned as to funnel all incoming vehicles into a single-lane trickle leading to a spot check. Mackay wound down his window as his interrogator stepped forward, clipboard and pen at the ready. He was a uniformed sergeant, polite, affable and with eyes like polished granite. His first question showed the form; Mackay didn't know his face, and played it straight.

'Your vehicle, sir?'

'Yes, sergeant.' He gave the licence number and proffered his wallet. 'Insurance, driving licence.'

The sergeant studied the various pieces of paper, his face impassive. 'Purpose of visit, sir?'

'I work here. Goldhawk Airfreight. Just over there.' He indicated the farthest corner of the agents building. The sergeant didn't look at the building; he checked a list. 'Room number, Mr Mackay?'

'Fifty-nine sixty G,' Mackay informed him. The sergeant nodded, and then surprised Mackay with one more request. 'Mind if I look in the back, sir?'

'Be my guest.' He turned off the engine and got out to unlock the rear door of the estate. He glanced at the police sergeant as the interior was revealed: one large cardboard box. 'Bit strong for a spot check, isn't it?'

'Just routine, sir. What's inside the box?'

'Video cassettes – for a closed circuit TV system I've installed.' He flipped open the lid of the box and the sergeant peered in, then drew back, satisfied. As Mackay closed the door, the sergeant put away his pen. Was it over?

'Pity some of the big boys don't have the same brainwave, sir.' The sergeant politely opened the driver's door.

Mackay slipped back into the seat with a nod of appreciation and as he started the car, he glanced ahead to where the major air freight warehouses loomed above all else.

'Is that what the trouble's all about?'

'Air France got done last night,' admitted the sergeant casually, then made it clear he'd give nothing more. 'You'll see it in the midday editions, I daresay.' He touched the clipboard to his cap and stepped aside.

As the car purred slowly forward, Mackay gave the nameless interrogator a small wave, but the officer had already moved to the next vehicle.

A business card that read 'Mike Mackay, Managing Director, Goldhawk Airfreight' didn't always stop the rozzers from getting nasty, but it helped; a straight face and a bit of sensible co-operation worked even better. He parked in his usual spot outside Building 521, and stared across at Air France. Imaginary headlines sprang into his mind: Cargo City Hit Again; Bullion Ripoff At Thiefrow. As a handling agent it wasn't his concern, but he couldn't help wondering what the villains had got away with this time. Then he remembered his own worries, and with the box of video cassettes under one arm, went in the service door to Goldhawk.

Bringing bad news to Jack Fenn was no joke. You had to stand there and tell it, and all the time those pale, watery eyes were watching you, giving nothing away, not even anger. He'd listen, and you'd talk; and if you got it wrong, God help you. It wasn't Sammy Berghoff's fault that he and the lads had come back empty handed, but he was nervous. If there was one thing that Fenn hated, it was a wasted investment. A pile of time and money had gone into fitting up this particular job; sorting out the right blokes, rounding up shooters and ammo and wheels, fixing just where and when to make the hit – all planned by Fenn, and skippered by Berghoff. But it had gone wrong. Somebody was liable to get topped for screwing it up. Berghoff liked staying alive, so he made certain the story came out right.

'It was a doddle,' he insisted, 'right up to when we opened up the strongrooms. Smooth as silk, no trouble – know what I mean, Jack?'

Fenn said nothing. His stocky figure sat hunched and brooding, his neat Italian shoes perched on the edge of the massive rosewood and black leather desk that formed the no-man's-land between him and Berghoff. The high-backed executive chair contained him like a huge black leather glove, but in spite of the room's overpowering furniture and decor – all wood, chrome, leather and smoked glass – Fenn was its focal point and king.

'It was Mickey Mouse time,' he said coldly.

The jibe stung, and Berghoff straightened. His powerful body took on an aggressive swagger that asked only for a target, man or woman, on which to prove himself, but he kept his mouth shut. He knew Fenn better than most, he'd worked for him for over ten years. The danger sign was when those watery eyes stared at you, and didn't blink; like being fixed by a snake.

'All that, for bloody nothing?'

'What could we do, Jack?' The big hands splayed out in a gesture of submission. 'We went there for gold bars and there wasn't any. So we got out.'

Fenn leaned back and studied the big man he'd lifted out of a back-street pub gymnasium over ten years ago. Then, hot-tempered, bone-hard, but slow as a turtle, Sammy had looked like having a great future as a human punchbag. Fenn had seen too many good boys end up with scrambled eggs for brains and vacant eyes that only came to life when someone threw a fist at their glass chin, but this bloke had something different. Take him away from Queensberry Rules and he was a killer.

With Fenn teaching him the rules of the game, Sammy had soon proved his worth, first as a personal debt collector, then as security manager at Fenn's Diplomat Club. Nowadays, the handsome, sullen face topped a smart, broad-lapelled suit, with a waistcoat that barely hid the barrel chest and its silken shirt, and Sammy knew he owed it all to Fenn. What's more, the manicured, big-knuckled fists still knew their business. Fenn only had to say the word, and those hands would do the rest, just so far and no farther.

'You did right, Sammy,' said Fenn, and sensed the big man relax. Sammy was no great thinker, but he had common sense. To get out had been just what Fenn would have done. The job had been geared to gold, and Fenn wasn't interested in the problems of fencing small-time rubbish. That was for amateurs.

But the laugh was on Fenn, and that he didn't like. He'd pulled a stroke and got away with it, but for all the good it'd done, he might as well have given a mattress full of fivers to the Police Benevolent Fund and then tried to claim it against tax. Jack Fenn had lost face. There had to be a way of making that good.

'Somebody pulled the rug away, Sammy.' Fenn swung his feet to the floor and, leaning forward to place his spread fingers on the desk, regarded them, thoughtfully. 'That's what I call a dirty trick. Like welshing.'

The hint needed no more explanation. When Jack Fenn set a limit to your losses, you stuck to it and paid up when asked. If you didn't, you had a visit from Sammy Berghoff – not to collect the money, but to teach you a simple lesson in basic communication. Do as Jack says, or else. Sammy gave that twisted grin of his and nodded. Message understood.

'Fancy giving us the wrong wrinkle,' he said. 'That wasn't very bright . . .' He clenched his right hand into a ball of knuckle, and ground it gently into his left-hand palm.

'If you can't trust a fingerman, who can you trust?' offered Fenn. He leaned back and set his heels on the desk again, regarding the gleaming toecaps with quiet satisfaction. 'But let's be fair. I'll talk to him first, OK?' A small, tight smile reached Berghoff from behind the shoes. 'Tonight, Sammy . . .' Sammy nodded but didn't leave straight away as was expected now that the post-mortem on the job was over.

'The lads, Jack . . .' As Number One on the Air France caper, it was Sammy's place to speak up. 'What about expenses?'

Sammy was right. The job had been pulled. But with no loot, there could be no cut – for anyone. Even so, Fenn had a responsibility. He waved a hand in casual agreement. 'Take it out of house money,' he said.

House money was the cream of the club take, spending money that the tax inspector never knew existed. What Fenn's tactful accountant liked to call below-the-line investment capital. The big man didn't look very happy, and Fenn reassured him. 'I'll square it with Queenie, don't worry,' he said.

'She'll moan,' said Sammy.

'I'll give her a bonus,' countered Fenn, and added with a chuckle, 'Something she'll appreciate, right?'

It wasn't until Fenn made a certain gesture that Sammy saw the joke. He walked out, laughing.

For visitors and formal inquiries, access to Building 521 was through the west-side foyer. Mackay took the simpler and more direct route, through the Goldhawk loading bay and warehouse, by way of the folding metal doors that opened on to the parking space outside. The storage space was little more than cupboard-sized when compared to the huge freighting sheds of Cargo City, but Goldhawk's prime function was to transit goods, not hold them indefinitely.The interior of the warehouse area was like the metal doors, all shades of grey; concrete floor, primed metal racks and shelving, emulsioned walls, with only a bright-yellow fork-lift truck for contrast.

There was no strongroom here as such, but Mackay was fully aware of the need for security even though Goldhawk only occasionally carried valuables, such as antiques, minor art treasures or maybe jewellery. Small items of real value were stored in Mackay's office, in the floor safe beneath his chair; the rest was covered by insurance and Mackay's own ingenuity. He closed the heavy folding door behind him, and shifted the box of video cassettes under his other arm. Almost instinctively, he glanced towards the top corner of the storage area, where a confused jumble of dusty rack shelving and untidy boxes helped to conceal the unblinking lens of the closed circuit TV camera. It had been there now for a full week, unknown to anyone except himself; cheaper than a nightwatchman and no National Insurance to pay. The bay was deserted. Lifting a heavy plastic sheet that acted as curtain, he stepped into the minute dispatch office, then through the door beyond into the noisy clutter of the administration area – the heart of Goldhawk. After the cool grey hum of the warehouse, it was like walking into the street market in Portobello Road.

'Morning, all!' he called out brightly, forcing the weekend blues to the back of his mind. The first glimpse of the organised chaos that was Goldhawk, cheerful and bubbling in response to his daily greeting, always helped. As he moved past the jumble of desks towards his own neat office, more personal hellos were exchanged: a nod and a wink from George the export clerk, his desk sinking beneath a deluge of documents and boxfiles; thumbs-up from Barney, the carrot-haired import junior, deep in an earnest telephone conversation; a crisp smile from Freda, trim, corseted and vaguely angular beneath her floral frock, as she bustled off to make Mackay's routine first cup of coffee.

'Hi, Mike!' Nik Andreadis, his top invoice clerk, flashed perfect teeth and returned to rotating the day's import arrivals. First names were the order of the day at Goldhawk, and Mackay was no exception to the rule, which was only fair, considering he had made the rule himself. They were as good a crowd as he could expect in this cut-throat business.

Real skill and experience was at a premium, and staff were liable to be poached at a day's notice; the only names you knew next door were on the company nameplates, and even those changed more often than was comfortable. Long-term accounts weren't easy to hold on to, with backhand perks and discounts taking the pricing market into something like gang warfare.

Mackay had fought hard to give Goldhawk standards in this wilderness, not just in cost effectiveness and delivery, but in security, insurance and good faith. At the beginning it had meant working anything up to twenty hours a day, sometimes seven days a week, but he had built a reputation second to none. Goldhawk was small but it was beautiful. Keeping it that way was the new challenge that made him tick. Unfortunately, it was also the millstone that threatened to drown his marriage.

When Joan complained that he loved his bloody job more than her, the kids and their home all put together, he had asked her to be patient. That had been the last straw, and the minefield of their daily quarrels had finally exploded into separation. Now even that uneasy truce was threatened, but Mackay was determined to forget. It wasn't going to be easy. As he turned the corner to his door, he caught a brief glimpse of one of the instant, nameless temps who were always drifting through, aimless, rootless and, more often than not, brainless. This one was pretty, knew it, and gave Mackay an automatic smile that left him cold. He nodded politely and she turned away. But as she reached yet again for the corrective fluid, Mackay tensed; the thrust of her lithe young body brought the realisation that beneath her blouse she was mother-naked. Suddenly, he was two hours in the past again, with Joan's pale body twisting underneath him, her gasping smile applauding him even as she made him the loser. The memory crumpled as a familiar voice brought the present back into focus, gloomily.

'Mike, we've got problems,' said John Swinford. Mackay wasn't surprised. A last look at the pretty typist showed her painting her nails with infinite care, as she waited for her correction to dry. Mackay shrugged, and led the way into his office.

Swinford closed the door after them, shutting out most of the background noise. He watched patiently as Mackay set down the box, slipped off his jacket and hung it up before settling into his chair. As manager, it was Swinford's privilege to have the first meeting of the day, a ritual where business wasn't discussed until Freda had brought in the coffee and the day's mail. Today the news couldn't wait.

'Gary's packed it in,' Swinford said.

The bald statement caught Mackay bending over the box he'd just brought in. He straightened abruptly and slammed down the cassette he'd been holding. Gary was Goldhawk's best driver, almost impossible to replace.

'Who poached him?'

'Mondial. Five doors along.'

'Bastards!'

'He had the grace to phone. Said he was sorry.'

'Sweet of him.' Sourly, Mackay asked the obvious question. 'How much more?'

'A grand, he said.' Swinford hesitated, then decided to go on. 'He sort of suggested we could top that . . .'

'Forget it,' snapped Mackay. 'Let him put the screws on somebody else.'

'It leaves us stuck, Mike.'

'We'll manage. I'll drive the bloody van myself if I have to!' If it came to the crunch there wasn't any job in Goldhawk he couldn't handle, no trouble. He'd come up that way, and knew what it was about. So did Johnnie Swinford. That's how they'd made it come good in the first place.

'No sweat for now, mate,' smiled the manager, wearily. 'Just pay me overtime, OK?'

It wasn't entirely a joke; Mackay could tell that from his eyes. Freda knocked and came in with the coffee. Swinford took his with a muttered 'thank you'. As Mackay moved the video cassette aside to make room for his drink, he made sure that Freda could see what the sleek plastic holder contained. He looked behind the upswept frames of her National Health glasses and saw her eyes register the information and frown. When she placed the folder of mail in front of him the frown had gone, replaced by her usual crisp-edged smile.

'No calls for half an hour, OK, love?'

'They shall not pass,' responded Freda, and went out.

He sipped the piping-hot, unsugared drink and stared across at Swinford.

'Having a bad run of it, John?' The query sounded casual, but held genuine concern. They had known each other a long time; the weakness was an old one.

'Half the bloody dogs run backwards when I pick 'em! Yeah, it's bad all right . . .' He looked up again and tried to grin; the mouth twisted up at the corners, but the eyes were dark with misery. 'It'll change, mate. You know how it goes . . .'

'Yeah, sure.'

It wasn't just the dogs, they both knew that. Swinford would bet on anything – dogs, horses, cards, the pools, roulette – the weather forecast, even. The trouble was, he'd win back just enough to keep him in dibs, but never completely out of debt. Mackay had helped him out whenever he was really skint, sometimes to the tune of forty or fifty quid a whack: not out of pity, out of friendship. Most of all, because he knew he could trust him not to make up his losses from the petty cash, and God knows he must've been tempted often enough. That trust had grown out of twenty years of friendship, ever since they'd started up a skiffle group together, back in the late fifties. But Swinford wasn't after a handout for old times' sake, not today; dipping into his coffee, he changed the subject.

'Have a good weekend with the kids?'

Mike looked at him, then into his empty cup, and set it down. He locked his fingers together, gripping tight, before he spoke. 'The kids were great,' he said quietly. 'Only Joanie decided to play the bitch, didn't she . . .'

Swinford thought he knew enough about Joan to guess the trick she'd pulled. Possession was nine-tenths of the law, and sex had always been pretty high on her list of ten commandments. She had a way of looking at you that put the goods on offer, then pulled the blind down once she knew you were interested. Now and then he'd wondered what she'd have done if he'd gone through with the pass, but his speculation had never been serious. The way things had worked out, Swinford hadn't seen Joan or the twins now for over a year. It was no great loss.

'Gave you the red carpet treatment this time, did she?'

Mackay half-grinned; embarrassed, he realised he needed to boast that he had scored. 'Lilac sheets and pale-blue pillowcases,' he admitted, then added almost apologetically, 'She was lonely . . .'

Swinford nodded. He was a loner too; he understood that sort of need; it could be desperate. 'Make the most of it, I would.'

'Why not?' Mackay said jauntily, but for all his bravado, he knew the grand seduction scene hadn't been his doing; he was the one who had been used. Eve and the apple, he thought, bitterly. Would it always be that easy? Brutally, he thrust all future promises from his mind and, flipping open the mail folder, concentrated on the letters it contained.

'Better start looking for another driver, John,' he said, offhandedly, then stared hard, reading and re-reading the brief third letter with growing anger. He hadn't expected this one. Swinford noticed, and knew it meant more trouble.

'What's up, Mike?'

Mackay said nothing, but pushed the letter across. Swinford cursed incomprehensibly under his breath. A documentary film company, one of their regular bread-and-butter contracts, had pulled out. Latest terms were not acceptable, overheads rising, state of the industry, better facilities on offer, thank you for your past endeavours, yours sincerely. Swinford pushed back the 'dear John', and scowled.

'Some pig has undercut our rates,' he muttered.

'Not for the first time, John.' He glanced down to the lower left-hand drawer of his desk. The files it contained were for his eyes only; contracts, special deals, discounts, prices – all the essential information that a rival firm would love to have, to put skids under Goldhawk. The drawer was always kept locked, but keys can be copied; certainly somebody had stuck in their thumb and come out with some plum trade tweaks. For a month now, he'd had his suspicions, but this latest let-down clinched it.

'We've got a sodding snooper, I reckon.' He stared hard into Swinford's unhappy face. 'But not for long . . .'

By the time Freda brought in the morning's third cup of coffee, Swinford had gone, the day's letters were answered and ready for typing, and Mackay was busily unpacking the last item from the bottom of the box. He looked up, guiltily. Freda could see him wondering whether to try to hide the plastic-wrapped device, but it was already too late. She set down the coffee and jerked her head closer, full of bird-like curiosity.

'Whatever is it, love?' she said brightly. 'One of those new pocket tellies?'

Mackay slipped past her and hurriedly closed the door. Then he stood by the package uncertainly, and suddenly ripped off the plastic outer cover. The two-toned metal device was about twelve inches long, five high, and three wide. The front end did, in fact, contain a tiny, three-inch television screen, with a neat array of five black control knobs beneath the opaque glass. Freda looked at it with innocent interest.

'Does it do colour?' she said.

'It isn't that sort of TV.' He ran his hand over the sleek, compact shape, and his face was serious. 'It's something special, Freda –' Now he looked her straight in the eyes, and frowned. 'You weren't supposed to see. . .'

'I didn't mean to pry,' she bristled, mildly. 'I was just –'

'I know, love.' He cut her short, apologetically. 'It was my fault.' He looked back at the portable TV monitor. 'The secret's out in the open now, isn't it?'

'Secret?' wondered Freda. 'I don't have to say a word, love. Not if you don't want me to, that is.'

Mackay looked hopeful. He put the monitor back inside the box, out of sight, carefully, thinking.

'Is it . . . spare?' Freda said.

Mackay shook his head, and gave a wry smile.

'Clean gear, Freda,' he said. 'It didn't drop off anything. On lease.' His face grew serious. 'But not through the firm's books.'

'I've never set eyes on it,' comforted the chirpy little secretary. 'Trust me, love.'

He studied her, thoughtfully.'Can I?'

'Of course you can! I won't say a dickie bird!'

'You're a darling!' Mackay's face showed his relief that the secret was in safe hands. 'Here – I'll show you what it's for.'

He took her arm and drew her towards the bookcase. A jumble of books and files filled the top surface, and Mackay carefully pulled a couple of books aside. Peeping out from this cunningly set recess was the lens of a camera. Bending to look at it more closely, Freda seemed a little flushed.

'Well I never!' Her voice sounded tight.

'See where it's pointing? Mackay indicated an imaginary line from the tiny lens, across the room, towards his desk. Its focal point was the locked drawer on the lower left-hand side. Mackay beamed at Freda like a boy showing off his first train set. 'Always on guard,' he said, 'Never off duty.'

'Candid camera.' Freda gave a small, nervous giggle.

'Something like that,' admitted Mackay proudly. 'It works on a time switch.' He checked, and laughed, resting his hand on her shoulder, the best of friends. 'Can't go telling you *everything*, love – now, can I?'

Freda gave her crisp smile and watched him carefully re-arrange the books to keep the secret TV eye from view.

'It's not the same as they have in the supermarket, is it?' she remarked. 'You can see yourself on the telly there.'

'Different system,' Mackay explained. 'Heard of what they call a regiscope, have you?' Freda shook her head, but Mackay was already continuing his lecture. 'It records visitors, or intruders, on tape.' He picked up one of the cassettes. 'Video tape, like this. They use it in banks sometimes. Everybody in or out, staff, customers or robbers – it all goes on to tape. Then they play it back, and they know who did what, and when.' The explanation seemed to hang in mid-air, as he took out the monitor set again. 'That's what this little gadget is for.'

'Like one of those tape recorders, only with pictures,' commented Freda with a knowing nod. 'I've got one o' them.'

'Bit more complicated, though.'

Freda pointed to the video cassette. 'But where d'you put one of them, to make it start?' she asked, all innocence. Mackay stared at her in mild surprise.

'That's the replacement tape,' he said. 'The video machine's been running for the past week, love.' He held up the monitor, as yet not connected. 'Haven't been able to see anything yet, mind – this last bit of gear's only just come through . . .'

'It'll take you a bit of time to look at a whole week, won't it?' It might have been a trick of the light, but there seemed to be a glazing effect over Freda's eyes. 'Or will you throw that first one away?'

'I know it's only a try-out,' admitted Mackay, 'but I reckon it'll work.' He became more enthusiastic. 'When I've got it all fixed properly, I'll be able to have instant replay!'

'Lucky you,' said Freda. 'When will that be?'

'This Friday!'

Freda picked up the empty box and moved to the door. 'I'll throw this away, shall I?'

'Thanks. Not a word, though, eh? Strictly "top secret"?'

'You men and your toys,' teased the secretary, briskly opening the door. 'Us women have got better things to do.' The door closed after her, quietly.

Mackay relaxed, glad that the charade was over. He'd laid the bait, it was now a matter of patience. He never enjoyed lying, least of all to someone like Freda. She was a good old stick and he was fond of her; blinding her with science had been a dirty trick. In fact, none of the CCTV units were connected, and the tapes were blank. But if the bluff worked, he'd be saved a lot of bother. A court case or police investigation would do no good to customer confidence or public relations; besides, industrial espionage – especially where filching simple facts and figures were concerned – was almost impossible to prove in a court of law. The CCTV in the warehouse was different, put there to record any pilfering of goods in transit; solid, actionable proof. But nothing from that locked drawer had ever been missing, unless it had been carried away inside somebody's head. Mackay sighed; it was a sad, dirty game. He looked at his watch and decided to stay late that night to fix up the system and get it going. Glancing at the monitor, he wondered – machines instead of watchmen? It seemed inhuman, science fiction taking over the world.

Suddenly he pulled a wry, unhappy face, not at the shape of things to come, but at something he'd remembered about Freda. She hadn't once questioned why the camera was pointing where it was, or what was so special about that particular locked drawer. Light dawned, and his vague earlier suspicion became cold, ugly fact. She hadn't needed to ask. She knew.

Detective Inspector Alex Tindall, CID, paced out the ground inside the warehouse for the tenth time, and at last came to a halt in front of his plainclothes sidekick. Hands in his pockets, he seemed to see nothing, even when he stared Jimmy the sprog full in the face. Jimmy Dalton kept quiet; in the seven months he'd worked alongside Tindall he'd picked up more than one of the guv'nor's old-fashioned values, and this one most of all: speak when you're spoken to, especially when the guv'nor's thinking. Tindall's craggy features always seemed ready to apologise for some regretted but needful act of violence, but the mind behind those mournful eyes never lost control. He shrugged his burly shoulders, and contact was re-established.

'The lads finished yet, Jimmy?'

'Packing up now, guv'nor,' answered Dalton. 'Nothing there, they reckon.'

'Stands to reason, lad. Pro job, wasn't it?'

'Made a proper balls of it then. They didn't take a thing.'

'Got their dates screwed up, didn't they?'

Dalton caught on, or so he thought. 'Not an inside job . . .' The bright remark trailed away under the dour scrutiny of those sad eyes. 'I mean – they'd've known –' Dalton stopped talking, aware he'd got it all wrong. Tindall answered him, typically, with a question.

'Reckon the villains knocked on that door at three in the morning, just on the off-chance, do you?'

Dalton wisely tried another tack. 'Somebody dropped a clanger,' he suggested. 'A bad tip-off . . .'

'That's more like it, clever Jim.' Tindall looked thoughtful. 'Hard men don't like being let down, either.'

'Nobody thumps nightwatchmen for a hobby,' observed Dalton cheerfully. 'No profit there!' He was suddenly aware that Tindall was staring keenly past him, eyes narrowed in recognition. Ask no questions, and don't look, unless the guv'nor says move: another rule learned through bitter experience. Tindall carried on the conversation, but his mind was on what he saw.

'It'll be on the street, lad. Bound to be.'

The thin, stooped driver clambered into the parked van, checked his worksheet, and threw a sly glance across at the huddle of uniformed rozzers outside Air France. The glance was more than simple curiosity: Tindall could smell the nervousness from where he stood, thirty yards away, unnoticed and screened by lanky Jimmy Dalton. The van driver started up his engine and flicked his stare away, and seeing that awkward cock of the head, Tindall put a name to the face: Gus Fulmer. Must be over sixty now, but a codger who gets around a lot, both sides of the fence. Light fingers, sharp ears; have info, will snout – for a quid or two or three.

'We'll just have to ask around, won't we, lad?' said Tindall, and gave an unaccustomed smile. 'Y'never know, we might get lucky.'

Catching villains was work, pleasure and holidays to Inspector Alex Tindall. More than that, a job committed on his patch was treated like a smack in the chops, a deliberate challenge; any villain who tried it on did so at his own risk. What Tindall called 'accidental' crimes by individuals under pressure – crimes of passion, domestic affrays, manslaughter, racial scuffles, even – had to be sorted out in terms of law and order, certainly. But they were human situations, emotional explosions. They just happened. Calculated villainy was different; it was a declaration of war. A villain who planned and set out to execute a crime against property or the citizen was out to prove himself better than the fuzz – and Tindall wasn't having any of that. The mob who'd pulled the Air France caper had come out of it looking like a bunch of 'nanas, but if they'd succeeded – and they'd come damn close – the laugh would've been on the Met. The Met, that is, and Alex Tindall, who took such acts of flaming cheek very personally indeed.

'Start the way you intend to go on' was a lesson he'd picked up twenty years ago in the uniformed branch. You had to make the rules, or somebody else'd make 'em for you. He'd taken that personal motto with him to Heathrow, when it had been brought under the Metropolitan Division, three years ago, and old acquaintances rehoused in Stanwell from East End billets knew exactly what it meant. Put dirt on Tindall's doorstep and you're asking for trouble. Maybe it didn't stop the real villains from going about their business, but at least everyone knew where they stood. They had been warned.

Tindall parked his car alongside the Customs and Excise offices serving the cargo complex, and strolled from there through the no-man's-land of vehicles that backed on to Building 521. Now, with statements made and preliminary reports sent to the DI, there was time for Tindall to come back to Cargo City – alone – and look up Gus Fulmer. The old codger would probably claim that he was going straight, they always did; but Tindall had come prepared for that.

He found Fulmer loading up a scarred van with small brown parcels labelled FRAGILE, and he almost dropped one when Tindall, coming up behind him on near-silent shoes, tapped him on the shoulder and shredded the old man's nerves.

'God Almighty, mate! What d'y'think you're up to?' Fulmer had spun round, mean-faced and aggressive in spite of his grey hairs. He glared at Tindall through bifocals: lips drawn back, he prepared to snarl a few ripe comments on Tindall's bloodline, but suddenly checked himself. He'd caught a whiff of Old Bill, and didn't like it.

'Bloody copper,' he muttered. 'I should've known.'

'No sweat, Gus,' said Tindall. 'You've forgotten, haven't you?'

'It's the smell I can't stand,' the old man growled, and moved back out of range. Still lively, and still a rat; corner him and he'd bite, when all the time he was scared half to death you'd tread on him.

'Don't be nervous, Gus,' soothed Tindall. 'No need to panic.'

'Done nothing, have I?'

'Did I say you had?'

'What you crawling round here for, then?' The old man stood up straighter, and settled his flat cap more cockily as he peered at Tindall.

'Plane spotters go on the other side!'

'You're talking very perky, old mate.' Tindall took a step closer, trapping Fulmer against the corner of the open van door. 'Not the way you should. Not to an old friend . . .'

The old man peered at him, acidly. 'I don't know you. Why should I?' he said. He took a closer look, and the sneer on his old, drawn lips tried to re-form into a desperate grin, but he wasn't laughing.

'Mister Tindall!' Suddenly it was old pals' time, then his face fell. 'Bloody hell.'

'I'm glad you've remembered me, Gus,' said Tindall gently. 'For old times' sake.'

'Been and gone,' protested Gus, licking his lips. He no

longer looked Tindall in the eyes, but watched his mouth as though waiting for the charge to be read out. 'They know, here –' He indicated the warehouse and offices above, behind the van. 'Prisoners Aid, all that cop. They'll speak for me, honest, guv'nor!'

'I'm not asking you for a reference, Gus,' said Tindall. 'It's your eyes and ears I'm interested in.'

'Eh?' Gus showed his stained teeth, pretending to be dense.

'Information,' Tindall prodded, patiently.

'I'm a driver warehouseman,' complained the old man. 'Not a flaming Citizens Advice Bureau!'

'Air France –'

'It's an airline.'

'They had a robbery. Last night.'

'Did they? Go on.'

'You know bloody well they did!' snapped Tindall. Fulmer saw the red light, and stopped being so cheeky.

'I heard they had a break-in,' he admitted. 'I didn't know anything had been lifted, though.' He looked sideways at the stocky detective. 'None of my business, is it?'

'It is mine, though,' insisted Tindall. 'You know the form, Gus. I want to know what's on the grapevine. Whispers in the grass. Anything like that.'

The old man stared at him, and Tindall mistook the fear in his eyes for greed. 'It could be worth a quid or two,' he murmured. The fear grew into anger, and Tindall wondered why. Gus waved his finger at the detective, and it shook.

'I don't know anything. You just leave me alone!'

'I'm asking nicely, Gus –'

'Get stuffed!' Gus lifted his head, defiantly, and pushed the glasses back on to his nose. 'Find somebody else to do your bloody grassing!'

Tindall sensed that the old man knew more than just a whisper. He decided to push harder. It could be worth it. 'Gus,' he put a hand on the old man's arm, gently dusting off an imaginary flake of dirt, 'some of my mates in CID . . . they've been hearing rumours about you . . .'

'I'm straight!'

'Like, if you want anything on the side – fags, whisky, perfume – dead stock, no duty, you know what I mean – ask Gus Fulmer.' He gave the old man a cold smile. 'They reckon you're bent as a nine-bob note, old son.'

The old man had stopped protesting; he seemed close to tears. Tindall was not moved. 'They're hard men, Gus. You know what that sort can be like. They'll prove it, won't they?'

Fulmer's hand shook as he wiped it across his mouth. He ran his fingers shakily up under his glasses, rubbing the suggestion of moisture from around his eyes.

The hand came down again, slowly. He straightened, but his voice was suddenly very old.

'For Christ's sake, leave me alone,' he croaked.

'Don't want to keep you from your work, do I?' said Tindall affably. 'Think about what I said, old son, eh?' He patted the old man's arm, sympathetically. 'I'll see you tomorrow.' He turned and walked away.

A moment later, the old man slumped, huddled and trembling, on to the sill of the van. Tindall couldn't see that Gus was weeping, helplessly, like a terrified child.

Dalton's throat was parched dry and his feet were killing him. At the end of a long afternoon he'd got nowhere, and he was fed up to the back teeth. So he'd found himself a familiar pub with a barmaid who didn't mind you staring at her sweater, and ordered himself a well-deserved pint of best brew. He'd hardly paid for his pint and received a smile when a voice drew his attention away.

'Timed that one badly, didn't I, James?' A lean, dark face was grinning at him, and Dalton forgot all about the beer.

'Bloody hell! Roy!' he yelped, and the two men pummelled each other, laughing gleefully. It'd been six months or more. 'Don't need to ask, do I?' Dalton beckoned to the barmaid, who this time wriggled her shoulders as she moved to take his order; she almost made him forget what he was asking for. 'Er – another of the same, please, love.' Knowing exactly what she was doing, she reached up to take a glass mug from the rack above her head, stretching her sweater to its limits. The effect was wasted; Dalton was already facing the welcome stranger again.

'Look at you,' he grinned. 'Fresh as a bloody daisy!' He poked Roy's ribs. 'Still on the cars, you must be!'

'Wrong, mate. I'm not.'

There was a small, uneasy silence. Both men seemed to concentrate on watching the beer foam into the tilted glass, but neither was thinking about beer or even the barmaid. Fragments of instinctive observation started to add up in Dalton's mind. The pale blue shirt and dark blue tie was a dead giveaway beneath his civvy top when a uniformed branch bod was wasn't in plainclothes branch either, he couldn't be, the look slumming it off duty. There was nothing like that on Roy. He of him wasn't right.

'Cheers,' said Roy, raising his glass to drink. 'Here's to freedom.' They both drank, slowly and deeply, and Dalton waited. He wanted to know why, but it had to come from Roy himself, in his own good time. You had to have a bloody good reason for resigning – either that, or it had to be the other. Dalton would've given his right arm that Lomas wasn't that sort, but you could never tell, these days. Roy gave him a sideways glance as he set his half-drained jar back on to the counter, and grinned, sheepish yet defiant. He knew what was going through Jimmy Dalton's mind. It was only natural.

'Resigned, didn't I?' he said. 'No prospects.' Dalton relaxed slightly but still looked puzzled, and Lomas added, 'Not if we wanted to get a decent place of our own, eh?'

Dalton nodded; now he understood. The copper's nightmare – marriage – had reared its ugly head. That was the difference between them – the Force was Dalton's life. If any bird ever hoped to take him on and change all that, she was in a for a hard time. He'd make a go of marriage, sure, it had its perks; but it had to be on his terms.

'Congratulations, mate,' said Dalton, and meant it.

'It hasn't happened yet – not legally,' admitted Roy. 'Got to start earning my living, haven't I?'

'Tell me when,' said Dalton. 'I'll be best man.'

'You'd better bloody be,' laughed Lomas, and they drank again, remembering old times.

They had been mates since they were police cadets together, and the bond had stayed good even after Dalton had made it into the CID. Dalton had an arrogance that didn't suit a uniform or beat-bashing. Going on the mobiles didn't interest him, neither did the legal side, or admin. But when it came to villains, that was different. To say he had a nose for it sounded a cliché, but it was true.

Roy Lomas, though, went strictly by the book, which was why he'd gone first to panda cars, then on to motorway patrol; he understood engines better than people. It was a different world, and Dalton wasn't surprised that he wanted out of it.

'What sort of a job you after, then, mate?'

'Would you believe a driver?'

'Round the village? Heathrow?'

'Better than taxis,' grunted Lomas, and Dalton nodded. Land the right number and Roy could double his old take-home pay – plus perks.

'Any luck so far?'

'You're joking. It's worse than being an ex-con!'

'You look straight enough.'

'That's it, chum. That and my impeccable references. Turned down yesterday, wasn't I? The firm didn't fancy taking on ex-fuzz. Could make for sticky employee relationships.'

'Sounds a dodgy firm.'

'Just my luck!' Lomas forced a grin. 'But are we downhearted?'

'Keep trying. There's always jobs going in security. You know the score.'

'No thanks.' Lomas finished his beer. 'I've given up playing sheriff, mate. I'm looking for honest, gainful employment and sensible hours, no sweat.'

'Can't help you then, can I? Strictly overtime, that's my lot.'

'Don't know how you stand it, James my son,' he said,

indicating their empty glasses to the barmaid. By now she'd found someone else to take a shine to and took her time coming over. Lomas noticed Dalton give her an appraising stare, and chuckled. 'You haven't changed!'

'Look,' said Dalton, seriously, 'keep in touch, eh?'

'Sure.'

'You know where to find me –'

'Copshop by the Main Tunnel?'

'Right. And don't be afraid to ask. I mean that.' Dalton flicked a cheerfully disparaging hand over Roy's jerkin. 'Even if you *are* Citizen Joe Soap – OK?'

'You're on,' said Lomas, and they drank to that.

The heavy mahogany door closed almost without a sound. It was the only exit, and Berghoff stood guard there, hulking and impassable. His hand in the small of Fulmer's back had thrust the old man stumbling forward into the centre of the room, where pools of light from three huge table-lamps intersected, surrounding him with soft, luxurious shadows. Out of the darkness beyond loomed the massive desk, and behind it, caught by an edge of lamplight, sat the dapper, lounging figure of Jack Fenn. Heavy drapes and the thick carpet underfoot muffled even the harsh rattle of Fulmer's dragging breath. Desperately, he tried to control the tremor in his knees.

He'd known that morning he was for it. When the news leaked out that the Air France job had gone up the creek, Gus had almost done a bunk there and then. But running had no future, not at his age. Besides, the rozzers would be bound to cotton on, and then there'd be two packs of hounds up his shirt. Tindall had scared the living daylights out of him, jumping on him like that. It'd taken half a bottle of duty-free best French brandy to settle his nerves, and for a while the end of the world hadn't seemed quite so close at hand. Gus even managed to persuade himself he wasn't in trouble. He'd done right by Fenn, passed on what he knew in good faith; what was wrong in that? Mistakes can happen. Airline schedules do change without warning. Only in this case, they hadn't. Old

Gus had been so bloody sure of his source, he hadn't bothered to check it. Fair enough if all you're hoping to do is to nick a few hundred quid's worth of watches, or even a certain piece of luggage, and it's only you and a mucker in it for the perks. But when it involves two million in gold bars and Jack Fenn's the guv'nor you get it right, by Christ, spot on, no gaffes or bloomers. But Gus's luck was out, and now the nightmare had begun.

Sammy Berghoff had arrived to pick Gus up from work, very polite; told him to leave his old saloon, he wouldn't be needing it on this trip. It had been a smooth, swift journey. At any other time, a ride in a Mercedes would've been a proper treat, and Sammy had been very gentle. No strong-arm stuff, only quiet instructions, with Sammy always in the rear. Not that Gus had any thought of making a run for it; the state his legs were in, he'd hardly make it to the bog, let alone leave town.

'Sit down, Gus,' the tight, rasping voice commanded. 'You don't look too well.' The watery eyes watched as Fulmer groped and found the chair. The old man sat, but he wasn't comfortable.

'I feel bloody awful, Mr Fenn,' he croaked. The flat cap was in his hands, never still. His bifocals had slipped down his nose, but he was too busy listening, waiting for the razor's edge to show. Right now, Fenn sounded too good to be true.

'Nasty shock, was it? The news?'

'I couldn't believe it, guv'nor!'

Fenn shook his head in a slow mockery of concern. 'All that hustle, and no return,' he said. 'Very upsetting...'

'I felt sick about it, honest!'

'Not half as sick as I did, Gus.'

The old man straightened in the slippery leather chair, and a small flicker of self-defence cracked his voice. 'These things happen though, don't they?' He started to make excuses, but Fenn cut him short.

'Do give over.' The reproof was almost a whisper, but filled with menace. 'You made a mistake. Didn't you?'

Fulmer looked down at the edge of his flat hat, and nodded

miserably. Fenn leaned forward, driving home the nails, one by one. Each phrase carried a little more hate.

'You blew it, didn't you? Ballsed it up good. Screwed my investment to bloody zero!'

The hat was still, held tight by fear-clenched fingers. He licked dry lips pulled back from those old, stained teeth, eyes drawn upward by the new purr of menace, to look at his inquisitor.

'It went so well, y'know, Gus. Every other department came up trumps, one hundred per cent, no snags.' A flat statement, cold as the grave. 'Except you.'

'I couldn't help it,' croaked the plaintive voice. 'It wasn't deliberate –'

Fenn's reply was like softly grinding ice. 'If I thought that, old son, you'd be floating in the Thames by now.' A note of cruel humour edged the threat. 'And you wouldn't be swimming.'

'I did my best, Mr Fenn!' The moan choked to a whisper as he swallowed back the pit of his stomach. 'I swear it. Honest to God.'

'You let me down, Gus.'

'I didn't mean to! I'd do anything to make it up to you, Mr Fenn –'

'Sure.'

'Anything! You just name it, I'll get it for you. I don't care what!'

Berghoff's scornful growl sliced across the shadows from the door. 'Like a million quid?' he taunted.

The old, drawn mouth gaped, mirthlessly, as Gus saw where they were driving him. 'What?' he muttered.

'Sammy's right, old son,' Fenn confirmed blandly. 'That's how much I'm short, after laying off the discount.' It was a weak joke but he played it, hoping it would make the old sod squirm a bit more. 'Can you find it, Gus?' The answer was what he'd hoped for: a cry of despair.

'You know bloody well I can't!'

'Shame . . .' drawled Fenn.

Fulmer decided to try one last tack. He'd got nothing to lose now.

'I didn't scarper, Mr Fenn. I stayed put, didn't I?'

'I'm glad you had that much sense, Gus,' came the cool reply. 'It isn't very pleasant, wasting a geezer your age.'

The bifocals glinted as the old man swallowed, hard; was it a reprieve? 'You're not going to top me, guv'nor?'

'Not this time.'

Gus lunged forward as a dog would to an offered bone. One hand left the cap and rummaged under the glasses, clearing the brimming eyes. He needn't have bothered.

'You're a saint, guv'nor,' he babbled, perched on the edge of the chair. 'I knew you'd understand –'

Fenn's laugh was like an angry snake. 'Listen to him, Sammy. He must think I've gone soft in the head!' He glared at the old man, viciously. 'You *owe* me, Fulmer...'

Fear began to heave at Gus's stomach once again. 'I can't pay,' he whispered.

'Welsher's talk,' said Jack Fenn coldly. Suddenly, Gus knew. They were going to put a mark on him, a lesson to the others, the bookies' warning. That had been Fenn's trade in the old days. Every track, dogs or horses, had had its frighteners. They hadn't used words; it was always razors, 'dusters, or broken glass. Panic spewed up inside him and he slithered off the chair on to his knees, pleading and grovelling, a jelly of anticipated pain.

'For Christ's sake, no! Mr Fenn, don't do that to me! Please...'

'Don't you drop your guts in here,' said Fenn, and made a small disgusted gesture of dismissal. Berghoff did the rest.

'All fixed up?'

Mackay answered Swinford's question by switching the monitor into flickering life and pulling the tired-eyed manager over to the far desk drawer.

'John Swinford... this is your life!' he bawled, in a bad

imitation of an Irish-American voice. 'Squat there a tick, and try to look like Jack the Ripper.'

Swinford obliged, kneeling at the desk and twirling an imaginary mustachio as he glared wickedly towards the concealed camera lens. Mackay opened the cabinet by the bookcase; the video cassette recorder gave out a faint metallic hum. He depressed the piano key switches, first stopping the tape, then rewinding it slightly, before setting it on 'replay'. A second later the miniature screen showed Swinford doing his spoof turn, in grainy black and white.

'Amateur night!' laughed Swinford. 'Take him off!'

'You'll never make a villain in a month of Sundays, John,' Mackay chuckled. He carefully reset the controls back on to 'record', then gave a last glance to check the timing device before closing the drawer. The monitor still flickered, but was blank now; Mackay switched it off, making no attempt to conceal its position on the top of the bookcase.

Swinford watched, as he tightened his tie. 'Will Freda tell the others, d'you think?'

'I'm not bothered. It won't hurt if they do know, now . . .'

'She doesn't know about the warehouse, though?'

'No, mate. That's strictly between you and me, OK?'

'Fair enough.' Swinford yawned, and stretched, slowly. 'We've still got time before the pubs close. Coming?'

'You're telepathic,' said Mackay. 'Let's go.'

They went out, making the usual end-of-day checks as they walked through the deserted offices. Once outside, Mackay locked the warehouse doors, and they strolled towards their cars. Mackay's was nearest, and he paused, fumbling for his ignition key.

'You go on, Mike – I'll follow, right?'

Mackay made no reply: he was listening. So was Swinford. They heard it again, the whimper of a desperate child, or an animal in pain. Then the sound broke down into a retching, choking cough and they knew it was a man. Light filtered down from the few first-floor offices still working, confusing the stark shadows cast by the mini-floodlights. The car park was almost empty, with no sign of movement, but the whimper came again, rising to a pitch of strangled agony. They exchanged a wondering look, all that was needed to set them into action. Running down the façade of blank freight doors, they searched the shadows between the few remaining vehicles. At first they could see nothing, but the sound was closer now. Beside the looming hulk of a familiar battered van, a sprawling figure lay half-propped against one wheel. Swinford flipped his cigarette lighter into flame at storm setting, and they saw and recognised the ghastly face.

'Gus Fulmer!'

'What in Christ's name happened to him?'

The flat hat was jammed comically on to the sagging head, with the bifocals still perched on Fulmer's nose, but broken and askew. The old man had just vomited, but that wasn't what clenched Swinford into a cold shudder. The skin of the left side of Fulmer's face, from temple down to jawline, had been ripped open by five vicious, blood-trickling weals. Mackay crouched closer, and his foot touched against the old man's outstretched leg. A squeal of pain bubbled from the cracked old throat, and the shadowed body tensed. Mackay pulled Swinford's hand and the lighter to cast the flickering light farther down, and Swinford had to turn away, retching at what he saw. Mackay got to his feet, grim faced.

'We'd better get a doctor, quick,' he said. 'He's been knee-capped.'

'What did the hospital tell you?' demanded Tindall. His concern for Gus was purely professional. If the old man had been done over because of what he knew, then Tindall needed to be told before anything worse happened. He didn't want the duffer flaking out just yet.

'Very neat, the doc reckoned. Considering what they used . . .'

Tindall grunted dourly. It meant there were hard men at work, and maybe more of the same to come. 'Can he talk?'

'Not yet,' said Dalton. 'Still in shock.'

It didn't make sense. Some of the reporters were making excited noises about gang warfare even though they knew it wasn't on. Heathrow was fair game for anyone who had the nerve; nobody squabbled over territorial rights here. But a kneecap job on a small fry like Gus smelled very fishy indeed; the tip of an iceberg, and not to be ignored. He remembered how the old man had gone to pieces when they'd had their little chat. Twelve hours later, Gus is found, roughed up. It needed explaining, and only the victim could oblige.

'The minute he's fit; OK, Jimmy?'

'I've already told the doc,' nodded Dalton.

'Good lad.' The approving comment was unusual enough for the younger man to take advantage.

'Why put the frighteners on an old bloke like that? What's he done, d'y'reckon?'

'That's what we'd all like to know. What have you found out about him?'

'Not a lot. He's a freight agent's driver and warehouseman. Slightly dodgy. Small-time pilfering, get you anything on the side, that sort of nonsense . . .'

'You might try Criminal Records,' observed Tindall, airily. 'A few years back, mind.'

Dalton gave him a straight look. Tindall knew the old geezer, after all; but that still didn't explain why all the fuss. 'Much form?' he asked.

'A good few years, on and off,' Tindall replied. 'Had a job at Tilbury Docks in those days.'

Dalton nodded, taking the point. 'He's got connections, then?'

'Rubbish, mostly. Small-time handlers and fences.'

'He's a long way from home.'

'Ships, planes, what's the difference to him?' said Tindall. 'They all carry nickable goods. Old game, new tricks, that's all.

'He hasn't been nailed here yet,' retorted Dalton. 'Only suspicion, no proof.'

'Knows what he's at, doesn't he? Years of experience. He's no fool at that game.'

'Even so . . .' Dalton brooded. 'He must've done something pretty spectacular to get his legs smashed.'

'Good point,' admitted Tindall. 'It isn't like Gus to tangle with the heavy mob. He hasn't got the elbow for it.' His mind went over Dalton's report yet again, always asking questions. If Gus had been done in the car park, why hadn't anyone heard the shots? Those two witnesses – how much did they know? Had they found him – or had they brought him there, after he'd been carved up? 'The two blokes who picked Fulmer up –'

'Mackay, freelance freight agent, runs his own firm, Goldhawk, room 5960, that same big building –'

'Not the old man's firm?'

'He works for Ferrywell, ten doors down.'

'And the bloke who was with Mackay?'

'Swinford, the manager at Goldhawk. They were both working late apparently. Finished locking up together, heard somebody in trouble, found Fulmer in a right old state.'

'What do we know about them?' Tindall wasn't particularly suspicious, he just liked to have details. A jigsaw with holes in was bloody irritating.

'Dead straight, sober citizens.'

'Same line of business, though. Did they know him?'

'Looks like everybody knew Gus,' responded Dalton drily. Tindall's mind was still on Swinford and Mackay. Anyone involved with goods in transit through an airport like Heathrow had to have a question mark by their name. And it was amongst the small independent firms that the fly-by-night merchants could operate best. Like house agents, anyone could put up a board, pay the rent and play their fiddle. Just how they made their score was their own business; Customs couldn't put a tab on everything. Plenty of them were clean as a whistle; but there were a thousand and one shades of grey between black and white, and Tindall was an expert in dirty linen. Dalton could see how the guv'nor's mind was working.

'Goldhawk keeps its nose clean,' he said. 'Customs rate their business OK so far. That's more than three years now, so it can't be bad.'

Tindall smiled. 'You have been a busy little bee, haven't you?'

'I thought you'd want to know, so I asked around.'

'Firms with tarted-up names always make me wonder,' said Tindall. 'I ask you . . . Goldhawk!'

'Bit too flash for you, is it?' Dalton asked with a deceptively innocent smile. Tindall was too busy pouring the old acid to notice.

'Sounds more like a James Bond TV series,' he jibed.

'Anything but, guv'nor,' smirked his junior, pleased to be able to put one over on his boss for once. 'Registered office is at Goldhawk Road, Shepherds Bush. Strictly on the up and up, no form.'

'Walking encyclopedia, aren't you? Let's hope our friend Gus can tell us half as much, when they let him have his teeth back in.'

'Can't see him talking, guv,' said Dalton, shaking his head doubtfully. 'Would you?' The duty doctor at the Accident Unit had spared nothing in his graphic description of Fulmer's injuries. As a warning to keep quiet, it'd make anyone think twice, and Gus was no hero. 'That duffing up was no joke.'

'Not just his legs, you said.'

'Yeah, that was odd,' frowned Dalton. 'His face was badly scratched all down one side. Like he'd been in a punch-up with a bird.'

'Fingernails, was it?'

'A handful. And deep.' Dalton watched the guv'nor's face take on that little smile that said he'd dredged up something useful.

'Five of diamonds,' he murmured.

'Eh?' Dalton was uncertain if his leg wasn't being pulled. Tindall could be like that sometimes.

'Meant as a marker, son. Before your time, it was. A bookies' rumble, some dog track or other up North.' Dalton still looked puzzled. Tindall showed him a clenched fist. 'A bunch of fives, right?'

'I can see that, guv'nor.' The fist opened out into a claw, fingers crooked and ugly. 'How come diamonds, though?'

'Because diamonds cut, lad. Anything.' Tindall pulled back his hand, and studied it, remembering history and the knuckle-duster days. 'It was nastier, then. A touch of the queer about it.'

The whole point of the mark was that it was there to be seen, a signature of violence. And it was done by experts. Old pennies slipped between the fingers, backed by a rolled up newspaper – 'What weapon, squire?' – razors, carefully mounted to cut open but not kill – acid, even; an armoury you didn't see much of these days, thank God. But the tradesmen were still around; Gus's scarred face would testify to that. Dalton took the wrong tack completely.

'You telling me that Fulmer's gay?'

'Not unless he's had a sex-change,' Tindall sighed. He went on to explain, scornfully patient. 'Gus was the target, son. It's the hit man that's got the nasty habits.'

'A specialist, then.' Dalton groped his way towards the obvious, and Tindall's slight nod showed him he'd got it right.

'A pro,' said Tindall, 'working for someone very rough.' The sad, craggy face looked at Dalton, ruefully. 'And that's going to make life bloody difficult. For everyone.'

Swinford felt sick, and no wonder. The memory of Fulmer's torn face was still with him; the shock of finding the broken old man, the scream of agony as the ambulance men had lifted him on to the stretcher, the statements to the police, no detail left unnoted . . . He went home to the cold, empty flat some time after one in the morning, and sleep refused to take him. There seemed no way to blot out the memory of Fulmer's pain, or the stark reality of that moment of violence; he had no tablets apart from aspirin, and only the last quarter of a bottle of gin. Drinking hadn't helped, simply given him a foul, jaundiced headache. There was no welcome in the bed, no warmth. Each fitful doze ended in a shudder of wakefulness, and the dawn felt that much colder when at last it came. Shaving clumsily, he tried to reason away his panic. It was someone else who'd been damaged, not him, so why should he be bothered? It was no use. He knew the answer. The sickening unease, that even now turned his guts over and left him aching, was naked fear. Fear that he could get the same as Fulmer. Fear of pain.

He sat hunched over his third cup of coffee, letting it go stone cold as he wished to God to be rid of this waking nightmare. Trembling, he relived the excitement of the tables. There he was one of the élite, everything else was forgotten while he played his chips against the numbers, never quite able to beat his luck. But forgotten or not, a warning had been given, that had been part of the deal. Swinford had shrugged it aside. As long as he was still inside his limit, he wasn't interested, the wins and losses would balance out, at worst he'd break even, at best scoop the pool. So what, if each time he played his limit got a little nearer; his luck would change, it had to, that was the law of averages. It was a lie he could believe in, and it helped. But last night, Swinford had knelt beside a maimed old man and known it could've been him. He was standing on quicksand, in it up to here, and if he didn't get out in a hurry, he'd had it. His despair became nausea, and it took him nearly an hour to pull himself together enough to drive to work.

When he did arrive, he looked – to use Nik's words – like death warmed up. Freda wasn't there to make the coffee and, clumsily, Swinford started to make his own. It was Mackay who saw the state his hands were in, and stepped in to take over.

'Come in and sit down, John,' he said and, carrying both their coffees, ushered him into the office, shutting the door firmly behind him. The others outside soon got their heads down again, but they all had their opinions. George reckoned it had to be the bottle, Nik swore the way that Swinford had walked in, it had to be a woman who'd left him so knackered. Barney wondered why not both, but when they decided to ask Freda for her mature, unbiased opinion, she was missing.

Freda was in the Ladies, trying to screw up enough courage to say what she had to say to Mike Mackay. It wasn't going to be easy, she was scared stiff, it was always the same. Doctor, dentist or bank manager, she spent more time in the loo than in the chair they offered her. Besides, she had a story to rehearse.

Mackay stared across the desk at Swinford, who with both hands around the coffee cup, still had the shakes. Mackay said nothing, but pulled open a drawer and took out a three-quarters-full bottle of whisky.

'Medicinal,' he said, pouring a good measure into Swinford's coffee, and the drawn face watched him, making no effort to refuse. Mackay replaced the bottle and shut the drawer. The tension inside Swinford slowly began to unwind as he sipped at the hot, pungent drink.

'You look shattered,' said Mackay. 'Drink that, go home, and get to bed.'

Swinford bristled, pathetically. 'Look – I can manage, I'm all right.'

Step gently, thought Mackay; this bloke could explode, any minute. 'What's it about, John?' he asked.

Swinford dropped his eyes and gave a small shudder. 'Last night,' he muttered.

'It got to you, did it?' Swinford nodded, and Mackay tried to reassure him. 'It was a risk Gus took, being on the fiddle –'

'He wasn't *that* bent.'

'He shouldn't't've crossed someone heavy.'

'Paid for it, didn't he?'

Mackay studied Swinford's haggard face. There was something odd here. John was no pal of Fulmer's.

'Why should that get up *your* nose?'

Swinford lowered the coffee cup and stared into it, wanting to explain. The words didn't come easily.

'I'm in deep with my own crowd, Mike. Near the limit.'

'Need something to hold them off? Mackay knew the ropes – or thought he did. What he didn't know was who John owed. Not your friendly High Street betting shop or trackside bookie, they wouldn't carry a dodgy customer like Swinford, not now. But he had got credit – of a kind. Gus was an example of the interest they charged. He started to explain, but already Mackay had pulled several large notes from his wallet.

'It's more than just a couple of bob, this time.'

'I can manage fifty.'

Swinford stared first at the notes, then past them into Mackay's face. There was no judgement there, no sneer, not even impatience. He accepted Swinford's weakness as just another hazard of living, like hay-fever or a touch of the bottle.

Mackay saw him hesitate, and pushed the notes across the table.

'Put these where they'll do most good, John. I need you in top form, OK?'

Swinford took the notes. He found himself almost laughing at the pitiable amount, but choked back the hysteria. Mackay's joking hint had given him an idea. Double or even treble it, and that neat little fifty quid would still hardly make a dent in what he owed. Make the money work, was the only answer. Make it grow. Use it. The insidious thought flooded through Swinford's mind like the whisky spreading its slow burn deep down in his gut.

'Strictly medicinal,' said Swinford with a grey, drawn grin.

'And the day off work,' insisted Mackay. 'No arguments, right?'

Certainly it was what he needed; now it also happened to be what he wanted. He rubbed his fingertips against his temple. The headache was still there, but easing now. A couple of hours' kip before the club opened and he'd be right as rain.

'You're the boss,' he said. He drained his cup and set it down, then stood slowly and moved towards the door. He looked better already, thought Mackay as he watched him go.

'And thanks, Mike.'

'Payment in kind, remember,' grinned Mackay. 'Tomorrow, you work your ass off.'

Freda was standing outside the door, hands primly clasped, and nervous. 'Sorry about your coffee,' she said. 'I had the runs.'

'The doctor will see you now,' Swinford chuckled into Freda's startled face. 'But make sure he warms his hands first, eh, love?' He walked out, leaving Freda staring in some confusion at Mackay. He questioned her, gently, sensing that this was going to be the crunch.

'What's the trouble, Freda?'

She stepped into the office and closed the door.

'I've come to give in my notice,' she announced.

'Sorry to hear it,' said Mackay without batting an eyelid. 'Why?'

'Personal reasons, Mike.'

'Aren't you happy here?' Mackay was determined to push the old duck to the limit; he wasn't going to make it easy for her, not after what she'd done. 'Is it you reckon you're worth more, love?'

'It's my sister,' she blurted out. 'I have told you about her, haven't I?'

'Never knew you had one, Freda love,' came the quiet comment. 'How is she?'

'Poorly,' admitted Freda. 'Very poorly.'

'Needs looking after, does she?' guessed Mackay. 'By you.'

Freda nodded, a martyr to this long-lost relative that only she could save from a living death. 'I'm all she's got . . .'

'That's a pity,' said Mackay. 'When's this likely to happen?'

'Tomorrow,' said Freda.

'Sounds desperate.'

'She's getting worse,' explained Freda, hastily. 'All the time. There's no telling what could happen if I don't go soon.'

'I wouldn't dream of stopping you, Freda,' said Mackay, and suddenly she saw from his cold eyes that he wasn't surprised. He'd been expecting her request, waiting for her; all he was interested in was hearing what sort of yarn she was going to tell him. Did he know the real reason? If he did, he might still turn nasty.

'I'll take my cards today, then?' she suggested, hopefully.

Mackay nodded. 'We'll have to send your money on to you . . .'

'Don't bother, Mr Mackay. Keep it in lieu. That's only fair, isn't it?' Her eyes were pleading with him; perhaps she really did feel a lick of guilt.

Mackay decided to rub in the salt. 'Got something put aside to tide you over, have you?' She stiffened, but he went on, bluntly apologetic. 'Can't claim redundancy pay if you resign, love. It'll have to be found from somewhere else . . . won't it?'

'I've got nothing extra due,' she insisted with a touch of dignity. Out of a job she had no value; until another sucker took her on, that is.

'You'll need a reference,' said Mackay. He had taken her by surprise, and her eyes glistened, wetly.

'I hardly deserve that,' she muttered. 'Letting you down at such short notice, I mean . . .'

'Something to remember us by,' Mackay smiled, 'and better than a year's suspended sentence, eh?' She stared at him, hardly daring to breathe. He waited before putting her out of her misery. 'We're small, Freda. A court case won't do us any good, the customers wouldn't appreciate it. And anyway, what's done is done.' He stood, dismissing her. 'The only sad thing is, I trusted you . . .'

He'd gone too far. Suddenly he saw that she was stiff with anger. His act of pseudo-Christian charity was just an easy way out, his soft touch a sly attempt to patronise the old dear. She exploded.

'You bloody sadist,' she raged at him, 'putting the screws on an old woman! I'm a pensioner, you know!' She stormed to the door. 'I hope this place burns down around your ears, you slimy bastard – and you, and all them with it!' The door slammed, and seconds later the outer office door as well. Freda had gone and she hadn't even said goodbye.

'Nice job, Sammy,' said Fenn, setting aside the last of the newspaper reports on Fulmer. 'Very tidy.'

'Don't thank me, Jack.' Berghoff was pleased, even so; he rolled his big shoulders inside the well-cut suit. 'It was Bloody Delilah took care of him.'

'Marked him good, it says here.'

'The five of diamonds, yeah.' Berghoff frowned. 'They didn't call it that though . . . did they?'

'What would they know,' said Fenn. It suited him fine that Fulmer's scars hadn't been given their trade name. As an advert, it was strictly for insiders. 'And I can't see our friend Gus going out of his way to explain, can you?'

'He'd be stupid to try,' said Berghoff.

'That's right,' agreed Fenn, smugly. 'He won't make a monkey out of *me* again.'

'Or anyone else,' grunted the big man. He watched Fenn carefully, biding his time. It came.

'What a bloody waste, though . . .'

'Definitely off, is it, Jack?' Sammy had settled with the lads and they'd all of them said the same thing: if Fenn fancied another crack at it, fine by them.

'We've missed our chance, baby. Delivery's been and bloody gone by now.' That's what was so annoying. A perfect stroke, and nothing to show for it. Damn Fulmer's guts, they'd've had it made by now!

'Must be other deliveries,' suggested Sammy hopefully.

'They won't let us in so easy next time, if that's what you're thinking, kid.'

'Other airlines might, Jack.'

Fenn's watery eyes made a careful appraisal of his perfect shoes, while his mind considered Sammy's idea. Maybe they couldn't pull an identical stroke, but who'd be expecting another hit so soon? It was a nice thought, very tempting; but there was a snag.

'We'd need a finger, Sammy.' Not an amateur, this time. For a proper job you needed an expert, someone who *knew*. With that sort of information, you could crack anything.

'Sammy,' said Fenn, 'what we need is an insider. Find me one, OK?'

'There's a bloke here asking after Gary's old job,' Nik announced without his usual gleaming smile, and that was odd. He stepped aside to let the guy into the office, and Mackay sensed something in the air but couldn't put his finger on it. Perhaps it was the way the stranger stood, a sharpness in his bearing, in the eyes, too. The drivers that Mackay knew were more casual; no slouches, but nobody bossed them about and it showed. This lad was used to discipline, a discharged soldier perhaps. Mackay thanked Nik with a nod and, reluctantly, he went.

'Sit down and tell us about yourself,' Mackay said pleasantly. He was in his shirt-sleeves, working on Swinford's documentation for the morning, and glad to find an excuse to give it a break. In the moment it took the stranger to decide against sitting, Mackay looked him over. Lean build, lean face, dark hair, mid-twenties: eyes that looked around and didn't miss much. That could mean he had some brains, or else that he was just plain nosey. After Freda, Mackay didn't want any more of that sort. He wondered at the stranger's moment of hesitation, and the explanation came.

'Can I ask a question first, chief?'

'Sure. Go ahead.'

'I'm an ex-copper. Any objections?'

So that's what had bothered Nik. He'd been on more than a few demos and rallies. He'd had some rough treatment; probably deserved it, he could be a stubborn bastard. He'd learned to smell the plainclothes blokes, as well as getting a dislike for the uniform. Just the thought of rozzers left him uncomfortable, even when the copper concerned was only helping old ladies across the street. Maybe he had too many bad memories about how it was back in his own sunny island in the Med. The rozzers there wore guns. Mackay looked at the stranger again, and wondered; somehow he didn't hang together like the usual beat merchant, on or off duty. What was this guff about being 'ex'?

'I've nothing against the fuzz,' said Mackay, 'if they're clean.' The stranger stiffened and Mackay saw the beginnings of anger at the back of the dark brown eyes. Then the face creased into a thin smile, and the lad sat down opposite Mackay.

'Makes a change.' The tension in the voice had eased. 'I'm Roy Lomas.'

'How d'you mean – a change?'

'Last place I tried reckoned having fuzz around could spoil things,' said Lomas.

'In what way?'

Lomas shrugged. 'Labour relations. Perks on the side. Things they preferred to turn a blind eye to.'

'That sort of carry-on bothers you?'

'Not my business, is it?'

'Even if it's against the law?'

'Look – I'm not a copper any more!'

'Why not?'

'I resigned, didn't I?' It was a flat, simple statement, but Mackay needed more than that.

'Before they nailed you? Or was it a whitewash job?' Mackay's voice probed sourly, and Lomas stood up; now he was boiling.

'Stuff your rotten job,' he gritted. 'It's your sodding sort that makes law and order bloody near impossible!'

'Don't you hang me in with the Save Our Criminals squad, mate!' snapped Mackay. 'And stop being so flaming touchy – I'm not A10, y'know!' Lomas turned back, stone-faced.

'I'm not bent,' he said. Mackay believed him, but now wasn't the time to admit it. He leaned back in his chair, relaxed but unsmiling.

'And I've got nothing against coppers,' he retorted. 'They do the best they can. But they don't drop out for no good reason.'

Lomas stared at Mackay then, satisfied he wasn't being sent up, went back to his seat.

'Two reasons, mainly,' he said quietly. 'To start with, where I'm at, it's pretty much a dead end, right?'

'Uniformed branch?'

'Motorway patrol.'

'What's wrong with getting a transfer?'

'What's wrong with better pay and conditions? Nobody seems to reckon we're worth it, do they?'

'Things are getting better. Seniority helps. Promotion, too.'

'I'm sick of bloody exams,' said Lomas.

'You don't look thick.'

'Look – the amount I use my noddle, I'm not much better than a park keeper on wheels,' retorted Lomas. 'I can do better than that. I need to, don't I?'

Mackay looked the question, and Lomas explained. 'I'm planning to get married. Lynn and me don't want a station house, we want somewhere of our own – and kids.'

'Not easy being a copper's wife,' agreed Mackay, with feeling. 'Rotten hours.'

'That, too,' said Lomas. 'And people don't care, do they? They want law and order, but they want it to smell of roses all the time. It ends up you want to get stuck in, but you daren't. There's always some berk who reckons that crime and punishment belong on the National Health.' He stopped and looked a bit sheepish, as though aware that he'd said too much. 'I reckoned I'd be better off out of it,' he said. 'So I went.'

'Pity,' said Mackay. 'But I should cocoa. They lose, I gain.'

'You'll take me on?'

Mackay offered his hand. 'The name's Mike,' he said, and they shook on it. 'First names, you'll get used to it.' Lomas half-smiled, but his eyes had flicked past Mackay, to the bookcase.

'All pals together . . .' He looked hard at Mackay. 'Is that why you've got closed circuit television?'

'I don't play Big Brother,' grinned Mackay. 'It's security. This can be a dodgy business, sometimes.'

'So I've heard. But there aren't that many in your game who cover it with electronic surveillance.' He flashed a sudden grin. 'How's that for jargon?'

'Never use the stuff,' Mackay commented drily. 'But it was recommended back in '74, and they've been talking about it ever since. I decided it was about time we made it happen, that's all.'

'Makes sense,' acknowledged Lomas appreciatively.

'Glad you think so,' chuckled Mackay. 'It was one of your top rozzers who wrote the perishing report.'

'Nothing to do with me,' said Lomas. 'I vote civvy now, remember.' He stood up; they'd talked enough. 'When do I start?'

'Like as from yesterday?' Mackay wasn't joking. He needed action now. That suited Lomas.

'You're on,' he said.

Mackay still had to sort out Nik.

'He's a civvy, Nik. Nothing more than that.'

'Oh, sure!' Nik turned away as though in despair at his boss being taken for a sucker. Patiently, Mackay explained.

'Nik – I've seen his papers. I believe him. Take my word for it.' They stared each other out; neither broke, and Nik frowned, genuinely anxious.

'You could be wrong.'

'You, too.'

'I've seen too many like that one.'

'In uniform.'

'CID as well. They're bastards, all of them. He could be a plant.'

'Not him. He's all right.'

Nik shrugged. 'If you say so.'

'You got it,' said Mackay, then paused before taking the plunge. 'And I need a favour.'

'Name it.'

'I don't want anyone else to know.'

'Oh, come on!'

'You know why.'

'He can stick up for himself, can't he?'

'You'll smile when I tell you what he reckons. He thinks an ex-con would get a better deal.'

Nik saw the joke, and laughed. 'Could be.'

'Is he right? Would you split on a jailbird, if I said don't?' Nik thought about it, and Mackay pressed harder.

'Fair do's, eh, mate?'

'OK,' conceded Nik, quietly. 'But it's up to him as well . . .'

'All he wants is a peaceful life. No sweat, OK?'

'Got a name, has he?'

'Roy Lomas.' Another pause, and then the real favour. 'I'd like you to show him the ropes, Nik.'

'What!'

'I'd do it myself, but I'm meeting a bloke at Terminal Three. So it has to be you. Will you do it?'

'It's a bit strong!'

'It's the quickest way for you to find out that he's human.' Mackay gave Nik a cheerful grin, a bit sly. 'Besides . . . you'd be standing in for John.'

'That's news to me.' Nik looked as though he was going to play hard to get, but he couldn't defeat Mackay's cheeky grin.

'It should be – I just made it up,' he said. 'King for a day, maybe it'll keep you sweet, eh?'

Nik shook his head and had to laugh. 'You should be a bloody politician,' he said. 'Or a barrow boy.'

'Is it a deal, Nik?'

'OK. I'll hold his hand, if that's what you want.'

Among the thinning crowd beside the carousel, Mackay waited, keen-eyed and alert. On the noticeboard that he held against his chest was a boldly printed name, inviting contact: MR HENDRICKS. This was to be one of those courtesy jobs that Mackay liked to provide for major customers – seeing in one of their VIP executives, and clearing him and his luggage through the complications of Immigration and Customs. Hendricks came into sight, burly and grey-haired, with big, square-fingered hands. Seeing Mackay's notice, he came across. His soft Midwest burr was almost lost in the bustle of passengers and flight announcements, and Mackay had to crane close to hear his greeting as they shook hands. Besides his personal luggage, Hendricks was travelling with a small but heavy aluminium case.

'Machine parts,' explained the American as he helped take the various items from the carousel. 'Jigs and templates. New model.'

'We'll need to clear them through MIB,' said Mackay, and led the way directly to the Customs examination lounge.

Mackay took charge of the formalities, and declared Hendricks' luggage and the metal container with its load of parts. The officer knew Mackay by sight and nodded pleasantly, without real friendliness. No favours here: that, all parties understood. The personal luggage was passed without question, but not the precious jigs. The inspection was painless and swift, but thorough. Like Mackay, Hendricks knew how to be patient.

'Good trip?' asked the agent, amiably.

'Didn't notice,' smiled Hendricks. 'I napped.'

'This won't take long.' Mackay reasured him. 'There's a

company car laid on. You'll be at your hotel in no time at all.'

'Glad to hear that,' the executive nodded. 'I could do with freshening up some.' Carefully, he relocked the aluminium case as soon as the Customs officer had snapped it shut and marked it through.

The pale blue eyes of Larry Liebermann smiled upon the world. The trip from Kennedy into Heathrow had been smooth, on time, and everything was fine, no complaints. Sure, he would sooner travel first class; but tourist economy was part of the job right now, just as the grade of hotel and his expense account. That was the system for courier delivery; he was just a transatlantic errand boy. Time got a little confused now and then when there was too quick a turnaround between trips, but Liebermann was a New Yorker, young and resilient. Besides, being on the move the way he was made for very convenient relationships, you know?

He'd had his share of casual breakfasts in strange apartments before returning to the cool, impersonal coddling of his hotel and journey back to the States. One day . . . one day, when he'd at last pulled off the big one . . . the stay-overs would be on *his* time, not the company's (man, he'd *be* the company!); the apartment would be his stop-over pad, not a hotel; and the travel would be marked Larry Liebermann, VIP, First Class.

Right this minute, he had his luggage and some excess baggage to collect. He waited, fresh and unrumpled in his cloud-grey lightweight suit. His eyes were serious, as his mind concentrated on the parade of passing bags and cases. This was hassle time; before he could properly relax, he had to pass through British Customs. His case and sack of deliveries appeared and, taking them up, he headed for the green aisle and the nervous formality of passport and baggage inspection.

Taking the same route as the other tourist passengers, he found himself confronted by a Customs officer on duty at the inspection benches. When patiently asked for the necessary declaration forms on his sackful of deliveries, Liebermann looked blank.

'You mean I have to fill in forms?'

'Yes, sir. The usual pro forma.'

'Can you help me do that?'

The official looked pained. He had enough on his hands without this helpless American cowboy. 'This way, sir,' he said and, waiting only for Liebermann to collect his gear, politely escorted him into the adjacent MIB lounge.

Liebermann was handed on to yet another calm-eyed official. He blinked, engagingly; the officer listened, impassive and aloof.

'I need forms, I guess, and some help. Do you have an agency here?'

'We're not a freighting service, sir,' commented the official icily, and caught the sharp-eyed attention of his senior. A quick, murmured explanation of the problem, and Liebermann was beckoned to struggle with his baggage, across the room. Mackay was just about to leave with Hendricks when his name was called.

'Mr Mackay – perhaps you'd care to get this gentleman sorted out?' Mackay excused himself, and Hendricks, seeing a fellow countryman in trouble, allowed him to go with a discreet gesture of those big hands.

'He needs documenting,' explained the Customs executive with a dry smile and left him to it.

Liebermann pounced on his new ally.

'You know all about baggage processing, right?'

'I'm a freight agent. It's my job, Mr –?'

'Liebermann – Larry Liebermann. Courier with Computer Interchange Incorporated –'

Mackay didn't want a life history. He cut in: 'Look, Mr Liebermann, I'm already dealing with a client . . .'

'Sorry to inconvenience you like this, sir.' The New Yorker beamed his boyish apology at Hendricks, who accepted it with a cool nod, eager to be away.

'I'll be a few minutes seeing him to his car,' explained Mackay.

'I can wait,' Liebermann reassured him, then grinned,

indicating the uniforms all around. 'Looks like I won't be going anywhere for a while, right?'

'I'll be back,' said Mackay, and ushered Hendricks out into the noisy concourse. It took only a few minutes to locate the waiting limousine, and the chauffeur did the rest. Mackay stayed at the pavement long enough to wave Hendricks away, then briskly returned to the MIB lounge, and Liebermann.

The New Yorker watched with artless admiration as Mackay tackled the sheaf of papers that made up the pro forma, a maze of questions, answers, and demanded information.

The sack was the most important item; it held something like twenty to thirty consignments. Each one had to be entered, with its valuation; Liebermann produced a neatly folded sheet of paper with the relevant advice. Mackay reached for it, but the American wasn't handing it over.

'If that's the contents list, I'll copy it –'

'I'll read it to you,' countered Liebermann. Mackay stared into the frank blue eyes and wondered why the American was holding back. What did he have to hide? But it wasn't his business to make an issue of it.

'Do it your way,' he said.

'Right,' acknowledged Liebermann, and started to dictate. The items were nearly all computer listings, contracts, and other equally duty-free packets. The valuation wasn't important in a case like this, but Liebermann dutifully supplied the figures; nothing over twenty-five pounds sterling, converted from dollar values in the same breath. Mackay glanced at the sleek blond head with new respect. The brain behind those clear blue eyes was as crisp and quick as a computer.

At last it was done. Now it had to be cleared. With Mackay as guide, Liebermann and the precious sack arrived at the Customs bench. As they waited, Mackay again sensed a hint of tension. The rules of the game were simple. Couriers and the firms they represented were supposed to be honest, but if there was any trouble, it was the courier that got the bullet. He was the guy in the front line. Either Liebermann knew his company was forwarding something dud, or he was working it himself. It told Mackay something about the New Yorker; that, even knowing that risk, he was prepared to chance it. The examining officer approached them and, right on cue, Liebermann's bumbling innocence welled up and swept away all suspicion.

'Sorry I wasn't prepared,' he said. The officer nodded, then glanced at Mackay and recognised him for a pro. Looking down at the pro forma, he could see his opinion confirmed. He marked the sack and cases, and it was over.

It wasn't until Mackay and Liebermann were standing at the bar of the departure lounge that the New Yorker let his relief show.

'Here's to good luck, huh?'

Mackay drank, then asked casually, 'You think you needed it?'

'Right,' was the laconic, straight-eyed answer.

The American drank his beer, and Mackay pulled back from asking unwanted questions. It wasn't his concern, just as it wouldn't've been had the Customs man pulled a couple of bars of bullion from the New Yorker's sack. If anything were in there, of course, it wasn't gold; the weight wasn't right. The Customs bloke had sorted that one out, ever so discreetly. Something light, perhaps. Ice. Drugs. Perhaps nothing; Mackay didn't have to be right on this one. But it didn't smell good, and if that's how Liebermann ran the game, then Mackay knew how he'd best have payment for his services. On the nail. Cash.

'It's been nice drinking with you, Mr Liebermann,' he said, 'but I've got an office-load of work waiting for me.'

'We need to make our deal, right?'

'Cash up front, if you don't mind.'

The merest pause before replying, then: 'Sure, why not.' He glanced at his digital chronomatic. 'How long did it take?'

'Call it an hour.'

'OK. How much?'

'Forty.'

'Dollars?'

'Sterling.'

Liebermann counted out the notes, in fivers, slowly – twice. 'Say . . . I'll need an invoice for this, right?'

'I'll send it to the company,' said Mackay.

'You'll need their address . . .' The blue eyes glinted with honest approval, and the smooth hand flipped a card at the agent. Mackay took it, but deliberately didn't offer one of his own. This was strictly a one-off job. Business was business, but he sensed that every time with Liebermann would be like this; either trouble in the making, or else he'd have to have someone hold his hand. But with the card taken from him, Liebermann still didn't move his hand away.

'You don't have a card?' he asked.

'Details'll be on the invoice,' countered Mackay.

The New Yorker beamed, but the hand still wouldn't go away.

'That's for company records,' he pointed out. 'This is for future personal contact. Right?' Mackay must've looked surprised; Liebermann hurried to explain. 'You were lucky for me today. I rate that.'

'It was strictly business,' grunted Mackay.

'I'm superstitious.' That Honest Joe smile again. 'It felt right . . . right?'

'If you say so, Mr Liebermann.'

'Larry,' insisted the American. The hand insisted, too. Mackay surrendered. He took out a Goldhawk card and passed it over. Liebermann studied it, full of boyish delight.

'That's great,' he said. 'We're surely going to do business here again!'

Mackay hoped not. The last thing he wanted was a dodgy courier who had ideas of using him as a rabbit's foot good luck charm.

Lomas had a pretty fair idea of the general Heathrow scene, but air freighting was a blind spot. It was a bit like sending stuff by British Rail; you dispatched it and, with luck, it got there. But how the process actually worked was a complete mystery. Nik showed him the company van that Gary used to drive. Just by the way Lomas looked it over you could tell he wasn't just a driver. He knew what motors were about, which was handy; these wheels had to take quite a beating, the miles they covered in a year.

'We deliver and pick up goods,' said Nik, keeping it simple. 'Packing, too – it saves time and aggro. Has to be specially done by the packing service inside the cargo complex, otherwise.'

Lomas nodded across at the big airline freight sheds, farther along. 'The airline cargo people?'

'We use them, but we have to stay landside,' said Nik. 'Airside gets complicated.' He gave Lomas a sideways glance. 'Security, you know?'

'So what does a bloke like Mackay actually *do*?'

'Mike, you mean,' Nik corrected him. 'We book space with the various airlines. They tell us about delivery deadlines, and we prepare the airway bills. If the customer hasn't made out a pro forma invoice stating value and contents, we do that, too.'

'Where do I come into it?'

Nik indicated the closed doors of the Goldhawk warehouse just behind them. 'We pack the goods and label them. You deliver to the airline warehouse. They do the rest.'

'Landside that is, is it?'

'Right. Each warehouse has two doors – import and export.' He grinned cheekily. 'Know the difference?'

'I'll look it up in the dictionary,' answered Lomas, his mouth showing a hint of amusement. Nik relaxed a little more. Maybe Mike was right about this guy after all.

'Once the shift leader at the airline warehouse has signed for the goods, that's practically it. Just a bit more documentation – post flight certificates to prove the goods have left, that sort of thing. No skin off your nose, though. You'd've done your bit by then.'

'Incoming goods, that's the other way about, is it?'

'More or less,' Nik nodded. 'Only we have to wait for Customs clearance before we can collect.'

'Sounds pretty straightforward . . .'

'You'll learn. And there's three of us to keep you right: me, Mike, and John Swinford.'

'Swinford –?'

'He's the manager. He's off sick today . . .' He gave Lomas a knowing look, and shook his fingers as though they'd been burned by something hot. 'A loner, y'know? Takes his kicks when he can.'

'Not a Saturday night regular, then?' said Lomas, straight-faced, and Nik laughed.

'You've got a delivery to make,' he said. 'Reels of movie film.' He hauled the metal door open wide enough for them to slip inside. 'Come on – I'll show you.'

Inside the cool warehouse, he brought Lomas over to where the pile of metal canisters were stacked, and looking at them, his face brightened. He picked up the topmost can and pointed to the title: *Cyprus Sherry – young wine, a trick or two.* He beamed at Lomas. 'A travel movie – that's where I come from, right?'

Lomas watched as Nik took the reel of film across to a darker corner of the warehouse. He removed a grey plastic cover from off a board with a 35 mm movie viewer set between two reel winders.

'Our very own Do-It-Yourself moviola,' he boasted, and began to thread the film lead into the machine and on to the empty reel on the right hand winder. 'We've had unmarked films sent through before now,' he explained. 'This helps.'

'We deliver movies, too?'

'These are commercial prints. Finished movies, ready for showing – business documentaries, usually, like this one. Adverts, that sort of thing, right?'

He switched on the low-powered bulb behind the viewing screen, and the felt-tip-marked leader code showed up, out of focus. He adjusted it, casually.

'We handle some of the big boys too, sure. Rushes – exposed negatives, the day's shooting, you know – stuff shot on location. That stuff can't be opened except in a laboratory.'

'So the Customs blokes daren't look at what's inside the cans?'

'They're not that dumb, mate. It's only random checks, but they seal the cans and sometimes put a bloke into the lab to supervise opening up and developing. Not often, though.' He looked back at Lomas, and grinned. 'Hey, what about this then, eh?'

The titles showed up and held for several seconds. Behind the plain lettering, a sunny landscape, filled with vineyards. It looked more like home movies than the real thing, Lomas reckoned; picture postcard, 'wish you were here' kind of crap. Then he blinked. The next scene was a bedroom. Cyprus Sherry? Cherie was there all right, and perhaps her landscape also came from Cyprus, but she wasn't interested in bottling up the fruits on *her* vine. Her ripe smile never faltered, as with eyes fixed boldly on the camera, she strutted in various stages of undress around the bed, focal point of the room and soon to become her personal wine press. Enter the virile harvester. To Cherie's obvious satisfaction, his immediate greeting was to test the ripeness and flavour of her grapes with his mouth. Just as the camera moved in for a shaky close-up, the image blurred, flickered, and finally froze in mid-frame. Nik, laughing in helpless disbelief, had stopped turning the winding handle. Lomas's face was like cold stone.

'It's bloody porn,' he said.

'Cyprus Cherie!' spluttered Nik. 'It's the Greek version of Eskimo Nell!' He started to wind on, still chuckling. 'Do you reckon he'll tread her grapes for her, Roy?'

'What's so funny?' demanded Lomas. 'Is that filth what you call good business?'

Again the tiny image ground to a mid-frame halt, with Cherie about to try a spot of harvesting herself. Nik had stopped laughing.

'It's a blue movie. We found it by accident, remember?'

'Yeah?' sneered Lomas. 'Regular shipment, is it?'

'How do I know?' Nik protested. 'We don't vet the goods –'

'Maybe you should.'

'Who do you think you bloody are – Snoop Squad?'

'So you're going to let it through?'

'Yes, Roy,' said Mackay from the doorway to the delivery

office, 'and that's *my* decision, not Nik's.' Tight-faced, he came over to the movie viewer. The frame still showing there said it all.

'Sorry, Mike,' apologised Nik. 'The can said Cyprus Sherry –'

'Feeling homesick?'

'Not for that,' denied Nik, indicating the moustached mouth poised over the thrusting nipple, all in miniature.

'You probably get more on the side than the rest of us put together, you randy sod,' grinned Mackay, and Nik didn't even trouble to deny it. Mackay looked at Lomas, and his eyes grew stern.

'This is the one with problems.'

'If I want that, I know where to find it,' muttered Lomas. 'What I don't like is playing greengrocer to some Soho porn merchant!'

'We'll make sure they collect this lot themselves,' said Mackay.

'You're going to let them make off with it? I thought this bloody firm of yours was straight!'

'Roy, I'm an agent,' said Mackay with quiet patience, 'not a judge and jury. That's a Customs job. They've passed this, without looking. They can't view everything. This one got through without anyone knowing – until Nik stumbled on to it. Be fair, eh?'

'Meantime, these pigs get away with it.'

'This one, yes. I've got no option, that's the contract.'

'A neat cop-out,' sneered Lomas. 'Blow you, Jack –'

'Don't worry. We won't be handling any more of their stuff. Not after this. And that's not to get *me* off the hook, mate.' He stared at Lomas, and the ex-copper knew that what he said was true. 'I don't need to handle dirty goods. It doesn't pay me any extra. It doesn't give me any kicks. And I don't enjoy being conned, either . . .'

Lomas nodded; glancing at Nik, he grinned, sheepishly.

'I got steamed up a bit,' he muttered. 'Sorry.'

Nik shrugged, and flashed those perfect teeth as a token of peace and goodwill. 'Tell you what, Roy,' he said. 'I'll rewind and run it backwards. Maybe that'll bring your temperature back to normal, eh?'

He started the flickering images into reverse action, and they all three gathered around the tiny screen to watch. Within seconds, they were almost doubled up, weak with laughter. Cherie retreated open-mouthed from her virile harvester, who was then hurled back from her grape-tipped bosom as though struck by a thunderbolt. Without breath to pause, he retreated like a clockwork toy, drooping violently as he disappeared. Magnetically, Cherie's skimpy clothing returned to her gaily cavorting flesh, until at last even her soft, unpouting lips retreated to that innocent first frame in the bedroom. Meanwhile, in Cyprus all was peace amongst the vineyards once again, and the three men wiped their laughter-wet eyes.

'Why don't they show all blue movies that way round?' spluttered Lomas. 'It'd be an education!'

Queenie was a landmark at the Diplomat Club, in much the same way as a bowsprit would be on one of Nelson's warships, all bulge and thrust. Somewhere over forty years, handsome, coarse, and painted, she was the club character. She knew the truth about the kitchen, about the clients, and most of all, about the money that rolled in, Gaming Act or not. Always ready with a rowdy greeting for the regulars, she had an eye and a memory that Sherlock Holmes would have envied. Strangers or gate-crashers didn't stand a chance. A wink from Queenie, and you were in; a jerk of that tinted hair, and you were bounced. Her throne-room was the cashier's cubby-hole that dominated the foyer entrance and the stairs leading to the upstairs gaming rooms. From here, Queenie ruled the club. Out of hours, it was her office, where she totted up the 'drop' – and most important of all, their current credit status.
the cash exchanged for chips – plus the clients' winnings, losses,

Queenie's blacklist was a short one, and nobody chose to stay on it for long. Keeping it that way was Queenie's pride and joy, and the weekly day of reckoning was Monday, the one day the club was closed. This week, her league table had showed a new geezer slipping into the danger zone. Checking him out, her card-index mind had come up with a wrinkle that Queenie hurried to share with Jack himself.

'Queenie . . . darling,' Fenn crooned in mock effection, 'why bother *me* about it? Sort it out yourself like you always do – OK?'

He didn't need to tell her the system. With the limit getting close, a short word of warning went out. Ninety-nine times out of a hundred, that was all that was necessary. For the big fish who ignored the bell a different sort of judgement had to be made: a forfeit demanded, no arguments. Payment in kind, a favour in lieu, and not always legal; sometimes a touch of pressure or privilege was expected, to turn a dishonest trick or swing a tender in the right direction. Only for the real all-time loser was the boot put in.

'You'll like this one, Jack,' said Queenie. Her painted lips glistened over pearly teeth. Fenn was interested now. Queenie had a real flair for spotting useful talent.

'What's so special?'

'A bloke who works in air freight at Heathrow,' she grinned. 'Interested?'

Joan opened the front door and straight away Mackay knew the house was too quiet.

'The kids are at their nan's,' she said, and stepped aside to let him in. His common sense ordered him to stay outside, play it cool, but too late; his feet had already taken him into the hallway, and Joan smiled at him as she closed the door. Her lips were still smiling as his mouth met hers; she tongued him, and the little shock of pleasure quickened the familiar reflex in his groin. His hands slipped downward from the small of her back, clenching the looseness of her buttocks, riding up her skirt and pulling her grindingly closer to him.

He had decided to play it her way, if that's how it went. Now, by putting the kids neatly out of sight and mind, she had given him the come-on that he wanted. Last time, she had used him; this time was going to be different. She'd wanted it to be like strangers, well, so did he, only this time he'd be the one to do the taking. His mouth and hands and body mauled her, and she pulled away, laughing breathlessly.

'We've only got an hour,' she said, and drew him after her, upstairs.

For almost the whole journey to the house, Mackay had planned, imagined and mentally rehearsed. Starters, positions, holding back, coming on; Joan as the plaything, Mackay as general, and the bed, her Waterloo. The minute he followed her into the bedroom, he knew he'd already lost. She'd been expecting him and what he'd try, all along. The curtains were drawn, the alarm set, and with a bright-eyed scurry she was undressed and waiting, naked and impatient between the sheets. Gone was the carefully planned romantic orgy, the ritual of disrobing, the eventual surrender to his urgent but controlled desire.

'Come on,' Joan said, her soft white body sprawled loose-limbed and inviting. 'Don't you want it?'

Fifty minutes later, the alarm rang. Half-asleep, Mackay reached out and turned it off. Joan was already out of bed and getting dressed. Fastening her bra, she smiled at him; her voice was a bold purr, like a cat who'd had the cream.

'I enjoyed that,' she said, stepping briskly into her dress and zipping it up. 'Didn't you?'

She knew damned well he had, so what was the point of answering. She'd met his determination with her own; he'd had his pleasure, she'd had hers, demanded more, and got it. The tumescent ache was satisfied, but lying there limp and naked beneath the crumpled sheets, Mackay felt drained and empty, body and soul. They had performed like sexual robots, turning each other on with pre-selected, programmed signals, touch-tuned by past experience. Each erogenous zone had received its share of stimulation, climaxes had been signalled and enjoyed, however separately, and not once, not until Joan's last patronising compliment, had they said a single meaningful word. He couldn't be sure if she'd called him even once by name. It really hadn't mattered.

Arm under his head, Mackay stared at the woman sitting at

the dressing-table mirror. She'd finished her make-up, and was now hurriedly brushing out her hair. Yes, he thought, she is a stranger. They'd enjoyed each other, without even the habitual cup of tea. She turned to him, crisp and neat and homely, her sensuality folded up and tucked away as neatly as the tiny hankie inside her sleeve.

'You haven't got much time,' she said, and moved to the door, picking up her handbag as she went and checking that her car keys were inside. 'I'm going to collect the kids and bring them home, now.' She paused on the landing outside, framed briefly in the doorway. 'Help yourself to tea and things,' she said, eyes laughing like a naughty child. 'You've earned it.'

She clattered lightly down the stairs. Mackay hadn't moved or answered, he felt thick with despair.

'Bye!' she called automatically, from the hallway down below; the door slammed, and she was gone, leaving only the ticking of the brass double-bell alarm clock to remind Mackay she'd ever been there in his arms. He sat up, and snatching the clock, gripped it in both hands, staring at it until the rage inside him blurred the Roman numerals on its face. Then he hurled it with all his force at the dressing-table mirror which minutes ago had held her primping image. Even as he threw it, he knew his shot had missed. He was right.

'My shout,' said Lomas, 'and no arguments, OK?'

'Just because you're earning real money now,' grinned Dalton. 'I'll have a swift half.'

'Busy?' asked Lomas, after giving his order to the barman. Dalton shrugged.

'Busy's like being on holiday, mate. We're rushed off our bloody feet.'

'Ten jobs at once . . . I know.'

'And half of them still up in the air. But what can you do, eh?'

'Anything heavy?'

'One job nearly was.'

'Nearly?'

'The Air France do.' Lomas looked blank. 'You must know. Last weekend. You'd've laughed, honest. The villains went home without a sausage.'

'That a fact?'

'Don't you read the newspapers, my son?' asked Dalton wearily.

'Only when I take home fish and chips,' countered Lomas.

The beers arrived, money was paid, and they drank up, thirstily. 'So you missed out on copping a bullion gang, eh?'

'It's still hanging about. Routine inquiries, you know.'

Lomas frowned, intrigued by this. 'Why's that? No crime, you said.'

'Breaking and entering. GBH. Two of the security staff got done.'

'Rough mob, must be.'

'That's what the guv'nor reckons.'

'Who've you got now?'

'Alex Tindall.' Dalton looked smug, and Lomas could understand why. He'd heard of Tindall's reputation even in Uniformed Branch. A right bulldog, that one.

'Doesn't let go, does he?'

Dalton grinned, swaggering in his guv'nor's reflected glory. 'You've heard about him, have you?'

'What's he like to work with?'

'Bloody marvellous. He can be a proper bastard, mind.'

'You don't surprise me,' chuckled Lomas. 'Rough luck.'

'Belt up, civilian,' Dalton laughed, aiming a mock punch at Lomas's shoulder. 'Just because you think you've made it off the dole!'

'Can't grumble.'

'Air freight outfit, did y'say?'

'South side, near where the big cargo sheds are.'

'What's their monicker?'

'Goldhawk.'

Dalton took a step back in overblown amazement, and laughed out loud. 'Good grief! You're kidding . . .'

'Know them, do you?'

'The boss man's a bloke by the name of Mackay?'

'Yeah. What about it?'

'Witness in a kneecap job, wasn't he? Him and his manager. What a bloody strange coincidence!'

'Small world,' said Lomas, shaking his head, before drinking. 'You had me worried for the minute.'

'You're all right there, son,' Dalton reassured him. 'They're clean.'

'I got that feeling, yeah.'

'Plenty aren't,' muttered Dalton into his glass.

'Too many,' agreed Lomas.

'Especially on the cargo side. That's where the real loot is, eh?'

'I suppose,' mused the Goldhawk driver, non-committally. 'We don't handle all that much in the way of valuables, mind.'

'But you get around a bit. Delivering and collecting, and that.'

'That's what the job's all about, yeah.'

'So you hear things.' Dalton's eyes were shrewd, and his voice had suddenly become softer, as though wary of being overheard. A flash of resentment went through Lomas.

'You what?' he demanded bluntly.

'You know what I mean,' Dalton persisted, not noticing the warning signs. 'Look, listen, evaluate –'

'And report?' rapped Lomas angrily. 'You can screw that, mate!'

'There's nothing to it, Roy,' he said. 'You know the score –' He looked surprised as Lomas turned on him, voice low and fierce.

'I am out of it, Jimmy! Remember? I'm not a flaming Jack any more!'

'I know.' Dalton tried to be diplomatic. 'That's the great advantage – can't you see?'

'You want me to be your bloody snout?'

'No!' disclaimed Dalton, trying to avoid the bother. 'Intelligence. Inside gen. On the side.'

'Acting unpaid bigmouth,' Lomas said, sarcastically. 'Or will I get the odd pint now and then, for services rendered?'

'Personal, Roy,' Dalton hastened to reassure him. 'A favour between pals.'

'You rotten toe-rag!' Lomas drained his glass and slammed it down. 'And I thought we were mates!' He started to go; Dalton put a hand on his arm to hold him back, but Lomas pulled free, roughly.

'What did I say?'

'If you want a sodding snout, pick one out of the bloody gutter. It isn't going to be *me*!' His face tight with rage, Lomas shouldered his way out of the crowded pub, leaving Dalton open-mouthed, the beer half-finished in his hand.

Sammy came up from the club, but not before he'd made sure that Fenn was on his own. Afternoons, Jack liked to reserve his time for dictation, behind closed doors. When there were no letters to be written, the same nimble, secretarial fingers would take on the duties of masseuse and physiotherapist.

Depending on the boss's mood, these inducements to his physical well-being could go on for an hour or more, during which time the business in hand took total priority, and everyone else kept their nose out. Today, Sammy saw, from the pleasure-bright eyes and bouncy strut of the departing girl, that the shorthand session had been a rousing success. He winked, and got a lip-licking, toothy smile in return; Sammy knew that Jack would be feeling on top of the world. It pleased Sammy that the Berghoff reputation for picking the cream of the talent was a valued asset – even if he couldn't take advantage for himself.

He forced himself not to watch those buttock-clenching hips swing out of view. He tried very hard not to cheat on his old lady. She was more than most blokes could handle, in or out of bed, and he never risked her temper more than he could help.

He paused outside the penthouse door, giving Jack another minute to slip on his post-therapy kimono, black silk with gold dragons and red flames. He knocked and entered at Fenn's crisp call. Inside, the guv'nor was about to take a draught of his favourite pick-me-up, raw egg in brandy. He'd read about it once in a magazine article by Barbara Cartland, and swore that it gave better results than oysters and ginseng put together.

'A snake, Sammy. A real wriggler. Bloody gorgeous.' He laughed, pleased with his own performance. 'Give yourself a treat there, mate.' His watery eyes twinkled. 'I won't split on you...'

Enjoying the compliment, Sammy gave Fenn the news that Queenie insisted he ought to know. Their pigeon had arrived and he was spending.

'Real money?'

'Changed a couple of ponies, she said.'

'Doesn't want to use up his credit,' brooded Fenn. 'He's getting nervous. That's good.'

'Queenie reckons somebody's subbing him. Not a cash merchant, usually.'

'So he's got friends,' Fenn shrugged. 'He'll still go down.'

'Born loser, Jack.'

'You reckon?'

Berghoff nodded, and looked smug. 'Found out about him, didn't I? He's nervous all right.'

'He owes us nearly two grand, that's why.'

'Better than that, Jack.' Berghoff paused, enjoying the chance of a punchline for a change. 'He was one of the two blokes who found Gus Fulmer the other night. It's put the fear of God in him.'

'That figures.' Fenn nodded, pleased. 'Did Queenie dig up details about what he does, all that guff?'

'Freighting manager – firm called Goldhawk. A few doors down from where Gus Fulmer worked.'

'Skiving lot of fat-assed bastards,' sneered Fenn. 'I wouldn't trust any of 'em.'

'This one's got no tickle, Jack. Even Customs say so.'

'Makes a change.' The comment was dry, but Fenn was sitting forward now, sharp-eyed and interested.

'Make a great cover,' Berghoff commented.

'Depends on our pigeon, don't it? What's his name again?'

'Swinford.'

'Can he be pushed?'

'Worth working on. If he saw the state Gus was in, he'd know what it's about.'

'What's he like at the tables?' This was one of Fenn's favourite yardsticks; you could tell a bloke's nerve or a dolly's taste by the way they played, and Sammy knew just what to look for, all the little signs.

'He plays like he thinks he's got a system.'

Fenn gave a half-smile and shook his head. The stupid bastards never learned. 'Sucker him in a bit deeper, Sammy.' Berghoff chuckled.

'He could do with a bit of cheering up, yeah.'

'The old hot and cold shuffle, eh?' They'd let Swinford find his luck; he'd win some, get cocky, and then they'd have him cold.

'Give him a bit of a lift,' acknowledged Sammy, with a knowing nod.

'Then pull the rug away, Sammy,' murmured Fenn. 'But nicely, eh?'

The Diplomat Club was a huge Edwardian house that had once stood in three acres of lawns and ornamental gardens. Now the flowerbeds and grass were for the most part buried three inches underneath the dull grey tarmac of the club car park, and most of the old stables and outbuildings had been converted into garages and workshops. There was a barbecue terrace and a token swimming pool, bar and all.

But it was inside the house that Fenn had been most lavish. The club was a legitimate, above-board enterprise; nothing like the seedy, backstreet dumps with boarded-up windows that Fenn had left behind him. This place was for the posh, the la-di-dah. It wasn't like up West, but it had class. Thrusting out from the heavy stone portico was a boldly striped plastic awning, designed to protect the ladies as they alighted from their Rollses and Jags. The foyer plasterwork was painted in shades of eau de nil; the floor was oak parquet with a deep wine carpet; all the doors were mahogany with gleaming brass locks and handles. Drama was important, Fenn reckoned; so the bar was predominantly red, the gaming rooms predominantly black, and the small, expensive restaurant so dimly lit that speculation as to its actual colour scheme was impossible.

Although many touches came perilously close to 'mock-casino' style, Fenn had cleverly allowed the sturdy air of Edwardian costly elegance to remain. The leather was real, not vinyl; the panelling was oak, solid, not veneer; the total effect was genuine, money-class respectability.

Swinford stepped back from the roulette table and immediately his place was filled. He stood for a moment uncertain what to do or where to go. An hour before, that fifty from Mackay had been on the verge of sinking without trace; then, on one card, it had all changed. The good times had come back at last; every play he made came up a winner. The fifty had been retaken, turned into a hundred, three, then *five*! Aware that he couldn't lose, Swinford moved to the wheel and started putting down a hundred at a time. Four calls later, each one on red, and he was over half way to clearing the two grand marked against him, with some of the regulars beginning to study his play. He felt good, then made his big mistake; he took a breather. Minutes later he watched in misery as his last hundred slid away across the table, raked into anonymity by the pretty, blank-eyed girl croupier.

A drink was offered to him, and he took it; faces and players filtered by, but he didn't see them. A laughing girl, not looking, bumped against him, spilling his drink and he was left to mopping up his shirt and jacket. He moved away to a quieter corner. There was still some drink left in the glass and he drained it; putting the glass down, he realised his hand was shaking and he plunged it deep into his jacket pocket, for sanctuary. If only *he* could hide that easily.

He began to stockpile all the things he'd done wrong that evening; the superstitions and omens he'd ignored, the bets he'd backed away from, the colours he'd stayed with too long, the sheer disaster of that last stupid plunge on a losing streak. Then he remembered. This had all happened with Mike's fifty. It had come, it had gone; but he wasn't sunk completely yet. He still had credit here, hadn't he? So – use it! He bustled his way over to Queenie's money cage, and put on a bold face.

'Fifty against the account please, love,' he asked. Her lurid mouth smiled politely, and her glossy eyelids drooped as she checked her tally sheet, set discreetly out of sight by her sturdy knees.

'Mr Swinford, isn't it?'

'That's the one.' He watched her anxiously. The eyes flicked up at him. The smile was still there, but there was a warning in the flatness of her voice.

'Twenty-five is all I can let you have tonight, Mr S . . .' She saw his disappointment, and gave him a slow, reassuring wink, flashing a bold silver streak of eyeshadow at him. 'Why don't you make it cash, save a lot of bother, that would?'

'Got none on me,' he mumbled. 'I'll take the twenty-five.'

'Up to you, duck,' said Queenie, and laid out five fives in a neat row before him. He moved off, eager to get to the tables again. Queenie didn't bother to watch him go; her cold eyes looked across to where Sammy Berghoff stood and, catching his attention, she beckoned him.

'Swinford's down to his last pony,' Queenie said. 'It'll finish him, this round.'

By the time Berghoff reached the table where he was playing, it was over; every last cent had gone. Swinford turned away. There was nothing more he could do, except go home and wait. He wasn't going to be given that long to square his losses, however; retribution was waiting for him just two steps from the table, in the shape of Sammy Berghoff.

'Mr Fenn fancies a word with you,' he said. 'Upstairs. Now.'

'Sammy,' said Fenn, 'fetch our friend here a drink.' He turned to Swinford, who was sitting in the chair once occupied by poor Gus Fulmer. It was probably just as well he didn't know. 'Brandy suit you, squire?' Fenn was all teeth and icy charm. He didn't wait an answer, but flicked the echo of his request across the room to where Sammy stood at the mirror-panelled drinks cabinet.

As they waited for the drink, Fenn pushed the large cigarette-box towards his guest, who shook his head in nervous refusal. It was easier than words.

'Very wise,' observed Fenn, taking one for himself. 'They kill you in the end.' Fenn lit the cigarette and smiled like a friendly shark. 'Drink up, Mr Swinford,' he said. 'It'll help settle your nerves. And don't panic,' he added with quiet concern. 'You're among friends.'

'I know my account's way over the top –' Swinford said, but stumbled into silence as Fenn cut him short with a gesture of the cigarette.

'Not kosher, is it, squire?'

'I need time, that's all . . .' He tried to sound businesslike and calm, but the liquid glowing in his glass shimmered with the trembling of his hand. 'Just a few days –'

'Time . . .' echoed Fenn, letting a drift of cigarette smoke seep between his narrowed lips.

'The old, old story,' said Berghoff. He was just behind the boss's chair, his presence a threat.

'It's not much to ask . . .'

'Time is money, squire – and yours has just run out.'

'Hold on, Jack,' said Berghoff, his big hand resting protectively on the back of Swinford's chair. 'He may have the two grand on him.' Swinford looked up at the quarry-faced hulk standing over him, and Sammy grinned down at him playfully. 'Go on,' the big man joked, 'tell the guv'nor you're having us on . . .'

'I can get it,' Swinford pleaded. 'Somehow.'

'I've heard that pigs can fly,' said Fenn, 'but I don't believe that, either.'

'At least let me try!'

'Not on, squire.'

Swinford gulped at the brandy and they watched him cough as the spirit seared his throat. Fenn waited patiently before laying out the sad, cold facts.

'Our little arrangement,' he said, 'is a contract between friends. A matter of good faith, right?'

'Bad debts are bad business,' grunted Berghoff.

'It's a responsibility that I don't always enjoy. I'm a fair-minded sort of geezer, but people take advantage.' He paused to blow out a slow stream of hazy smoke. 'They never learn,' he said, and stubbed the barely used shaft of tobacco as though it, too, had crossed him. The gesture said it all.

'I'll pay –' insisted Swinford, unnerved by the quiet chill in Fenn's voice. 'I promised I would!'

'Sure you will, squire. But how am I going to put a stop to any other mugs getting ideas about making a monkey out of good old Jack Fenn?' He stared hard at Swinford's clammy face. 'Tell me that, squire.'

'I don't know.'

Fenn was ready to oblige with a simple explanation. 'By making an example, of course,' he said cruelly. 'It'll mean you getting hurt a bit, but it'll buy the time you need.

'You were in the papers the other day, squire, weren't you?'

The nightmare was getting closer, and Swinford drained the glass of brandy. He tried to say 'It wasn't anything' but his mouth was on fire. 'Gus Fulmer thought different.'

Swinford waited; it was the only thing left to do. This was the dead end he had always dreaded. Now it was here, in the same room, he felt strangely numb. A small murmur of defence crept from his mind, instinctively.

'Why me, if you've already duffed *him* up?'

'Did Sammy say it was anything to do with us?' Fenn spread his hands wide in a gesture of injured innocence. 'Violence like that? Wicked!'

'Needs to be done, though,' insisted Sammy. 'Put it down to experience, eh?'

'You're younger than Gus,' said Fenn. 'In pretty good health, too, I reckon, don't you, Sammy?'

Berghoff looked him over carefully before replying. 'He should heal all right. Delilah's a pro, no messing.'

Swinford shuddered inside. Fenn noticed, and was slyly sympathetic. 'It's no worse than going to the dentist, squire,' he smiled. 'Over in no time . . .'

Swinford's fear gave out one short squirt of pale bravado. 'Can't I have an anaesthetic?' he joked. It was all he could do to stop the shaking in his legs, and it wasn't laughter. Fenn grinned, though.

'Another brandy, Sammy – a double.' He lit another cigarette, staring into Swinford's tensed face. 'He's got guts, this one.'

'He'll need to have when he starts to learn to walk again.'

Berghoff's jibe was the last straw. A sudden surge of memory brought back Fulmer's choking cry of agony, the scarred face, those blood-sodden, broken legs . . .

'For Christ's sake,' whispered Swinford, and he began to sob, harsh, dry gulps of despair.

'I thought you were going to be brave, squire,' mocked Fenn. Swinford could only shake his head in a wordless, choked denial. He huddled tighter into himself, rocking in a parody of childish grief.

'Pathetic,' said Berghoff.

'Shame,' smiled Fenn. They watched and waited as Swinford's face crumpled and contorted into blubbering tears. Words finally came, pitiful and staccato.

'I can't . . . stand . . . pain!' he gasped. 'For God's sake . . . give me . . . a chance!' There was no reply. 'I'll do *anything*!' The last phrase was almost a scream. He peered at Fenn, and saw him look at Berghoff, thoughtfully. The fingers that held the smoking cigarette rubbed gently against his dark, shaven chin.

'What d'you reckon, Sammy?'

'Dunno, Jack. Maybe.'

'Payment in kind?' Fenn's chilling, watery stare switched to the huddled figure in the chair. 'But no rubbish. It's up to you, squire.'

Uncoiling himself, Swinford leaned forward with hands tightly clasped between his knees, as dignified and eager as a labrador taking an obedience test.

'What do you want me to do?'

Her hair was pale straw, with ash-blonde streaks, framing a face barely coloured by her make-up. Big, suspicious grey eyes.

A small nose, almost snub. A girlish, unfashionable mouth; the long upper lip jutted, bow-shaped and sullen, over its smaller, rosebud underpart. The tip of a pink tongue slipped out and hurriedly moistened the nervous lips. Mackay found himself wanting to see that sad mouth smile. The clouded eyes stared at him, defensively, and he wondered if she'd ever laughed aloud in all her life.

'Angela Collins,' he said, checking the fact against the details laid out before him on the desk. She was the third applicant already he'd interviewed that morning. Mackay wasn't interested in passing trade. He needed someone who'd be permanent enough to make training them worthwhile; the difficulty was getting someone good who shared the same long-term idea. This girl looked as if she'd been running all her life.

'Married?' he asked casually, and she nodded; but there was just a tiny moment's hesitation before she spoke.

'That's right.'

'It's a full-time job. Normal office hours,' Mackay said pointedly.

'No problem,' the girl said, reading his mind. 'I – we haven't got any kids. No ties like that.' Her voice was clear but muted, low-pitched but not from trying to sound 'come-on', more as though she was used to being shouted down. Flat, resigned and sad.

'Long at your last job?'

'Until the firm went bust. Two years, about.'

'What sort of machine?' This would tell him how skilled she was; with any luck she'd be used to an electric.

'Olympia SGE 50,' she told him, flatly. 'An Adler before that.'

He nodded, satisfied. He'd been right.

'You'll be doing more than just letters. Know anything about invoice pro formas?'

'I can learn,' she said.

He glanced at her sharply, drawn by the challenge in her voice. The grey eyes stared back, daring him to call her a liar. He tried to nudge her out of her iron-clad wariness; she'd have to show up brighter than this; a wet blanket amongst the lads in the outer office would be a disaster.

'What did your last boss think about your coffee?'

He'd taken her by surprise, and for a moment she was flustered, uncertain whether to answer him in kind.

'He never sent it back, if that's what you mean.' The corners of her mouth dimpled, then grew serious again.

'As long as its hot and sweet and strong,' smiled Mackay. The grey eyes cleared, and he could've sworn she was holding back a smile.

'That's what the girls in the office used to say.'

Mackay blinked, then caught himself wondering if it was only *his* mind which had seen the innuendo, or whether it was meant to be shared. But she sat prim and straight, waiting for his next daft question, her crisp, unbuttoned raincoat telling him nothing about her figure. He tried not to make his glance obvious, but guessed that her shape and walk would match her muted face. What was the key that would make her come to life?

He glanced at the references she'd handed him, then looked back at the girl, and the clouded eyes seemed to grow darker still. Carefully, he laid out each brief but complimentary testimonial, side by side. No raves, but they all reckoned her to be good at her job, honest, trustworthy and responsible. The trouble was, she'd used the identical typewriter for all three references. He pointed to each sheet in turn, each one with a different business heading, each with a different date.

'Same machine,' he said.

She flushed, and as her dull eyes grew bright with anger, Mackay felt a snag of disappointment. She was alive all right, beneath that hard-done-by mask of bitterness she wore; unfortunately, she was also bent. At least Freda had never been that clumsy.

She stood up, snatched the papers back from him, and stuffed them angrily into her handbag.

'All right, clever dick,' she snapped. 'You've caught me out, isn't that great?'

'I wasn't meaning to,' he said, trying to be gentle, 'but why try to con me?'

'Because my bloke's inside the nick with another seven to go,' she said. 'D'you think anybody's going to give me a job with *that* sort of reference? Like hell they will!'

'Your family history's got nothing to do with it –'

She cut him short, thumping the handbag on the desk top, hard. 'No? Wife of a villain, doing time? Think you can trust me?'

Mackay stared at her, fascinated by her mouth, its new liveliness, its almost sensual mobility. Luckily, she couldn't read his mind, although for a brief second, he wondered.

'Like the rest, aren't you?' she sneered, and her mouth framed utter misery. 'Play it safe and sod giving the kid a bloody break!'

He said, 'You can have the job.'

She was half way to the door, but stopped in her tracks, head tilted, questioning and not believing what he'd said.

'Do what?'

'Your typing's OK, you're sharp enough to be able to stand up for yourself, and you look clean and healthy,' Mackay replied. 'I'm willing to give you a try.'

'Christ!' she exclaimed, and sat down again, very quickly. Her mouth dimpled and for the first time that afternoon, she really laughed. 'Honest?' Suddenly, she was all her name suggested, a happy angel.

'You'd better believe it,' grinned Mackay. 'And if I see you without that smile again, you're fired.'

Tindall didn't like hospitals. They weren't as bad as some open prisons he'd been to – prisons without bars, more like holiday camps without the redcoats – but every time he'd found himself pacing those echoing, disinfected corridors and wards, it had been at the expense of someone else's pain or misery. Mates, more often than not, injured in the line of duty; villains occasionally, for questioning; mercifully few relatives; and just one soul whose quiet anguish he'd learned to share because he'd known her body when it was young and smooth and perfect: Kathy, his wife. That was years ago, but every new visit brought back echoes of those months of waiting. Kathy had been twenty-four. By the time they'd finished filling her up with drugs and bombarding those fragile bones with radiation, she'd looked more than double that. The sight of that sallow skin and frail-limbed body had hurt Tindall less than missing her richly flowing hair, once so soft and fragrant, deep chestnut brown, a delight spread just for him upon her pillow. It had gone; that was what the treatment did, they told him. She'd cried over that more than all the pain; but once she knew that it had all been for nothing, she never cried again. Always her eyes shone for Tindall, even when her mind was tucked away beneath its daily blanket of anaesthesia; it was her love and only her love that had made that long death bearable. He never saw it fade or flicker; his last visit had brought him blundering into the ward just as the meat box was being deftly wheeled away, and it wasn't until he'd seen the empty bed that Tindall had realised.

Since then, nothing and no one had taken the place of work. Kathy was just another memory, like childhood, brought to life for a brief instant now and then by a scent, a sound, a familiarity of place or timing. Hospital was the dark side of that memory, but twenty years had made Tindall an expert in burying emotion.

Gus Fulmer was in a side ward, and the staff nurse had just finished taking his temperature and blood pressure.

'Won't be a minute,' she smiled as she added her markings to the chart at the foot of the bed. Tindall nodded, amiably.

'Morning, Gus.'

'I want her to stay,' croaked Gus, knobbly fingers endlessly working the hem of the bed sheet. 'She's my witness.'

'I'm not here to charge you, old son,' Tindall murmured reproachfully. 'Besides, you can see Staff's busy . . .'

'He always gets cross when people come and see him,' she said cheerfully.

'I'm not staying here alone with fuzz!' Gus protested feeblv. He might as well not have bothered.

'You look after him too well,' said Tindall, holding the door for the Staff to go out. She paused and glanced back at Gus, and her eyes were serious.

'Somebody needs to,' she said, then stepped outside into the corridor. 'Ring if you want anything – and don't be too long; he gets tired.' The door clicked shut, and Gus was even more alone.

Tindall moved up the side of the bed, and the old man drew away, scrunching himself deeper into the pillows. The weals down the side of his badly shaven face were beginning to heal, but still looked ugly. Pointedly, Tindall stared at them, and Fulmer turned the left side of his face against the pillow. The crisp, starched pillowcase thrust forward and hid half the ageing features; one solitary eye stared at Tindall with defiance.

'What you staring at? Leave off!'

'Five of diamonds.' Tindall shook his head. 'Nasty.'

'Dunno what you're on about.'

'Must've stung a bit.' No reply. 'But not as much bother as your poor old pins, eh, Gus?'

The old man's tongue flickered over dry lips, but his grimace remained, defiant and sour. 'It was an accident,' muttered the old, crooked mouth.

'Shame,' said Tindall, and sat on the bottom left-hand edge of the bed. Gus flinched as though expecting him to go for the weak spot, but Tindall was careful where he sat and placed his hands – for the time being, that was.

'Bloody lot you care,' mumbled Gus, still half afraid.

'Don't like to see old friends get hurt, do I?'

'Friends! Christ!'

'We all need friends, Gus,' said Tindall carefully. 'You especially, by the looks of it.' He stared at the shape of the legs beneath the blankets. 'Tell us who, old son,' he said, 'and let us put 'em away – eh?' Tindall gave a tired, kindly smile. 'Then we can all relax . . .'

'You must think I'm bloody stupid, Mr Tindall,' the old man whispered. His eyes closed tight, remembering. He looked frail and haggard without his precious spectacles; not that he really needed them, but their executive styling gave the old geezer a touch of bravado. 'Isn't having my knees done bad enough?'

'What did you hear, Gus?' demanded Tindall gently. 'What was so special, they had to mark you for it?' He had assumed all along that Fulmer's going-over was in some way connected with their earlier chat; for that much, he felt responsible. Now Fulmer's curt reply came as a surprise.

'Who said it's got anything to do with you?'

If Gus hadn't been caught with his ears flapping, then what *had* he got himself into? He stared at the old man, thoughtfully. Gus was saying nothing, but that one miserably staring eye gave the whole game away. He was scared sick. Somewhere deep inside Tindall's brain, a tiny bubble of intuition floated to the surface and popped. Air France. It had to be. Gus had seen something, heard something – a face, a name. That was why someone had bothered to shut him up, all right. And by the look of it, they'd succeeded. Tindall didn't rate his chances of persuading Gus to alter his mind, but it was worth a try.

'Protection guaranteed, old son,' he said confidently. 'Just give me a name. No one'll know.'

'*They'd* know,' whispered Gus. He turned away now, not bothering to hide his face. That mark was all the explanation needed, but Fulmer's fear went deeper than pain. The twitching, clutching fingers drew the sheet up higher, almost to his chin. 'They'll top me next time, Mr Tindall,' he said, then turned to look for sympathy and, seeing none, flared into anger. 'You wouldn't mind that, would you? Well, I'm not having any! Get stuffed!'

Tindall turned to find the Staff nurse in the open doorway. Her face was stern.

'He needs rest and quiet,' she said reproachfully. 'You'll have to go.' Tindall's stony face disturbed her with its cold authority, but she insisted. 'Please.'

Tindall didn't even trouble to look back. 'I won't bother him again,' he said, and left.

Mackay had been out all day and it was late afternoon, almost evening, before he made it back to the office. Swinford was there, and Angela. Everyone else had done their stint and packed off home. Mackay was still inside the warehouse when he heard Swinford's impatient voice; he smiled, realising that poor old John was having trouble getting through. He never did have much patience with women, business or pleasure.

'No, no, no!' he was saying, 'those figures go into *this* column, Angela!' A tired sigh. 'You must be blind!'

'Shouting won't help,' responded Angela's pert voice.

'Look – it isn't *that* difficult. Just concentrate, for Pete's sake.' John sounded his old self all right, Mackay decided. That day off had obviously done the trick. He made a small, deliberate noise to herald that he was about, then cheerfully came into view. They didn't notice him at first.

'I'm tired,' said Angela, then clammed up as she spotted Mackay.

'Don't expect to get it all in one day, love,' he said, then threw a quizzing glance at Swinford. Behind her back, the weary manager raised his eyebrows as if appealing to heaven for strength to carry on, but Mackay could tell it wasn't all that bad. Anyway, he was prepared to make allowances. Much as John knew about the business, he wasn't much cop as a teacher; luckily, Angela was a bright kid, she'd soon pick it up, regardless. Mackay mentally kicked himself for being a muggins. He'd had to hand her over to John because his own day had piled up with appointments and on-the-spot documentation. What he should've done was to share the workload better; John the paperwork, and Mackay the girl. Looking at Angela, sullen and withdrawn though she was, he'd sooner have her company than any of today's clients, awkward sods the lot of them.

'Can't seem to get the hang of it,' said Angela. 'Worse than one of my mum's knitting patterns, this is.'

'You'll do,' said Swinford grudgingly, 'but you'll probably drive me bonkers on the way.' He gave a tired grin and jerked his head at Angela, slumped in the chair beside him. 'At least she looks a damned sight prettier than Freda, eh?' he said, and stretching, gave a great yawn. Angela stared at him, uncertain if he was paying her a compliment or sending her up.

Mackay looked her over, taking in what he'd been missing. She wasn't elegant, or stringy, or poised; she had all the right curves, but her shape was muscular, almost sturdy. Strong, thought Mackay, and started wishing that her languid sprawl was for his benefit alone. She wore a simple button-up dress today, sleeveless, revealing bare arms up to where the first firm curve of shoulder slipped out of sight. Suddenly her glance shifted, and those cool grey eyes met his. She straightened, rubbing her arms as though she was chilled, defending her lightly tanned skin against the casual boldness of his eyes. Swinford hadn't noticed; he was too busy shrugging on his jacket, ready for the off.

'I don't know about you, Mike,' he yawned again, 'but I'm whacked. Coming for a jar?'

'You need to sign some letters first,' Angela chipped in firmly. 'I didn't type them for fun, y'know.'

Mackay grinned. One day and she was already getting him organised. 'Not tonight, John,' he answered. 'Need to finish off here, don't I?'

Swinford was already at the door and leaving; he obviously wasn't bothered.

'Just don't let her get stroppy with you, mate,' he grinned. 'Sharp as a razor, she is. Makes great coffee though. See you.' This last phrase was lost in the slam of the door. Within seconds, his footsteps had faded out of hearing. Angela stood, and picked up the file of letters to be signed.

'I just wanted you to know I'd done them,' she said. 'I've missed the post, anyway.'

'I know. My fault.' He was glad she'd stayed on.

'Coffee?'

'Something stronger for me,' he countered, taking the file and drifting into the office. She didn't follow him, but stood in the doorway. Nervous, he thought, and felt vaguely disappointed. Reckons I'll make a pass at her, I suppose. He turned casually and made a tippling gesture, grinning broadly. 'Fancy a nip of the hard stuff?'

She frowned, and his stomach sank again.

'Booze?'

'Scotch.'

Out of nowhere, that all-too-rare smile spread from the corners of her mouth, and Mackay found himself grinning back like an idiot. 'Terrific,' she said, 'but sign those letters first.'

He pointed to the drawer where the bottle was kept. 'Help yourself,' he said, 'and pour one for me, OK?' She quickly found the glasses and poured a stiff helping into each, while Mackay went briskly through the letters, nodding and signing as he finished reading each one. She watched him, anxiously, still holding the glasses.

'All right, are they?'

'Like John said, you'll do, love.' He smiled, not joking now. 'How're you finding it?'

'Not bad,' she said, and handed him his glass. 'This helps.' He frowned, and she looked embarrassed. 'I don't mean –' She stumbled over her words. 'I can take it or leave it, you know?' Mackay nodded. He knew; a bottle was never your friend, but it never answered back, either. 'It's being on your own,' she went on. 'You've got to have something . . .'

'Yeah,' he said. It was his turn to explain. 'This isn't how I get my kicks, y'know. It's for VIPs – special cases –'

'Like us,' said Angela. 'Cheers.'

'End of the day,' responded Mackay warily, and they drank. 'Purely medicinal.'

'Wish my GP'd prescribe it on the National Health,' Angela gave a small apologetic giggle, then stared into her glass. 'Valium's all he ever gives me, y'know that? I get depressed, see,' she explained.

'Smile and drink up,' Mackay replied, trying to push her off the edge of misery. 'Tomorrow's another day.' He drank again and so did she, her cool gaze watching him all the time.

'It's all right for you,' she said. 'You've got a wife and kids, haven't you?'

His silence bothered her. 'The others told me, when we were

chatting,' she said. 'I didn't pry.' She paused, then added meaningfully, 'I told them that my feller was on long-distance lorries. Got a giggle, that did.'

Mackay closed the file of letters, his face shadowed. Angela wondered if he objected to her lie, and put it to him, bluntly. 'I had to say something, didn't I?'

'We're not so very different,' said Mackay. She questioned him silently and he answered her, carefully. 'I don't live at home. Not any more.'

'Divorced?'

'Separated.'

'That's a daft way to live,' she said. 'Bloody lonely, too.'

'Sometimes.'

'Christ!' she murmured bitterly. 'Only sometimes! You lucky bastard...'

He watched her drain her glass; he wanted to explain everything, the hate, the hunger, the self-disgust, but how could she possibly understand? She caught him staring at her, and she smiled, sheepishly.

'I'm off,' she said, 'before I start telling you the story of *my* life.' Her eyes were too bright, close to tears perhaps?

'What about food?'

'Fish and chips.' That elusive smile haunted the corners of her mouth again. 'I'll manage.'

'No,' he said. 'With me.'

She stared at him, soft-eyed and serious, her hands slowly rising to enfold her crossed, bare arms. 'You don't have to,' she said. 'You've done enough already.'

'Do as you're told,' he grinned. 'Just remember who's stamping your cards, right?'

'You bloody fool,' she said and, moving round the desk, bent over him and kissed him on the mouth. Feeling for the desk top he set the unfinished whisky down, and he was trembling. Before he could reach for her, she'd slowly drawn her lips away. He almost moaned at the soft, reluctant parting, and as she started to speak, his hand found her arm and drew her to him, his mouth covering hers, fiercely. He didn't need to hold her close; she slipped on to his lap, her head bent, arms laced about his neck, meeting the movement of his lips with hers.

His hands slid downwards from her waist and she squirmed against him, the urgent movement rucking up her dress, baring her knees and thighs, inviting, commanding him to fondle her. They broke the kiss, both gasping, only to kiss again and again; the rest was a burning confusion of eager movement. His hand met hers, both unbuttoning the dress; the bare flesh beneath came to his mouth, as she wriggled from his lap, eager to uncover him, in turn; the chair couldn't hold the desperation of their bodies, and somehow, still clinging tightly, they found their way to the floor, breathless and laughing. At last their half-bare bodies met, in a feast of wanting and taking.

'It's been so long, Mike,' she gasped, her mouth pressed wet against his ear. 'Don't let me down, lover – please don't let me down . . . !'

'It's wrong, isn't it?' said Angela. Leaning on one elbow, her head on her hand, she looked down at Mackay with serious eyes. She was naked beneath the bedclothes and the swell of one breast came temptingly close to his mouth. He kissed her there, gently, but she didn't respond or move away; her body was comfortable and satisfied, at least for now. Mackay lay back and felt good, but Angela persisted. He had to smile; it was a change to have someone alongside him like this, who actually wanted to talk. He hadn't yet caught the drift of what she was on about, and murmured contentedly:

'What is?'

'Adultery.'

'Huh?' he grunted. The good vibrations slowly started to slip away. They'd enjoyed each other; was she going to spoil it all? Mackay thought briefly of Joan and her passion for technique, and now it left him cold. Love-making with Angela was completely natural; it just seemed to happen, there was no aggression, no competing about who was going to score. Why did she feel guilty?

'We're both married, love, remember?' He looked up at

her, hoping to see that smile, but her face was just as it was when she'd first stepped inside his office: sad, almost sullen. 'It's all my fault,' she whispered, and turned away, falling back on to the pillow, her arm across her face.

He moved to her, holding her tight; there was no sensuality in the embrace, but the attempt at comfort couldn't stop the little sobbing shudder that pulsed along her body. He went to kiss her, but she turned away, not from rejection, but plain misery. 'Bloody stupid, aren't I?' she whispered, then turned to him, wet-eyed. 'And you're so good to me, Mike . . .' She kissed him, gently, but stopped him when he wanted to go on. He tried to make it right with words, but she'd caught him off-balance. Whichever way he put it, they were lovers.

'We haven't hurt anyone, love,' he said.

'It's cheating.'

'For God's sake, it's not a crime to love somebody!'

'I wanted you to so much,' she said.

'It takes two,' Mackay retorted with a grin, and kissed her ear, hoping to tease her out of her mood. She moved her face away, and shook her head.

'It's no good, Mike.'

'It's very good.' He was trying to placate her, but she turned on him, eyes flaring angrily at the smooth-sounding compliment. 'The best . . .'

'Don't you bloody score me!' she snapped, then saw his expression of dismay and hugged him to her, burying her face against his naked shoulder. His hand went to the nape of her neck, stroking and soothing the short, tangled hair. There was only one thing he could say, and the words came more easily than he'd ever thought possible.

'Don't be daft,' he said. 'I love you. Just you. Not anybody else, that's what makes it right . . .'

She pulled back from him, her anger gone, the tears barely under control. 'All right,' she said, 'so you've got it made. You're separated, your wife doesn't give a damn what you do, and it's all roses.' She looked into his face and he suddenly realised that she was afraid. 'But if my bloke finds out about me,' she whispered, 'he'll bloody kill the pair of us.'

He kissed her firmly on the mouth; it was an order, shut up, stop moaning, listen.

'You've got a right to something good. And *I'm* not going to tell him. Are you?' She shook her head. 'Seven years, you told me –'

'Four with remission.'

'Then for Pete's sake, what are we worrying about?' He lifted her chin and laughed into her face, almost happy. 'Four years!' At last the smile came back, and her eyes sparkled.

'Think you'll get tired of me by then?' she demanded cheekily.

'I'm going to have a bloody good try,' he murmured, and started to kiss her neck and shoulders. He didn't get far, although she wanted him to. The phone rang.

'Let it ring,' Mackay said, between kisses. She pushed him away, laughing softly.

'Answer it,' she said, 'go on, I can wait.'

'You better had,' he said, and picked up the phone, determined to lose the caller, fast. 'Yeah? Who is it?'

'Hi, Mike!' It was Liebermann, phoning direct from New York. Mackay pulled a face and shook his head in mock-desperation; Angela, looking puzzled, had to laugh. 'You OK, Mike? You sound a little far off.'

'It's three thousand miles, Mr Liebermann,' said Mackay, and spluttered, eyes flicking wildly at Angela. She was stroking him and he didn't know how much longer he could hold out. His spare hand retaliated and she liked it, but that didn't help his long-distance conversation.

'Right,' said Liebermann, 'I'm going to do something about that.'

'I don't understand you, Mr Liebermann,' said Mackay, getting desperate. Angela had kicked the covers back and began to show her appreciation of what she saw.

'I'm arriving at Heathrow Saturday, Mike. Pan-Am flight 296. About midday. Right?'

'Right,' answered Mackay, gritting his teeth against the pleasure. Angela's crooning assault was too much; he was going under fast.

'I have a deal you can't refuse, Mike,' crowed Liebermann, then added jauntily, 'shall I tell you about it?'

'On Saturday, Mr Liebermann,' said Mackay, and putting down the phone, turned to make his reckoning with Angela.

The list that Swinford handed across the chrome and smoked-glass desk was everything that Fenn had wanted. Flight numbers, delivery dates, goods carried and insurable values, each consignment listed against the relevant airline.

'Bloody Aladdin's cave!' he chuckled. 'You've done us proud, squire!'

Sammy, standing behind Fenn's chair, added his approval. 'Proper little Santa Claus.'

'Checked it, have you?' Fenn demanded, suddenly cold-eyed. Swinford nodded, quickly.

'It's accurate,' he insisted. 'I confirmed it with our flight-schedule book.'

Fenn's eyes greedily scanned the shopping list. 'Just take a look at this, Sammy my son.' He pointed at various choice items that caught his eye, and couldn't stop the rasp of laughter bubbling up. 'Currency four hundred grand, silver a million and a quarter . . .' His voice dropped as he searched past the less interesting jumble of small rubbish. 'Fine art miniatures, not our kind of market, three oil paintings by Picasso – that's not on, for starters!'

Sammy laughed, but Swinford didn't see the joke.

'What sort of goods are you after?' he asked, fidgeting nervously.

'The best,' grunted Sammy.

'Bullion, squire,' said Fenn. 'Gold, silver, platinum –' He smirked like a satisfied hyena. 'Anything over a million, I'm interested.'

'Got to be worth the bother,' added the big man hulking in the shadows. 'We got overheads.'

'The greater the value, the tighter the security,' Swinford was quick to point out. From the look in Fenn's eyes, he knew he'd spoken out of turn.

'Just you mind your own, squire, right? Just button your lip!'

'Jack means keep mum,' Berghoff explained in kindly fashion. 'Or else.'

'Understood,' Swinford replied, hastily.

'The security side's for us to sort out,' said Fenn.

'You mean I've done my bit?' asked Swinford hopefully. If that were so, it'd been almost too simple. But Fenn never let anyone off the hook *that* easily. The watery eyes stared at him and glinted with mock-surprise. The voice was soft, but shadowed with menace.

'You haven't finished yet, squire. Not by a long chalk. Goodbye is when it's done and we're in the clear. Not one minute before. OK?'

Swinford nodded, and swallowed hard, as Berghoff's big hand rested on his shoulder. The heavy had moved up to him like a cat, pouncing playfully before Swinford could react.

'Don't go sloping off, eh?'

'I'm not going anywhere. But I don't see what else there is I can do to help.'

'We'll think of something, squire,' said Fenn. 'And if you're good, your cut'll cancel out what you owe us, and a bonus on top. Any complaints?'

'I don't want any part of it!' Swinford blurted out. 'I'm not in it for that!'

Fenn took the outburst calmly. He'd got Swinford by the 'short and curlies', so it wasn't surprising the poor sod felt like squealing now and then. 'Easy, squire. Go home and think about it.' He gave a small, almost paternal, wave of dismissal. 'Sammy'll be in touch.'

Berghoff moved to the door and opened it, guiding Swinford forward by his elbow. 'Better still, give yourself a night out,' he said, 'on the club.' Swinford still looked nervous, the way he always did when Berghoff stood so close – within striking range. The big man had a second thought and, smiling, put the record straight. 'Not at the tables though, my son. Food and booze only. Compliments of the management.' A gentle push propelled him outside, and the mahogany and brass door shut Sammy and Jack Fenn from view.

Swinford leaned against the wall, for a moment too weak to move on. What he'd just done had seemed so simple, hardly a criminal act at all. Now it was up to Fenn and his heavies to do the actual graft; that meant clean hands for Swinford. With luck, he'd be off the hook with dibs to spare and nobody would ever know who'd done the fingering. Right now, that dream felt pretty shaky, and Swinford desperately needed a stiff drink – but not here. He knew he couldn't take Queenie's forbidding eyes, and the tables behind her cashier's throne, green and tempting. More than that, wherever he stood in this scabby pot of gold was a reminder that he was bound to Jack Fenn, body and soul. It sickened him, not so much how they'd treated him, but that he'd let them. Pigeon, they'd called him. Eat out of our hand, they said. Damn them, he'd sooner starve, they couldn't make him, he had that much pride. They hadn't bought him; he'd sold out through fear. He stumbled down the stairs and out the back way, into the night. It was raining.

Fenn leaned back in his chair, and beamed. There it was, the stroke they needed: bullion, gold bars, topping two million, delivery at the Air India freight shed, ten days from now. The joy was, Fenn already had a sleeper in the security firm who'd be handling the consignment, and that gave him an extra edge in timing the job just right.

'It'll be a doddle, Sammy,' he said. 'Sort out what we need, and fix up with the lads, OK?'

'Sure, Jack,' Sammy replied, but from his face he wasn't happy. Sammy Berghoff was a key man; if something worried him, it had to be important.

'What's up?' asked Fenn, narrow-eyed. 'Something got a bad smell?'

There was no easy way of saying it, but if he didn't, one way or the other Sammy'd be up the creek without a paddle. 'It's the date, Jack.'

'Ten days is long enough to get everything fitted up, it's got to be, my son. I'm not missing the bloody boat again!' The big man shook his head, as though clearing it from a punch. Fenn began to realise that something more personal was bothering his number one. 'Come on. What's got you so screwed up?'

'It's awkward.'

'Don't you balls this one up, Sammy.' There was no threat. There didn't need to be.

'No sweat, Jack,' the big man protested, miserably.

'So what are you giving me, you great berk?'

'I got an operation booked.'

'Operation?' The watery eyes stared. 'You doing jobs for someone else, on the side?'

'Not a fit-up, Jack. Medical.'

'Since when have you been sick?' Fenn gave a sour laugh. He knew the last time Sammy had been off, having treatment. It still made Sammy sweat. 'They don't cut it off just because you've caught a second dose, kid. You ought to know that.'

'Vasectomy, Jack. Doc Rogers is fixing me up.' Sammy's face showed his desperation. 'I daren't dodge it any more, Jack. You know how the old girl gets . . .'

Fenn knew all right. A real snapper, he'd had his share years back, before the big man had married her. She'd been on the game then, a class chick, up West only, telephone number with the best hall porters; twenty a trick, a hundred the night, guaranteed clean as a whistle. It was Molly who had gone to see Doc Rogers in the first place, on behalf of Sammy; she found out all the answers, the how and why and wherefore about vasectomy and what it could do for a marriage bed, and from that moment, Sammy didn't stand a chance. Now, on the very same bloody day he was due to have the op, Jack was ready to pull the big one, a stroke that could set them up for life.

'I don't know what to do, Jack,' the big man mumbled. He stood there, so bothered by what Molly was going to say, he couldn't even think. As usual, Fenn did the thinking for him.

'Change the flaming date of the op, Sammy my son,' crooned Fenn with gentle, icy menace.

'She'll kill me.'

Fenn sighed. 'Not if you have the op done *first* . . .'

He watched Sammy brighten as the sheer brilliance of the answer filtered into his bony head. 'Yeah, she'd go for that. She really would.'

'Great,' said Fenn. 'Fix it with Doc Rogers.'

'Supposing he can't?'

'They tell me it takes a quarter of an hour,' Fenn said. The watery eyes glared, and the voice rasped bitterly. 'Can you spare a quarter of a sodding hour, my son? Can you? You better bloody had!'

Anything that Molly had fixed had to be handled delicately. Sammy knew she just had to be pleased, bringing the date forward, but with Molly you never knew. Pregnant women were tricky, anyway.

'Change the bloody date?' she screamed, sitting up in bed and clutching his pillow.

Sammy was standing on one leg, desperately trying to unhook his toe from his Y-fronts. He had decided he would tell her just before getting into bed, then he could take her mind off it if she objected, not forgetting to point out how eager he was to have it done. That was a laugh, anyway, because he was as scared as hell. He still didn't like the idea of a blade going anywhere near him down there. He'd heard of accidents before now, and a fat lot of use he'd be to Molly if *that* happened.

'Ya don't let me say –' he appealed desperately.

'Now you listen to me, Sammy Berghoff. It's me gone to all the trouble. Me who's been and fixed it up with Doc Rogers in the first place, and I'm telling you . . .'

'Lemme tell you. Not change it –'

'– by one bloody hour. That's what.'

Sammy sweated. He sat down, naked, on the cold, cane-seated chair. Her hand was too close to that sodding clock, and any minute she'd chuck the thing at him. Marble it was, too.

'You've got some chick dated up, that's what it is,' she decided, the flush of her anger rising in her neck. She tried it again, on a higher note. 'You've got some chick . . .'

Oh, Christ, he thought, that's knackered it. She thought he'd dated a tart for the same night as the op, when he wouldn't be able to touch it with a feather duster. Now she wouldn't let him budge it, either way.

Then Molly got out of bed. That, in itself, was ominous, because once in bed, and with Sammy naked, there was usually no shifting her. The trouble was that she brought the clock with her.

Molly was a big, handsome woman, and had a temper that matched her bouncy, just-darker-than-auburn hair.

'Molly!'

'You tricky bastard,' she howled, and she went for him.

It was too much. Sammy fled. Fleet of foot, and unencumbered, he made the kitchen ten yards ahead. And there he stopped, cornered. Where the hell could he go, with no clothes?

She came in through the kitchen door like a tornado. Sammy had to admire the entrance. The class, from the old days, was still there. Just a few muscles had developed here and there, and an ability to shriek him down. And Lord, how that temper had blossomed!

'Now, love . . .'

'Don't you come that with me. You and your soft-soaping. We ain't courting now.'

But she had left the marble clock behind. Maybe the sight of him running off like that, everything swinging free, had given her ideas. He backed into the corner between the sink and the washer, holding one hand up in entreaty and one down, and leering warily.

'Don't you wish we was?'

Her temper usually went as it came. Now it hovered.

'You make me sick. All the trouble I've taken, and now you come whining like a sick dog.'

'Just let me tell you, Molly . . .'

She sat down suddenly on the chair beside the table, her bosom almost jolting free from her nightie.

'How many times've I got to go through it? It ain't gonna hurt. The doc said that – only a bit, anyway.'

'There's been times . . . Mistakes've happened.' He licked his lips. Just when he'd built himself up to it, she had to go and remind him again. 'I've heard about 'em.'

'Since when has Doc Rogers produced any forty-year-old sopranos? Look at you, the great big strong man, shivering in his shoes. If you had any shoes on.'

The plastic tiles were as cold as ice. 'You know I've always been enough for you, Molly. Ain't I?'

Oh, he had, he had. Molly almost permitted herself a smile. But she suppressed it, and managed to look contemptuous. It didn't do to encourage him.

'Don't think I haven't seen better. Look at you.'

'What d'you expect, when I'm cold?'

'I oughta take that as an insult. Nobody's got any right to be cold when I'm around.' But he'd been good to her, satisfying, and Molly had to admit that; though she'd seen better, she hadn't enjoyed better, or more consistently. It was the last bit that mattered, the consistency, so to speak, and the regularity, and Molly wasn't going to have anything wasted on cheap tarts, anywhere, any time.

'I've always put you to rights,' he said awkwardly, feeling she was coming round.

'You put me in the club,' she shouted. 'That's what you did. Three of 'em, all girls, and another on the way. And you . . . you stupid fool, you won't do anything about it.'

That was unfair. He'd braced himself for it. Out of a sense of injury, he burst out: 'You could go on the bloody pill!'

And that was a distinct mistake. They'd argued it too often, and too noisily. Sammy wished he could choke it back. She was half out of the chair, her eyes blazing, her hands reaching. When she went, she exploded, and anything was possible. The last time, it'd been right there in the kitchen, and she'd been frying chips. The whole pan, chips, fat and all, had come flying at him, and he'd had to dive full-length under the table.

'They do things to you!' she screamed.

'And so does a bloody knife.'

'One little cut, you yellow bastard.'

'Which I said I'd have,' he yelled into her face, and she reached up for his eyes.

He just managed to catch her wrists. There'd be teeth in a second, he knew. 'I said I'd have it,' he shouted over her screams. 'I'm gonna. It's just the date, Molly. Listen, will ya!'

She was struggling like a tigress. 'You got a tart lined up, you randy bastard.' And God, how she'd mark her if he had, and break his arm for a bonus.

'Nobody'd dare!' he hissed.

'They laugh at me! Behind my back. Come on, Sammy – I can hear 'em saying it – let's see what keeps Molly happy. And your mates, that Fenn . . .'

He flung her wrists away, suddenly beaten. He didn't want to know about Jack Fenn. Fenn and Molly, it galled him still. And the mention of Fenn reminded him . . .

She was coming round the table. 'Jack'd laugh his head off,' she cried. 'He'd find the tart for you himself. Oh, I know him. He'd wheel her in on a trolley, and he'd laugh . . .'

'He bloody envies me!' he shouted.

She stopped. 'Jack does?' Still?

'They all do. Damn it, there's a standing joke . . .' And Christ, he'd done it again.

'Joke?' Through her clenched teeth.

'Nothing.'

'Joke!'

He shrugged. 'Not funny. Well . . . they say you move too fast for me, that I don't get time to find the French letter . . .'

She tucked in her lower lip, and now her eyes were shining.

'Sammy!'

'Now what?'

'Oh, Sammy, you bloody idiot.' And she was laughing in his arms.

He didn't know what had happened. The edge of the cabinet was cutting a groove in his buttocks, but he said nothing. She was sighing, and making those swinging movements he knew so well.

'Sammy!'

'It's just,' he whispered, 'that there's something on. *That* night. You know I'll be useless for a couple of days, after it's done, not be able to move right. So I thought . . . a bit earlier. What you say?'

She held him at arm's length, watching his greedy eyes, her mouth now amused, teeth just showing.

'Sammy, carry me to bed.'

'Up them bleeding stairs? You ain't no lightweight.'

'You can do it. And you've already got a bit of extra support.'

Doc Rogers raised no objections, especially when Sammy offered him an extra pony for the favour. To anyone else, the surprise in the dry Australian voice would've sounded more like a sneer, but Sammy had known Doc for years and the hint of mild scorn never got up his nose. Not much, anyway.

'You want it done *earlier*?' Rogers had said over the phone, with a laugh that sounded like an angry goose.

'Can you do it, Doc? It's an emergency. Holiday arrangements, you know,' lied Sammy. Rogers wasn't fooled, but it wasn't his way to ask questions.

'No skin off my nose, friend,' said the Doc. 'It'll still be six months before you're in the clear though – y'know that.'

'Yeah, I know. When?'

'Friday suit you?'

So it was fixed, and Berghoff felt better; better for having put himself in right with Jack Fenn again, that is. He had three whole days of worry ahead of him. Luckily, he also had a job to do: the fit-up.

When it came to offering a spot of work to a mate, Berghoff liked to make it face to face. That way you could drop the bait, see the geezer's reaction, and if he fancied the deal, shake on it there and then, details later. On the phone you never knew quite where you stood; no face to look at, you never knew who else was hanging round, or like the plumbing, where the leak might be. On a phone you had to be a bit windy; you never knew what the filth'd get up to these days. Phone-tapping might be illegal, but who was to know? You'd never find out until it was too late, and a fat lot of good that was. Besides, Sammy liked to be seen around, he liked the greetings and the glances, the nods and the winks. He was doing all right, in the money, and you'd better believe it. There were risks, of course; nothing was that safe. But Fenn had been a good teacher, he knew how the fuzz worked and thought almost as well as he knew his own mind, and he made Sammy understand what cover meant. Camouflage. Decoy and double decoy. If you wanted a word with one particular geezer, make sure you chatted to a dozen, so nobody knew just which one you were putting your money on. Where there were villains, there were snouts, and the quickest way of being put to rights by the law was to drop your guard. Being pulled in for questioning was no joke; for a start it meant you were losing your touch, and no one was happy working for a loser. Worse, it meant the fuzz had got their beady eye on you, so you had to step twice as softly. Sammy kept his nose clean, and never even fiddled a parking meter.

Getting this fit-up together was a snip, though. The lads were already on standby, only waiting for him to give a passing nod to know the job was on the boil again. If they were on, they gave him the wink, and a simple question clinched the first meeting. What did they fancy for the 3 o'clock on Thursday? The venue, unnamed, would be the club; they knew that and they'd be there. Only two were a bother; Henry, away on holiday in Teneriffe, and Bev.

It'd all gone so well until then; Alan, who'd been providing the wheels, George, Vic and Hodge, the muscle squad, Cyril, who was minding the shooters – they were all OK. But Bev was the fly in the ointment. He'd heard bad news.

Bev was a welder by trade and ran a small repair yard just off the New King's Road. He saw Berghoff coming and didn't stop work, a patch-up job on a cracked chassis that when finished would last just long enough to beat the used-car guarantee that covered it on the forecourt. Sammy wasn't very pleased at having to dodge looking at the piercing blue-white flame; it didn't take long for him to realise Bev was using the job to keep his head down.

'Got a minute, Bev?'

'Eh?' The masked face glanced briefly sideways, then threw out an explanation. 'Rush job.'

'Turn that bloody thing off!' shouted Sammy above the hissing roar. Bev didn't seem to hear, so Sammy turned off the cylinder cock himself. Bev protested as the flame died, but he was nervous.

'Quit playing stupid games, will ya!'

'I'm here to talk, Bev. Be polite, eh?'

'I'm listening, OK?'

There was no one else in the yard, but Sammy played it cool, even so.

'Got a weekend job on, old son. Interested?'

'Don't fancy it, Sammy. I'd sooner you got someone else.'

Sammy was surprised. Bev was never one to hang back when there was work to hand. 'Anything up?'

'It's in the wind already.' Bev fiddled with the nozzle in his hand, his eyes avoiding the big man's sharp reaction.

'What is?'

'Alex Tindall's asking a lot of questions.' Bev didn't need to explain, it meant trouble wasn't very far behind.

Bev fretted, awkward and apologetic. 'You know what he's like.'

'Thanks for the wrinkle, Bev,' the big man said. 'What else?'

'Isn't that enough?'

Berghoff said nothing more, but gave a small gesture of farewell as he moved away, thinking hard. Behind him, there was a snap of igniting gas as Bev went to work on the sub-frame, but the sound hardly registered. Sammy's mind was full of the bad news and how he was going to tell it. Fenn wasn't going to like it whichever way it came.

The silence in Fenn's office was like a thundercloud, looming and oppressive. Standing at the window, the neat figure looking down into the floodlit car park hunched its shoulders like a frustrated vulture. The voice rasped back into the shadows of the room to where Berghoff waited.

'So it's Tindall asking around, is it?' said Fenn. He knew him from years ago, their paths had crossed more than once, leaving neither of them exactly happy. Fenn had wriggled off the hook, but he had nothing to crow about. He'd never managed to pull a really smart stroke on Tindall's patch, and life hadn't got any easier until Tindall had moved his manor.

'I found out something else, Jack.' Berghoff paused. Fenn would like this even less. 'He's in charge of the Air France investigation.' He waited for that to sink in before the real bombshell. 'And he's been to see Gus Fulmer in hospital.'

Fenn sat down, stiff-backed, eyes glazed with hate. Now it all made sense. Fulmer was the weak link in the chain, the only possible Judas. For a moment, Fenn considered the possibility that the old bastard had set the Air France deal up as a trap; but if he had, it'd gone wrong just as much for the fuzz as it had for Sammy and the boys. If Tindall had gone visiting the old creep, it must've been because he had a reason – he wasn't in the Red Cross. So far, nothing had happened; Gus only knew about the Air France caper, not about the next stroke. But he did know names. If the fuzz got those out of him, there'd be aggro for certain, apart from putting the kibosh on the bullion caper. Fenn took a cigarette, lit up, then looked at it with hooded eyes, dispassionately.

'Poor old Gus,' he said. 'He's becoming a liability.' He flicked off a fragment of ash.

'Top him.'

Gus stood in the open doorway of his scruffy bungalow, watching the ambulance that had brought him home drive away. They'd wanted to come inside, make him comfy, settle him down, but he wasn't having any. He'd had enough trouble getting clear of the hospital; he knew his rights, knew he could discharge himself, and did. In there, too many people could get at him, nurses, doctors, fuzz – he'd had enough. More than that, he had this feeling that whatever he'd said,

Tindall would be back. Well, he'd never get past the front door here!

Gus lurched indoors, still awkward on his elbow crutches. He didn't need them in the hall; it was so narrow he could use the walls as support. His legs ached, but he knew what he must do before he could ease up; bolt the front door, top and bottom, and put on the chain, then he'd be safe. He found he couldn't do the bottom bolt, and he left it. He paused for a moment, breathless from the attempt to bend, and looked along the dim passageway leading towards the kitchen. Home sweet home, he thought bitterly, but better than doing 'bird', or another day in that bloody hospital bed. That little tart of a nurse – always grinning, flashing the bedpan, hoping to have a peep at his privates. Christ, if his legs had been good he'd've shown her all right! She'd've liked it too, he'd seen that twinkle in her eye. In spite of the greyness of the hallway, he chuckled at the impossible dream and, taking up his crutches, made his clumsy way towards the kitchen. Reaching it, he poked the door wide open and lurched inside. He paused, puzzled. He hadn't left the curtains closed, but they were. Somebody had been here while he was away. Wrong, a small voice inside his tired head warned him; someone *is* here – now – waiting for you. The unease churned over in his gut and welled up into helpless panic, as the shadow that was sitting on the corner stool stood up and moved into view, deliberately. Gus knew the face but it was the gloved hand he feared; he tried to think what he had done to deserve it. He tried to name the intruder, but fear brought up the bile, gagging his throat with its sour, burning acid.

'Hello, Gus . . .' purred the shadow, and kicked away the crutches.

'Seems the old geezer gassed himself, then, guv'nor,' said Dalton. He glanced at Tindall, slowly pacing at his side as they walked away from the meat shop, and wondered why he seemed so bothered. It wasn't as if Tindall had never been a visitor before to that gaunt room with the refrigerated drawers;

Dalton had put in only half as many years, and stiffs didn't trouble *him* that much any more.

Dalton had learned to look on the chilled flesh and bone simply as evidence; wondering who they'd been or how they'd lived was less important than knowing how they'd died, and why. Feelings had to be kept out of the way, you couldn't mend a corpse by wishing it better. The only real reason was: had the law been broken? If it had been, find out who, and nail them. That was the only service you could render to the dead. All of which brusque realism left Dalton even more puzzled over his guv'nor's reaction to Fulmer's pallid, shrunken body. It was obvious what had happened. The old feller had been done over, had his legs smashed, lost his job, and at his age, with no prospects, simply chucked it in. Motive – depression; method – the gas oven; result – suicide, straight and simple.

'Suicide, my ass,' said Tindall sourly, as though reading Dalton's mind. 'Not with Gus. No way.'

'Accident, then. Easy to be clumsy on those crutches.'

'You don't draw the curtains to have an accident, lad. Especially when you can't reach them properly.'

'He could've drawn them on the night he copped his knee-cap job.'

'Just in the kitchen?'

'He was a funny old bloke, guv'nor. Maybe his kitchen was overlooked from across the back –'

'Was it? You tell me.' Tindall stared at the youngster, dourly challenging him to remember.

Dalton frowned. 'No . . . it wasn't.'

'I know the front door was bolted –'

'Only at the top, guv'nor. Couldn't bend down to the bottom bolt, could he?'

'Which makes it look as though he couldn't get down to lighting the oven, either, once he'd turned it on –'

'Right,' said Dalton, pleased that the guv'nor was following the same line of reasoning. Two minds with but a single genius thought.

'So when he found he couldn't light it, why didn't he turn it off?'

'Forgot,' offered Dalton lamely, then recovered. 'All right, not an accident. It had to be deliberate. So – suicide, like I said, guv'nor.' Dalton opened the door leading outside to where their car was parked. 'Right?'

'Wrong,' said Tindall.

'Why?' demanded Dalton, peeved that he'd obviously missed something vital. Tindall sounded so certain, he had to be right. He usually was, when he did that little rocking backwards and forwards on his heels. Dalton unlocked the car door and held it open as Tindall sat in the passenger seat, staring ahead with saddened eyes. He never bothered with a seat-belt, said it gave him indigestion. Dalton waited patiently for the answer to his question.

'He was a Roman Candle, wasn't he?' said Tindall. He glanced up at Dalton, still standing there holding the car door. 'You know about them, do you?'

'They reckon suicide's a sin.'

Dalton flinched at the bitterness in the older man's sad voice. 'RCs rate killing themselves as one way to eternal damnation, my son!' rasped Tindall. 'It's the one sin you can't take to confession, isn't it?'

Dalton had to smile at the black joke: pardon me, Father, for I've just committed suicide. A voice from the grave. Impossible. Which in the context made it funny. But Tindall wasn't laughing, and his next words gave Dalton some idea why. 'Gus believed in God, lad. Going to heaven mattered to him.'

Dalton started to smile at the thought of that sour old man, bent, shady and protesting before St Peter. The smile slipped out of sight as Tindall carried on talking, as much to himself as to his companion.

'Confession every Saturday, communion every Sunday. Even while he was in hospital . . .' There was a pause while Dalton shut the door, came round and clambered into the driver's seat. Fishing for the car key, he glanced at Tindall, still gazing out through the windscreen with sad, thoughtful eyes. 'He didn't want to die, Jimmy. He was too afraid of what he might find. He'd sooner emigrate to Borneo.'

Dalton put the key into the ignition but didn't turn it. 'So you reckon someone topped him?'

'Can't prove it,' said Tindall. 'Don't know who. Don't know why. Not yet.'

The last two words weren't only for his own satisfaction. He had a score to settle. He owed Gus Fulmer that much at least. 'Drive on, lad,' he said crisply. 'We've got work to do.'

Berghoff picked up the newspapers that Fenn shoved towards him across the desk, folded them one by one, and placed them in a neat pile ready to be taken away and dumped.

'Good riddance,' said Fenn, and he didn't mean the waste-paper.

'Saved everyone a lot of trouble, discharging himself like that,' commented Sammy with an appreciative roll of his shoulders.

'Gus could be like that when he put his mind to it,' Fenn smirked. 'Considerate.'

'Hadn't even changed his cooker over to North Sea Gas.'

'Thoughtful to the end,' said Fenn, and lit up a fag. 'Easy, was it?'

'No trouble, Jack,' Sammy confirmed. 'That's the end of it then.'

'The end for Fulmer, sure.'

'I meant the bullion job,' said the big man. 'We're up the creek with that one. Shall I tell the boys that Sunday's off?'

'Did I say that, Sammy?'

The big man looked surprised. Jack had always been a shrewd operator; a bookie, not a punter, safe bets, no risks, and always hedge the odds. Yet here he was talking about going on with a caper that was already on the whisper.

'You mean we let it ride?'

'Why not?'

'Tindall, for a start-off.'

'What does he know? Nothing.' Fenn stubbed out the cigarette, half-finished and almost immediately lit another. Berghoff knew that sign; it meant the boss was high, the old brain-box had come up with something special, a new wrinkle, a cunning stroke. 'The Jack wanted Gus to stool for him, right?' said Fenn. 'So *that's* a dead end. Tindall's nowhere. Forget him.'

Sammy took Fenn's word for it; he'd personally be very happy to lose Sad Alex permanently, but even Bloody Delilah would look twice at that sort of contract. It was true, wasting the fuzz had no future; still, with any luck Tindall might drop dead one day from natural causes. It'd be worth having a whip-round for a lily and stinkweed wreath when *that* happy day arrived! But Sammy was still feeling bothered. 'We can't pull the Air France caper again, Jack,' the big man said. 'You said so yourself.'

'Good rule, kid,' complimented Fenn drily. 'Never repeat yourself.' He let out a long stream of cigarette smoke, and watched it fade, with smug satisfaction. 'So we make changes.' More smoke, drawn back almost immediately. 'Little changes. Air India, not Air France.'

'Almost neighbours, Jack.'

'And we don't hit and run, Sammy.' He paused, savouring how this would grab the big man. 'We leave the loot behind.'

Sammy blinked. 'You mean we don't take anything?' Fenn chuckled.

'We lift it all right, but we stash it somewhere safe. At Heathrow. Pick it up later when the heat's died down.'

Sammy remembered Swinford, and his big face beamed.

'The pigeon,' he said. '*His* warehouse.'

Dalton's feet were very sore. The guv'nor had said he wanted more news from the street, which meant a lot of leg-work. This time was nothing to do with Air France. That was getting stale anyway. Bullion, too; Tindall was happy to let that simmer for a bit. He'd made it known that he was interested, thrown his bread on the waters, and with luck, some of it would come back, perhaps with interest. For that he'd have to wait. What he wanted Jimmy the sprog to pick up on today's trek was what the grapevine said about Gus Fulmer. A snout getting roughed up was one thing; being blown away was something different. With someone that heavy around, who was safe?

Nobody wanted to know. The kneecap job on Gus had shaken the regulars; now, with Gus dead, the most that Dalton could raise was a 'Rest in Peace, poor bastard,' and several promises to light a candle after the funeral. Enemies? Silence. Trouble? Silence. Associates? *Stumm.* Dalton did his best; he realised how important it was to dig up something, to please the guv'nor. Gus was on Tindall's mind for some reason, and finding out who'd wanted him dead would've meant a real breakthrough. Jimmy visited old friends and more than a few unlikely new ones; he waved some green around, even tried carrots other than money, such as the Nelson touch over a charge pending; as a last resort, he even leaned on one or two nervous individuals whose line of business wouldn't be improved by a van-load of rozzers stamping all over the place in a best-boot and truncheon raid.

'No luck, guv,' he reported. 'Gus getting his has put the curse on everything.'

'Someone has to know.'

'Knowing's one thing. Telling's another,' he said wearily.

'A bloody ballerina could take more punishment than you can, flower,' grunted Tindall. 'Didn't you hear *anything* else?'

Dalton eased himself more comfortably in his chair, and chuckled. 'One bit of gossip, if you fancy a giggle. Not much use, mind, guv'nor.'

'Amuse me,' sighed Tindall.

'Remember Sammy Berghoff?' Dalton saw his chief respond, and continued, 'His missus is expecting number five.'

'That's funny?' queried Tindall. He knew about big Molly and Berghoff. Tarts and heavies didn't often make a go of it; these two were a happy exception, and Sammy had sobered up a lot since the old, wild days. But neither of them were what you'd call comedians.

'That isn't the punch line,' explained Jimmy, pained at Tindall jumping the gun. 'His old lady's threatened to walk out unless he has a vasectomy.' Dalton chuckled. 'And he's going to!' His laughter fizzled into an apologetic splutter as he saw Tindall was not amused, only thoughtful. 'Well, *I* reckoned it was funny,' he said defensively.

'Vasectomy,' muttered Tindall, 'Doc Rogers . . .'

'What's so interesting about Doc Rogers?' Dalton asked warily. He sensed that Tindall had stumbled on to something that he was keeping to himself, and seeing that it was he who had given him the lead, that was hardly fair. 'Tell us, guv'nor, eh?'

'He's . . . an acquaintance, lad,' said Tindall innocently. 'I might pay the old sport a visit.'

'I don't get it.'

'There could be a connection. Berghoff used to be a customer of Gus – the bit of unmarked loot, on the side – booze, perfume for his old woman, that sort, you know –'

'Nothing to nail either of them with, though,' frowned Dalton.

'Couldn't even prove they'd ever met,' agreed the inspector. 'But you know Sammy . . .'

'A hard case,' Dalton nodded. 'But no trouble now, for years.'

'Nothing that we know of, lad,' corrected his guv'nor. 'But I wonder when he's having that op done . . .' He got up and walked jauntily out of the office and along the corridor to the men's room. He was humming to himself all the way, and that really made Dalton steam. When he took to music, it was only because he felt the angels were on his side, and Dalton – and the rest of CID – would have to wait.

The outside of the terraced house could only be described as 'scabby'. Twisted railings guarded the basement area; the peeling paint and flaking stonework made the tall, once elegant, frontage look like a cripple with leprosy. Most of the close-parked cars that lined the road seemed just as seedy and uncared for, thought Tindall.

If Rogers had been straight, and taken rooms in Harley

Street, he'd've been GP to the stars and all the other lovely people; as it was, he had a shady past, a shambles of a pad off Westbourne Grove, and a clientele that numbered more first-class villains than Parkhurst and Holloway put together.

The manor hadn't changed much, Tindall thought, as he walked up the front steps. Unhealthy, and not very likely to recover. He'd hardly rung the greasy bell – no nameplate – when it opened, giving a glimpse of a shadowed hall behind a soft-sheened golden head. The sun-blond hair framed a perfectly boned, tanned face and young but wary eyes.

'Yes?' The light, sensitively modulated voice had hardly spoken before Tindall had pushed the door open and shouldered his way in. No fluster or struggle; just a quiet, firm pressure, and no arguments. The young boy-god in the pale silk medical tunic started to protest, retreating as he did so.

'You can't come in. Not without an appointment –'

'I'm an old friend of the Doc's,' said Tindall, bending the meaning of the word 'friend'. 'He'll see me.'

The silk and gold figure hovered, uncertain as a ghost, in the rich purple shadows of the passageway. The pad may have looked seedy on the outside, but its guts had class. Not so, golden wonder-boy. Just the opposite.

'I'm not supposed to let strangers in. Please go away.'

'Tell him Alex Tindall's come to say hello,' said the Inspector, and looked to where the answer came, from the white-painted stairway farther along the hall.

'Let the Inspector in, Francis,' drawled the bitter voice. 'And shut that flaming door.'

The boy stepped aside to let Tindall past, staring at him warily. Doc's hand was not outstretched in greeting; it only indicated where to go: the waiting-room.

'In there.'

Tindall went ahead and Rogers followed, pausing only long enough to give a curt order to the boy outside. 'Don't let anyone else in, understand? Put the chain across.' A soft, incomprehensible apology. Rogers's voice lost its bitterness and grew more gentle. 'It wasn't your fault. Pigs like this one eat little boys for breakfast.' The door closed; Rogers stood facing the CID inspector, and the bitterness returned.

'What d'y'want?'

'You haven't changed much,' said Tindall, then indicated the room, 'but you've had the place redecorated.' The Australian's shrewd, world-weary eyes followed Tindall's gesture, and took in the languid richness of the décor; genuine, but not too expensive, Edwardian furniture, a carefully blended, patterned colour-scheme, a few exotic but sensitively placed ceramic ornaments; evidence of a taste and style more than likely wasted on Rogers's clients, and not having much appeal for Tindall either.

'I like it,' drawled Rogers, 'but I know you'd prefer it done out in Woolies' plastic best.'

'Cost of living,' grunted Tindall. 'I don't have your income, do I?'

'Money doesn't buy good taste,' Rogers drawled, lording it. 'You and that modern fart-house up the Edgware Road deserve each other. Tarted-up pig-bin,' he added.

'Left it years ago, sport,' said Tindall. 'I'm at Heathrow now, aren't I?' He sat down and crossed his legs comfortably. Rogers remained standing, and frowned. This wasn't Tindall's manor any more, but he was here, and it wasn't for medication either. Answers or information weren't on, if that's what he was after; Rogers might not be on the medical register any more, but his code of conduct – total confidentiality and privacy – was what had made him, and he'd never break it. Tindall knew that.

'Nice lad,' commented the CID man, with a nod that indicated the golden boy outside. Rogers straightened the slight droop of his shoulders, and alarm bells rang inside his head as Tindall smiled, gently. The bastard, Rogers thought, he's going to put the knife in!

'Relative,' he grunted, curtly.

'English?' asked Tindall.

' 'stralian.'

'Working?'

'I look after him,' said Rogers. 'Like an uncle.'

'You'll have all his documents, then?' Tindall's eyes were cold, knowing bloody well what he was doing to Rogers. 'Passport.' He paused. 'Birth certificate, even.' Rogers sat, and glared; his tanned, perfectly manicured hands worked slowly together, the fingers interweaving, stroking, tangling with frustration and despair. Tindall had come knowing his weak spot from the old days; he'd put it under threat as neatly and cold-bloodedly as Rogers would insert a hypodermic. Francis was the latest in a long history of 'nephews', the most beautiful and for now, the most loved. And Tindall could end all that.

'Not that it matters to me personally,' said the sad-faced copper. 'But I sometimes forget about Immigration or the Social Security people.' He stared at the elegant, anguished Australian and pushed the needle deeper. 'They like to keep their records straight, I hear.'

There was the deal. He'd forget golden-boy Francis, if Rogers talked. The smooth, cared-for fingers locked together and were still; there was no other choice.

'Don't expect too much, copper. I'm not much good on details.'

'We'll see,' said Tindall gently, then added as though changing the subject totally: 'See much of Sammy Berghoff these days?'

The question took Rogers by surprise, but having given in, he saw no reason to beat about the bush. Berghoff was no talker; Rogers knew nothing about him other than the medical treatment that had been arranged. Tindall would have no joy over this one.

'He's a patient.' He corrected himself, quickly. 'A visitor. I advise him in matters of health.' Advice was safely on the right side of the law; prescription or any other practical form of medicine was strictly inadmissible after what had happened in Melbourne over twelve years ago. Tindall seemed not to have noticed the slip, or at least, didn't seem to care.

'Like vasectomy.'

The warning bells rang again. The knuckles on Rogers's hands grew white with tension and quiet rage, but his voice remained calm. 'It's his choice, isn't it?'

'Very wise, too, from what I hear about his old woman,' said Tindall. 'Simple operation, is it?'

'Fifteen minutes. Any capable GP can do it in his own surgery.'

'Painless?'

'There's discomfort afterwards. Local anaesthetic's all that's needed for the cut.'

'Like at the dentist.'

'More or less.'

'But –' Tindall paused, carefully '– suppose you had someone who didn't like pain. Someone who was nervous of being cut. You'd give them something extra, wouldn't you?'

The bastard, thought Rogers. He knew damn well. 'If the guy asked for it I would,' he admitted.

'And you'd use intravenous valium. Like some dentists do.'

'Yes.' It was a whisper. Rogers understood at last. Given intravenously, the valium had the same effect as eighteen gin and tonics. Berghoff wouldn't know a thing. He wouldn't even know that he had talked his head off like a fool, or what he'd said, or who had heard. And that's what Tindall was counting on.

'When's Berghoff due to be done?'

'It was going to be a week from now, but he's brought it forward to this Friday – tomorrow. Family holiday arrangements,' he added, unnecessarily. Tindall looked thoughtful as he stood to go.

'I'll be back,' he said. Rogers didn't get up, and Tindall opened the door himself. 'Don't go spoiling anything, will you, Doc?' he said.

'What you're asking me to do is strictly unethical!' shouted Rogers in a sudden burst of helpless fury. Tindall took the point and paused for a second before moving on, but he wasn't sympathetic.

'Ethics is a big word,' he said coldly. 'You should try explaining it to Francis.'

Mackay stood to take the big man's hand, and was impressed. The grip was gentle, no nonsense, and yet not pushy. A bloke with a fist that size could've cracked walnuts between his knuckles, but he didn't try to, and that pleased Mackay. He noted the smart suit, the fine silk shirt and tie and the cuff-links; they had to be gold, no rubbish. No briefcase; this guy wasn't a salesman. He announced himself in a hard, curt voice that made it clear he wasn't used to being mucked about. He meant business and Mackay was hooked.

'I'm Bernie Samuels.'

'Mike Mackay, Mr Samuels. Won't you sit down?'

'You handle freight.'

'That's our kind of business, yes. We don't fly it ourselves –'

'Sure, I know,' grunted the big man. 'You do the paperwork. Customs. Delivery. That right?'

'Correct.'

'I've got a consignment due from Hamburg. Ships' spares. Compressors, mostly. Can you handle it?'

'We'd be glad to, Mr Samuels. If you'll give me details –'

The big man thrust a typewritten list at Mackay; a glance was enough to show the freight agent that everything he needed was there. An efficient customer was too good to be true.

'I hear you're OK,' said Samuels. 'Prove it, and we can do regular business. Is it a deal?'

'Terms, Mr Samuels,' said Mackay. 'Our rates –' he started to explain.

'I'm not looking for cut-price delivery,' said Samuels bluntly. 'Just service. The best. You have the invoice ready, that's all. Payments COD, right?'

'Right,' said Mackay, drawn to his feet by the big man looming over him, his business complete, ready to be on his way.

'Any problems, get me on this number.' The big hand thrust a tiny card at Mackay; it read BS Marine Maintenance Ltd. It was a piece of quality printing and Mackay nodded appreciatively.

'Nice to do business with you, Mackay.' A brief handshake

and he was at the door, moving like an athlete for all his craggy bulk. 'I'll be in touch.'

'My pleasure,' responded Mackay, and the visitor had gone. He sat down, delighted yet bemused with the speed of the transaction. There it was, in black and white.

Swinford edged in, looking vaguely nervous.

'What was that about?'

'Would you believe – a customer?' laughed Mackay. 'Only in here two minutes, and we've done a deal – and more to come if this goes along OK!'

Swinford tried to sound enthusiastic.

Mackay brought out the bottle, and poured out two small shots, grinning cheerfully.

'Let's drink to that, John,' he said. 'To BS Marine Maintenance and Mr Samuels, good on him!' They drank, but Swinford kept his eyes down, troubled at what he knew, and Mike did not.

Swinford looked up from his desk to find Nik hovering by him, an import invoice in his hand, but his eyes fixed firmly on Angela as she made more coffee.

'Fly me, Nik,' said Swinford, and broke the spell.

Nik grinned, unashamed; he liked a girl with enough meat on her bones and Angela carried it with style. Ever since the boss had given her a lift to the bus stop one evening, she'd been a new woman, a real woman. It was now part of the day's routine, Mackay collecting her after work. It hadn't escaped Nik's beady eye that the boss often brought her in to work of a morning. Wickedly, he wondered just how far they travelled together, and he didn't mean on wheels. All the way, with Mike Mackay, lucky sod.

'This the consignment you wanted me to look out for, John?' he asked, coming back to reality.

'Ships' spares . . . right,' said Swinford, trying to sound casual. He didn't know the details of Fenn's plan, he'd only done what he was told; he didn't have to like it. He didn't have to ask questions, either; Berghoff had made that clear. Just smooth the way, act normal, and when Mr Samuels arrived to do business, don't stand there looking like a goof. So here it was, the delivery pro forma telling Goldhawk the flight details and the fact that the goods now only needed Customs clearance for their removal. Fenn had said don't worry, the consignment was clean, nothing more nor less than what the documentation said: ships' spares, compressors. Swinford felt nervous in spite of that, and Nik's next snide comment only needled him more.

'Hamburg, John? Ships' spares? I haven't heard porn called *that* before!' Nik chuckled. They'd had nothing blue themselves from the Hamburg route, but they all knew the trade existed. Customs cut out a fair percentage, but they couldn't spot it all. He laughed out loud as he spotted the article description. 'Hey, look at this – compressors! It has to be a load of dildoes! This I got to see!' It was meant to be a joke, but Swinford exploded.

'Keep your stupid nose out of it!' he snapped. 'You've got a mind like a bloody sewer!' Nik gasped as Swinford snatched the documentation from him. 'It's new business and it doesn't come from Cyprus!'

Swinford suddenly realised that everyone bar Mike, who was away, was staring at him. Perhaps it was something in his face, the edge in his voice that suggested nervous strain. Nik held his temper and stalked back to his desk. The moment passed, and the others got on with whatever they were doing, not knowing what had pushed Swinford over the edge. He'd seen the letter-heading that identified the firm as Berghoff's cover: BS Marine Maintenance. But what had jolted him had been the company mark. A group of pips, arranged as though on a playing card: the five of diamonds.

It was 9.30 am and a fresh, clean morning when Sammy arrived for his appointment. Francis had been cautious, not unchaining the door until the visitor had identified himself by face and by name.

'I'm Sammy Berghoff, kid. The Doc's expecting me.'

He'd followed the boy down the hall and into the lush waiting-room, his nervous mind wondering playfully at the boy's natural grace.

Sammy shrugged the thought away, it wasn't important. As far as he was concerned, the quack was a straight bloke, and what he did at 'beddy-byes' time was nobody's business but his own.

Rogers came in to collect the big man personally. He never used a bell. For one thing there was never a queue because he spaced his appointments well apart. He could afford to; besides, not everybody wanted to meet old pals on a visit to Doc Rogers. That meant questions, and questions meant answers, and there were some subjects nobody wanted to wave the rag about. He also did straight medicine on the side, but nobody'd believe you if you came up with *that* tale.

'All fit?' he asked genially.

'Fit as I'll ever be,' Sammy responded, nervously watching Rogers work his supple fingers into readiness.

'No trouble after this, friend,' smiled the Doc, reassuringly. 'You'll be coming back for a bromide, to hold you down.'

'You won't let it hurt me, will ya, Doc?' asked Berghoff. 'I wouldn't like that.' His face made it clear he wasn't joking. Rogers took the only chance he had. If he could only persuade the big man not to bother about the valium, he could meet Tindall later with a clear conscience and nothing to tell him.

'You won't feel a thing,' said Rogers. 'In fact, with local anaesthetic, you can sit back and enjoy the show. I'll talk you through it, if you like.'

It was the worst thing he could have said. Just the idea of a knife carving up his balls turned Sammy over; to have the chance of actually *seeing* it happen was too much.

'Christ, no!' he exclaimed, his palms sweating. 'I'm not a bloody pervert!' He wiped his neck with his handkerchief, and his eyes grew dark and determined.

'You put me out properly, Doc,' he said firmly. 'I don't want to know a thing, OK?'

Rogers nodded, resigned. They'd discussed it all before, but not with the dilemma now hanging over Rogers. Berghoff never went to the dentist without having gas, or a 'knock-out' injection, even for a simple filling. Rogers could hardly hope to get away with giving him less, not in these circumstances.

'Don't worry,' he said. 'When you wake up, it'll all be over.' As he led the way to the table in the surgery, he prayed that whatever he heard in those next fifteen minutes of delirium, would be useless, incoherent rubbish. The prayer was hopeless, and he knew it. What he needed was a miracle.

Tindall had told Doc Rogers he'd be back, and so he was; sitting in an unmarked car across the road a few doors down. He'd got there well before Sammy Berghoff was due, and not simply because he was afraid of missing him; finding the right parking space was more of a problem, since this section of the cluttered road was for residents only. Tindall had known of surveillance jobs when the stake-out car had been jumped by an energetic Panda cop, alerted by an outraged local citizen. And apologies are wasted once the cover is blown.

Tindall sat and waited and the gods were kind. No traffic wardens, and the big black Mercedes bringing Berghoff to his appointment was dead on time. Berghoff walked in looking nervous; the Mercedes remained outside, double-parked. The headrest in the driver's seat blocked Tindall's view, but he wasn't bothered. He wasn't even interested in Berghoff except to smile slightly as the big man came out twenty minutes later, down the steps to the Mercedes, more gingerly than usual. The fact that Sammy also looked a bit woozy pleased the watcher even more. It never for one moment crossed Tindall's mind that Rogers would pull a fast one; the Australian had too much to lose. The Mercedes surged quietly away, and Tindall went in.

The door was on the chain, but Francis opened up without a word and took the Inspector directly to the waiting-room. Tindall stood at the net-draped window impatiently staring at the street outside. At last Rogers entered, and he didn't look happy. His hands worked restlessly, as though he was still cleaning up after the op.

'How did it go?'

'Perfectly straightforward.'

'Sammy looked fine,' said Tindall. 'A new man.'

'Let's hope his missus appreciates it,' responded Rogers drily, glad to keep the subject at small-talk level. It couldn't last.

'You gave him the shot of valium.' A curt nod from Rogers, and Tindall continued, more pointedly: 'And he talked.'

'Crazy stuff, mainly. I didn't get it all.' The immaculate fingers were still for a moment. 'I was busy, remember.'

'Tell me,' said Tindall quietly.

Rogers slumped into a chair, reluctant but compelled by the stare of those sad, merciless eyes. He answered in fragments.

'Bullion. Gold. A million, mebbe.'

'Where from?'

'The South Side.'

It had to be Heathrow, the cargo village, one of the big air freight sheds there. But which one?

'Names would be handy,' said Tindall.

'He didn't say,' Rogers lied. 'He laughed a lot. Didn't make it easy.'

'To cut, or to listen?'

'He wasn't very coherent. He rambled a lot.' Tindall waited for more, and Rogers was obliged to explain. 'About Molly – how she'd make it up to him for having the op done – how the six months' wait and check period would fit in with her being pregnant – for the last time, I told him –'

'Did he say when?' asked Tindall.

Rogers chose to be deliberately obtuse. 'Normal term,' he said. 'Six months from now. Let's hope it's a boy.'

Tindall wasn't amused. 'This bullion rip-off,' he insisted coldly. 'They have to have a date.'

'It wasn't mentioned.'

Tindall sensed the Australian getting prickly, and knew he'd do better to be more casual. There was no advantage in making Rogers angry. One more answer should do it.

'When's Sammy going on holiday?' he asked pleasantly.

'Next week,' responded Rogers, somewhat surprised. Then his handsome face tightened, and the smooth hands thrust into his jacket pockets, as he stood. He'd had all he could take. He was about to say as much, but Tindall got there first.

'That's all, sport,' he said. 'Not very painful, was it?' He started to go, then turned. 'Or am I pinching your line?'

'It's arrived,' said Fenn, putting down the phone. He stared across at Queenie with his shark-tooth grin. 'The stuff from Hamburg.'

'Like the pigeon said it would,' nodded the henna-haired cashier. 'Works at it, don't he?'

'Nothing like incentive, darling,' crooned Fenn, pleased with himself. 'Cleared by Customs, stashed away in Goldhawk's storeroom . . . just waiting.'

'Time we did something about it, then,' said Queenie.

Fenn looked at his watch, lit a cigarette, and brooded. He wasn't ready to give the green light yet. Queenie waited, her painted eyes never leaving his face. He blew out a long strand of smoke, and studied the glowing ash of the fag.

'Don't make it too near home, darling, eh?' he said. 'Wouldn't want to make life too easy for the pigs.'

'West Drayton nick?' suggested Queenie. It was just north of Heathrow, handling most of the petty cime that the Met rozzers at Heathrow couldn't be bothered to waste their time on. Fenn nodded.

'A nice crowd there,' he said. 'Like to go by the book, don't they? Just the sort of elbow we need.'

Queenie brightened up. 'Take it downstairs, shall I, Jack?' she said. Fenn waved a casual hand at the four phones on his desk; cream, blue, green and black.

'Be my guest.'

Queenie smiled; her livid, arching mouth revealed teeth that were slightly too large and even to be natural.

'Black,' she purred, 'my favourite.' She turned the telephone towards her.

'West Drayton Police Station. Can I help you?' A brusque

but tired voice, sounding experienced – the desk sergeant with a bit of luck. Queenie pitched her throaty voice a shade higher, giving it an edge of venom. Fenn couldn't help smiling at her tasty performance.

'Is that the police?'

'Yes, madam,' replied the patient voice. 'What's the problem?'

'I'm not telling you twice, so listen.'

'Who is this, please?'

'Listen fuzz, I said!' said Queenie. 'Heathrow – the agents' building. Next to Cargo Village. Firm called Goldhawk.'

'Easy does it, missus – I'm trying to get this down –'

'They've got a load of dodgy gear in their warehouse. Stuff *you'd* be interested in.'

'Stuff? What like?'

'Use your bloody brains, copper! But look for it tonight. It'll be gone by tomorrow morning.'

'I need more –' Queenie wasn't listening. She'd put the phone down, hard. Whatever the copper fancied having, he'd have to make do with what she'd given him.

Sammy was feeling uncomfortable; not just from the soreness and after-effects of the vasectomy, but because word had trickled back to Fenn that rumours were still floating in the wind about Sad Alex. Tindall had got his teeth into something, the grapevine said. Maybe to do with the Air France caper. Maybe to do with a new heist. Something big, something soon. The berk was asking questions again, dangling carrots, putting the squeeze on. What's more, when he put down the bait, he always mentioned two things – bullion, and the end of the month. Still no names, but he was getting far too nosey for comfort. Fenn wanted to know why.

'He's not bloody telepathic,' he rasped. 'He must've had a tickle.'

'He's guessing,' suggested Sammy hopefully. 'He got wind of something when he was hanging round Gus Fulmer.'

'He's too bloody close!'

'Bluff, that's all it is, Jack. You said yourself he's working blind.'

Queenie arrived, looking swanky. Her painted eyelids hooded the smug glance she threw at Berghoff, and he felt a tiny prickle of bother. She was ready to crow. She liked being in good with Jack, it reminded her of the old days. She'd had her turn then, but she knew her flesh didn't reckon a second glance now, compared to the dollies that Fenn tumbled for his kicks. So her pull with him was different, and she liked to rub that in, to keep Sammy in his place.

'Gus didn't tell him,' she purred, 'but I got a bloody good idea who might have . . . Sammy,' she said, and gave a nasty chuckle.

'Don't be bloody stupid, darling,' said Fenn. But he gave Sammy a hard look, all the same. The big man clenched his hands, uneasily; he knew Queenie had to be joking, but who would Jack believe?

'Bollocks,' grunted Berghoff. 'Pull the other one, it's got bells on.' He didn't shout at Queenie, no one ever did that; but his eyes made it clear she'd better quit spreading the poison, double quick.

'You wouldn't know, Sammy,' she said, her throaty voice syrupy and dangerous. 'You wouldn't remember.'

'Remember what?' Fenn rasped.

'This morning.'

Berghoff appealed to the dapper, hunched figure behind the desk. 'What's she talking about, Jack?'

'The state you were in when you came out of Doc Rogers' place,' she said.

'What sort of state was that, Queenie?' Fenn demanded, dangerously quiet.

'Pissed,' she said. 'As a newt.'

'It was the op!' Sammy protested. 'The dope Doc Rogers poked into me –' He stopped short. Queenie smiled, content that both Sammy and Fenn had got the message. The big man groaned, softly, angrily, his face twisted with dismay. 'Oh, Christ!' he said. 'Sweet bloody Jesus!'

'Rogers,' said Fenn. The watery eyes stared into space,

seeing neither Queenie nor the big man standing so pathetically before him. Groping automatically, Fenn's hands found and lit a cigarette, while his mind conjured up an image of the lanky, silver-haired Australian. He recalled the dry, jibing voice, the elegant hands, the golden boys forever hovering; that was what had screwed Rogers up.

If Fenn had wanted something from Rogers, something that Rogers would never normally give, he'd have done just the same. Yes, it was Tindall's touch all right, the pig. Fenn refocused his mind on here and now, and Sammy in particular. 'Never trust a queer,' he said coldly.

'He'll pay for it,' said Berghoff, aware and thankful that he was off the hook for now at least. But Rogers had nearly fixed him, and that Sammy didn't like.

'Let me put him down, Jack. He deserves it.'

'Maybe he didn't hear about Gus Fulmer,' said Queenie. 'Someone ought to tell him.'

'Just a warning,' brooded Fenn.

'Top him, Jack,' insisted Queenie, her bold mouth relishing the phrase, gleaming brash red over those all-too-perfect teeth. 'Sammy's right. It's what the bloody poof deserves!'

'That'd pull Tindall in too tight,' said Fenn, shaking his head and blowing out a wavering pennant of blue smoke. 'All I want is to put a stop on Rogers,' he murmured. 'Something to make him see sense.'

'Mark him,' suggested Sammy, and Queenie nodded in agreement, bright-eyed and leering.

Fenn didn't answer straight away. He seemed intent on rubbing out the glowing end of his cigarette into the bowl of the gleaming smoked glass ashtray. Slowly, thoughtfully, he twisted and finally broke the half-finished stalk in two.

'Not Rogers,' he said. He didn't need to explain. Find the weak spot and hit it hard; Tindall's way, just as it was Fenn's way. Doc Rogers would understand. There wasn't any option.

Joan was sullen. 'What kind of time do you call this? Why couldn't you get here earlier?' It was the middle of the afternoon and she was wearing a button-up house-coat. Mackay guessed she was wearing next to nothing underneath, and kept his distance, warily. He needn't have bothered. Her frustration had soured into anger, and that, plus the lack of time before the kids came home from school, had turned her off completely. For the time being. She was just as likely to try to have him there and then on the carpeted stairs, than let him get away scot-free. She'd been looking forward to an afternoon of fun in bed, and ended up with nothing.

'Work,' he said. 'Remember?'

'You can pick your own hours. You're the boss.' Her eyes became sly and, taking his hand, she rubbed it against her, slowly, showing him it pleased her. 'Come upstairs to *my* office,' she purred, 'and I'll show you how to enjoy a business conference.' She was getting high, and moved in closer. 'You do the dictation, and I'll practise my shorthand . . . eh?' She began to show him how, but he pulled away.

'There isn't time.'

'Whose fault's that?' She was angry and flushed, seething at being turned away even though she knew that what he said was true. He knew he only had to touch her in a certain way and she'd boil over into lust. He also knew he didn't want it. Even the feel of her body forced against his hand had left him cold. An uneasy elation filled him: he was free, he didn't need her flesh against him any more, he'd found the real thing and it was good. But now wasn't the time to tell her, and he continued to lie.

'How do I pay the bills?' he asked, lightheartedly. 'By kissing the milkman?'

'That's my line,' she said, and laughed, a little too brightly. Her eyes met his challenge, and she swaggered. 'Why not?' she said. 'I might have to one day, and he hints at it often enough.' She smiled, sweetly, testing him. 'One way of giving you a holiday,' she teased. 'Shall I?'

'If you like,' he said, and meant it.

She decided she'd managed to hurt him and, satisfied, tried to make it good. She cornered him in the far end of the hallway, and the handle of the broom cupboard pressed hard into the small of his back.

'Quit,' he said. 'You're being stupid.' This time when he pushed her back, she stayed away. Her mouth was parted in surprise, her eyes wide and unbelieving. Another second and she would fly into one of those sickening rages. Hoping to avoid the tempest: 'The kids,' he said. 'They'll be home any minute.' She slumped, and the surprise turned into a shrug of resignation.

'I suppose you want a cup of tea.'

'I wouldn't mind,' Mackay answered thankfully.

Her eyes grew dark and sly again. 'You pig,' she said. 'I ought to make you wait till bedtime . . .' She smiled, and the heat was off. 'I'm not letting you off, you know,' she said, and brushed her hand against his groin as she pushed past into the kitchen. 'I'll hold it against you till you've paid off what you owe – understood?'

He flicked on an automatic smile, feeling safe as the clatter of children's feet raced up the driveway to the front door. He didn't tell Joan that he'd only be staying until the kids went up to their bath, and that while she was with them, he'd leave. No goodbyes: no point. Angela would be waiting. He didn't intend disappointing *her*.

In the days after his separation from Joan, most evenings Mackay used to eat alone at the Duke's Head, his local pub. The bar there had a micro-oven that toasted everything from sandwiches to garlic-flavoured pizza in about ten seconds flat, and although the taste wasn't very special, the grub was hot and fast, and if you were on your tod that was all you needed. Tonight was going to be different. Angela was going to be with him. The heady routine of work, lovemaking at Mike's place and then a snack and a beer later, was getting her down, she said; she wanted a change.

'A bit of posh nosh,' she said with a giggle. 'To keep my strength up. And yours, too.'

Mackay agreed. There were times when he felt his feet hadn't touched the ground since the night before; jumping in at the deep end with a bird like Angela was all very well, but you had to come up for breath *sometime.* They'd ignored the expected rituals of courtship; the uneasy, nervous overtures, the half-serious, half-joking cuddles and touching; the snakes-and-ladders game of romance, with the final throw ending in someone's bed. That was for beginners, teenagers, newlyweds. This new relationship had made Mackay too worldly-wise to be anything but realistic, he thought. They'd met, they'd seen each other's need, and they'd answered it. Now they could relax, have fun, play a more sophisticated kind of game, where you didn't have to guess will she, won't she, he loves me, he loves me not. This evening out together was the icing on the party cake; they already knew where the night would end.

During the time they'd known one another, Angela had bloomed; tonight she looked even better. The ash-blonde hair was soft and sleek, the pallid skin now had a glow that wasn't entirely the blush of make-up, and her eyes were sharp, even wicked now and then. She wore a plain black dress that might have cost a fortune; it made her bouncy little body look lithe and promising, and Mackay felt smug at the thought of his hand eventually zipping open the bundle of pleasure it contained. The restaurant was something better than a steak bar; muzak, candles in red-glass shades on every table, smooth Italian-cum-Spanish waiters, and a well-stocked deep freeze. Drinks in the bar beforehand, a hundred per cent mark-up on the wine list, and the menu in 'kitchen' French with subtitles. Angela, already on her second rum and coke, hadn't even bothered to look; she knew what she wanted.

'Steak,' she said, eyes gleaming over her clinking glass. 'With all the trimmings.'

'Starters?' queried Mackay. His personal style of bachelor eating might be plain and basic, but Goldhawk contacts and VIPs had to be entertained in a more de luxe fashion. That didn't mean he wanted to educate Angela into high living; he just wanted her to enjoy herself. 'Melon? Avocado?'

'Not fussy. You choose for me.' Her eyes danced. 'Have you ever tried kissing with ice in your mouth?'

Mackay shook his head and laughed. He felt good, higher

than he'd been for months. He'd found a dream of a lover, he'd cut free from Joan at last, and Goldhawk was beginning to take off into a turnover figure that could make living a real pleasure. Even the thought of Larry Liebermann seemed promising; maybe he would be the transatlantic breakthrough that Mackay saw as the next step towards expansion.

He looked at Angela as she finished off her drink; she was his mascot, part of him now, and of his future.

'I feel great,' he said, and touched her bare arm with the tips of his fingers.

'I'm famished,' responded Angela. 'Do we have to wait long?'

'Not once I've ordered,' said Mackay. 'Another rum and coke?' She nodded, then flashed the dimpled grin that turned him on so easily.

'You won't get me drunk, y'know,' she said. 'And anyway . . .' she nuzzled against his shoulder, 'you don't need to . . .'

'I'll drink to that,' he said, and they leaned against each other, bubbling over with soft laughter.

'That last drink we had,' said Angela, leaning back against Mackay. 'What was it called?'

'Sambucca,' answered Mackay. They were in his bedroom, standing in front of the dressing-table mirror, and very slowly, inch by inch, he was unzipping the little black dress.

'Those little black nutty things floating in it.'

'Coffee beans,' chuckled Mackay. 'Supposed to make you randy.' She turned to look at him, dark-eyed, twisting in his hands. The dress, still not properly undone, pulled away from her honey-skinned shoulders, revealing thin black straps.

'Think I need it, do you?'

Her mouth found his before he could speak, and answered the unnecessary question for him. Breaking the kiss very slowly, she nestled tight against him as he completed the unzipping ceremony, all the way down to the small of her back. His face was pressed against her hair, but his eyes watched his hands at work, reflected in the mirror. His fondling led gently along the descending curve and swoop of her spine, creamy, dimpled and tempting in the soft gleam of the table-lamp behind her, the sheen of sensuous golden down was like silk beneath his fingers. She moved away from him, but only to allow the dress to slip rustling dowward to her hips. His hands helped the unwanted covering on its way, then stroked upward again to the restraining catch on the thin, black cross-strap. She giggled as he fumbled, confused by the reverse image in the mirror.

And then the phone rang.

He tensed, but she held him close.

'Forget the phone,' she said. 'It's probably only that funky American git, anyway . . .'

MacKay laughed, even though the catch defeated him; he remembered Liebermann's last call with pleasure. He fell back on the bed, pulling Angela down with him, and reached across to take the phone. 'You did all right last time,' he said, 'try again . . .'

He picked up the phone, and she knelt over him, giggling and eager to delight his sprawling body. She didn't get far. Suddenly his hand came down on hers. He sat up, his face stone-cold sober, and pushed Angela back on to her heels; she was angry at first, then concerned, when she saw his face.

'Yes,' he was saying, 'I'll be there. Give me half an hour.' He put the phone back. 'That was West Drayton police. They want to open up the Goldhawk warehouse, and I'm the key-holder.'

'At this time of night? What the hell for?'

'Information received,' he said bitterly. 'Some bastard's fingered me for smuggling.'

It was obvious the fuzz didn't know what they were looking for; to be on the safe side, they covered the lot. Eager to be first, the specially trained sniffer dogs whined and yelped with quiet frustration until they were given their leads. They drew a blank on drugs, firearms and explosives, and that included the office, the warehouse, and the patch outside regularly marked by visiting mongrels. At last, a nod from the uniformed inspector in charge dismissed them, and the handlers withdrew. Now the real graft began, with the remainder of the snoop squad turning over Goldhawk the hard way. Every box, packet, crate and carton was opened, emptied, inspected and cleared. Mackay could only stand by and watch; tidy though these blokes were, they were lousy when it came to repacking gear back to the necessary standard. Mackay said so.

'We do our best, sir,' clipped the inspector. 'Gift wrapping isn't part of the job.'

The search continued; slow, methodical, meticulous, wall to wall, with nothing missed, not even rubbish on the topmost racks. One clambering constable uncovered the concealed video-camera. The inspector was quietly impressed. Less so when he realised that the whole search was being recorded. The word soon got round his lads, and now every movement became formal and correct, strictly by the book.

'Sorry if it's a bother,' said Mackay, taking some satisfaction from the fact that with the video eye watching them, they couldn't skimp anything or pull any tricks.

'You could switch off, sir.'

'It's on a time switch,' said Mackay, determined to be bloody-minded. The inspector, not easily put down, had his own simple answer to that one.

'Conceal it the way it was,' he told the constable who had shifted aside the camouflaging boxes. 'The best you can – more or less,' he added, pointedly. The constable got the message. He concealed the camera all right, blocking the lens. For the rest of the search, the video was blind.

The snoop squad relaxed, but the search was, if anything, even more rigorous. Now they came to the BS Marine crate, with its bold, five-diamond marker, and Mackay was bothered.

'Compressors,' he explained. 'They've already been cleared by Customs.'

'Have they really, sir?'

The crate was opened, the compressors removed and stripped, and inevitably the reassembling and packing was bodged. One of the constables gave a small exclamation of discovery, and Mackay's heart sank. He had recognised the consignment from the airway bill number and the addressee label; was it going to turn out to be a dud, like the Cyprus Sherry porn movie? He breathed again as the constable held up a small, clear plastic bag that had held several spare connections. False alarm. The one and only. Two hours later, the snoop squad had finished and were fed up to the back teeth. So was the inspector, but he refused to show it.

'You'll be pleased to know the place is clean, Mr Mackay,' he announced, his watchful eyes never looking away, this time at his lads as they trooped outside.

'It was a bloody hoax,' said Mackay. 'You've turned the place inside out for nothing.' He looked around bitterly. To an outsider, everything had been left ship-shape, neat and tidy; there were no signs that a police search had ever taken place. Mackay knew otherwise. It would mean a full day's work just to check everything and repackage where necessary; time and labour he could ill afford. He glared at the braided official, and the sheer blankness of the man made him boil over. 'Don't trouble to apologise, will you?' he said.

The inspector stared at him. 'We don't like it any more than you do,' he said quietly. 'A waste of time and money – for us as well.'

'You don't run the business. A few more tricks like this one, and we'd be right up the creek.'

'It could be worse,' said the inspector. 'Think yourself lucky we didn't find anything.' He touched his leather-covered baton to the peak of his cap; a smooth, impersonal salute, normal PR in the circumstances. 'Thank you for your co-operation,' he said. Mackay looked at his watch: it was past four in the morning. He might as well stay and put the place to rights. For once this week, Angela would have to sleep alone.

Mackay usually worked on a Saturday, all day if necessary; today, the thought sickened him. It was a day to pick up lost time, catch up on paperwork, work out any problems that needed his personal attention, a chance to clear any log-jams that had piled up during the week. If there were freight due to arrive or be delivered, either John or Nik would be on call to handle it; they held off from bothering Mackay with that sort of grind, that was the system. But today was going to be a stinker. He'd phoned the flat, and had had a short, tired row with Angela; they'd both been acid, turned off and frustrated. She didn't offer to come in to help tidy up and that made him sour. He'd have told her not to bother anyway, but he resented it that she didn't seem to care. He had said so, and she'd put the phone down on him.

With that on his mind, trying to put the warehouse to rights was too much. The echo of how it'd been with Joan brought back a vague dread that now he might lose Angela as well. That hurt. He had phoned the flat again, but there'd been no reply. Either she was being bloody-minded, or she'd gone back to her own place. He couldn't reach her there, she had no phone.

Nik arrived to find Mackay drinking coffee laced with the remains of the VIP scotch, and in a very bloody mood. 'We've been turned over by the fuzz. Clear it up.' Nik didn't wait for an explanation. He went into the warehouse and stayed there, methodically working through the consignments to be sorted, checked and repacked. It was going to be a long job, and he could understand why Mackay didn't want any part of it.

By the time Swinford had arrived and walked through to the office, he'd been briefed by Nik about the raid and how Mackay was taking it. It didn't leave him very happy.

'But why, Mike?'

'Some bastard's got it in for us. That's why.'

'The cops didn't find anything?' It was a statement of hope and a question all in one. Swinford still didn't know what was really in the crate that Berghoff was sending through Goldhawk, or why. Fenn had to have a reason, and it probably smelled as high as Billingsgate on a Monday morning. But a plant of anything illegal would only discredit Goldhawk; why should Fenn want to bother? Then there was Mackay's puzzling reply.

'Nothing, John. That's what's so bloody stupid. We were clean.'

'A hoax?' Swinford understood it even less, and felt more and more uneasy. 'What sort of joke is that?'

'Ask the bastard who pulled it. I'll half kill him if I ever get my hands on him.' God forbid you should tangle with Fenn or Berghoff, prayed Swinford silently; the last person he wanted to drag into the quicksand was Mike; he owed him too much. Somehow, Mike had to be kept out of it for the next forty-eight hours.

'Leave it with me and Nik. We'll tidy up. Get away from it this weekend, eh?'

Mackay looked at him, nodded appreciatively, then shrugged. John meant well, but where was there to go? He'd finished with Joan, and he was in the doghouse with Angela; he wasn't going to crawl and, he suspected, neither would she. Getting together again wasn't going to be easy, but equally he knew he had to get her into his life, perhaps even for good, somehow. The brief, bitter memory of the night before flitted through his mind; the meal, the laughs, the eagerness to be alone. The sight of her cream-and-gold body in the mirror, and the phone-call that had ruined everything. That reminded him of the earlier call he'd taken on the very same bed, and its very different consequence; it also brought back Liebermann. He was arriving today, probably on another shady assignment, but this time with a proposition that could make the New York connection more profitable and worthwhile. Straight or bent, Mackay needed some good news, anything to help him kick the present feeling of gloom.

'Maybe you're right, John,' he said. 'I've got to meet this guy Liebermann at twelve. Maybe I'll take him on the town and swing a little business our way, eh?'

'I never eat much lunch,' explained the American, picking at his salad. 'I like to keep in shape, right?' Nothing had been said so far about the proposition; the trip, the weather, service at the hotel, the computerised menu – all garnish for the momentous deal that was taking so long to be laid on the table that Mackay was beginning to doubt if it had ever existed.

The idea of wining and dining friend Larry sank without trace, once the American announced his schedule. Mackay felt both envy and relief. Envy at the good time that Liebermann had planned, and relief that he didn't have to face sharing it with him.

'It's kinda tricky, y'see, Mike. This girl – well, she's twenty-six, maybe twenty-eight, you know – she's throwing a party, wild, you know, that's her style.' He crunched his way into a stick of celery decorated with tired-looking foliage. 'A ginseng tea-party. D'you have that kinda shindig over here?'

'We're still into pot,' confessed Mackay. 'Not my scene, Larry.'

'You prefer it straight, right?'

'Right.'

'Straight's kinda nice, now and then,' said the New Yorker sincerely, 'but her kind of trip gets me really horny, you know?' He grinned, boyishly arrogant. Any minute now, Mackay decided, he's going to start boasting how many times this bird took him in one night.

'It's great while you're young,' he said. 'Hadn't we better talk about the proposition?'

'You should meet Jan. She'd like you. You're cool.'

'Perhaps she has a sister,' joked Mackay, only to find the New Yorker taking him seriously.

'Why no, she hasn't,' he said. 'But hell, I can fix you up –' He took out a slim black leather-covered notebook, and waited, pen poised in his other hand, for Mackay's requirements. 'Just tell me, Mike. I got phone numbers here to suit the whole United Nations, if you know what I mean.'

'Business,' insisted Mackay.

'Suit yourself,' grinned Larry, and put his personal contact (female) file away. Mackay waited as Liebermann composed himself; when the pitch came it was short and sweet. 'You're a pro,' said the courier, matter-of-fact and shrewd. 'I rate that. Better still, you have status here. You get along with your British Customs officials. That's a facility I require as of now.' Mackay looked modestly impressed until Liebermann uncovered the hook. 'I'm forming a courier conglomerate. Strictly executive standards. No questions asked, and what we carry is at nil risk to the sender.' He grinned excitedly at the sheer excellence of his brainchild. 'Top rates for top risks, though, right? That's our insurance. We use kids – international students – Jan can fix up that angle, she's got contacts all over. And you handle the paperwork this end.' He paused. 'Does that grab you, Mike?'

'Documentation for bent couriers,' said Mackay, shaking his head in disbelief. '*That* is a deal I can't refuse?'

'It's a smash. It can't lose. Not with the right team – right?'

'Count me out,' said Mackay, and started to get to his feet.

'There's ten grand in it as a retainer. Dollars, US.'

Mackay sat down again. 'You're joking, Mr Liebermann. You haven't got that kind of currency.'

'I'll be back here in ten days, I'll have it then.'

Liebermann was serious. 'How?' asked the agent. 'You mean you've got backers?'

'Ice,' said Liebermann, shaking his head. 'Dividend from my own investments. This trip is *pour moi*.' Mackay went cold; it fitted all right. Diamond smuggling, small packets either inside the regular courier bag, or somewhere on Liebermann himself. With luck, a bloke could pull off any number of runs without getting caught. But he needed a cool brain, and a hell of a lot of luck. He also needed the cover of a respectable company, a set-up with a high credit rating in legal trading, someone A1 at Lloyds and with HM Customs. Goldhawk. Mackay. A pigeon, for a price.

'No deal.'

'Twenty grand,' countered Liebermann. 'In Deutschmarks, right?' Mackay stared at him, and the New Yorker leaned across the coffee cups to slide home the *coup de grâce*. 'And a percentage of each UK consignment,' he said. 'Up front.'

It was mid-afternoon when Mr Samuels arrived to look over the BS Marine crate as arranged; confronted by the sleekly tailored bulk of the big man, Nik suddenly felt nervous.

'Mr Swinford won't be long,' he apologised, hoping that John would appear on time to explain about the open crate. Hope didn't last as Samuels strode over to the clutter of compressors and packing, still waiting to be reassembled.

'What the hell's going on?' he demanded. 'This was cleared by Customs. Who's had it apart?'

'We got done by the Law,' confessed Nik. 'Some pig tipped them off we had drugs or something. A real dirty trick.'

'Come out of it clean, did you?' Samuels sounded surprisingly relaxed, almost sympathetic. Nik wondered. If it'd been his crate that'd been ransacked and left like that, he'd've been doing his nut.

'Not a mark against us,' said Nik. 'Sorry this wasn't put back in time for you –'

'No sweat, my son,' said Samuels. 'Now I'm here, I'll fix it myself, shall I?'

Nik was about to protest, but the big man was already peeling off his jacket. He seemed bigger still, without it. Even so, it wasn't his job, it was Nik's. If Mike got to know, he'd shout for sure, especially the mood he'd been in that morning.

'If you don't mind, Mr Samuels –' Nik tried to insist.

'I know what I'm doing, tosh. Kindly don't interfere.' Nik swallowed hard, ready to protest and ignore the unspoken threat, when Swinford's voice cut across the warehouse.

'It's all right, Nik. I'll help Mr Samuels. You've done more than your fair whack, mate.'

'There's still plenty left to do,' answered Nik, 'but if you're sure –'

'Have a good weekend,' said Swinford. 'I'll finish off. See you.'

Nik nodded, pleased to be away. 'Monday it is, John,' he grinned. 'Bye, Mr Samuels . . .'

Alone with Berghoff in the greyness of the echoing warehouse, Swinford was afraid, as he always was, of the unobtrusive threat of those massive hands. He'd been waiting for this meeting ever since Mackay had gone across to Terminal 3. There was nothing he could hope to do except make sure

Berghoff was in the right place at the right time, with that craggily handsome face pointed in the right direction. There'd be no cries of 'Watch the birdie!' or 'Say cheese!'; just as long as the video camera could catch Berghoff full frontal with his drawers down, so to speak. Whatever Berghoff was up to here at Goldhawk, it'd show when Mike reran his tapes. Swinford would be in it as well. That was important, because it'd prove that Swinford hadn't fingered Berghoff. That way, there was just a chance of coming out of it unmarked. Squeal beforehand, and he might as well be dead.

'Stop bloody daydreaming, and give me a hand,' grunted Berghoff. He explained what was wanted; forget about reassembling the stripped compressors; roughly put together would do. Just make sure that, in the packing that surrounded the useless pieces of mechanism, there were five neat spaces left, each the size of a small brick. Swinford listened. Within minutes, he'd got what he wanted: the big man facing in the general direction of the hidden camera, casually dumping the clutter of disassembled mechanism into the crate any old how. After that, it didn't matter. Swinford played his part, asked the obvious question, and received the expected reply.

'But what are the spaces *for*?'

'Mind your own, and just do it!'

Swinford did it. Five neat spaces, ready to take – what? The job was almost finished, with Berghoff about to replace the lid of the box, when Mackay walked in.

'Hello, Mr Samuels,' he said wearily. 'John's told you about our troubles, has he?'

'Yeah,' said the big man. 'Rough luck.' He went to set the lid of the crate in place, but Mackay's hand checked him pleasantly.

'Let's see if John's made a decent job of repacking,' he said, chuckling. 'You know what these managers are, especially on a Saturday.' He'd meant it as a joke, but Swinford didn't laugh. When Mackay looked inside the crate, he wasn't smiling either.

'What kind of a cock-up is this, John?' he demanded. 'It's a complete bloody mess!'

'That's how I wanted it, my son,' said the big man and hit Mackay, once, very hard, with the edge of the wooden lid.

Perhaps it was the more modern class technique that he'd been taught, but Dalton liked to list what he had on a blackboard. Tindall preferred to use his brain box; it was less messy, and you could carry it around with you, no trouble. Dalton had responded by scribbling on scraps of paper, but the compromise had only resulted in a tattered jigsaw that blew on to the floor every time Tindall opened the window for fresh air, which was often. Dalton went back to using the blackboard; it was safer and clearer, even if it did mean having to suffer the guv'nor's needle. Besides, it looked good whenever the DI came through.

Today, Dalton came in and couldn't believe his eyes; Tindall had added a line of his own, a date, bold and underlined in thick red chalk: Monday, August 10th. It was neat, precise and important – very different from the usual ribald comments scribbled across the dusty board. Tindall was surveying his handiwork.

'Great stuff, guv'nor,' said Dalton, and grinned. 'Go to the top of the class.'

'You'd better believe it, Jim-lad,' retorted Tindall. 'That's jackpot day.'

'Straight up?'

'It's not my birthday.' Tindall put his hands behind his head. 'But it could be, if we pull that lot in.'

Dalton looked at the board and the jumble of information scribbled there. It had started from virtually nothing; but by leg-work, odd tickles of gen here and there, the odd bit of guff from the collator's office and, most of all, the wrinkles that Tindall kept coming up with, it had begun to build into a solid picture. A bullion job. Heathrow. One of the main cargo sheds. Monday the 10th – only two days away! Names of the villains who might be involved: Sammy Berghoff, Tommy Long, Bev Ackermann, then three question-marks. A job like this would have to be mob-handed, six at least, including a driver. But it was still a dodgy bet, with no solid proof to back it up.

'Are we going to cover it, guv'nor?'

'God and the CI willing, yes.' Of the two the Chief Inspector was the most likely to be difficult. This sort of job, with so many unknown factors, demanded manpower; and that was very valuable, not to be granted lightly. If Tindall was to get the force he wanted, he'd have to present something better than a 'spec' whisper.

'Something we can bring on could help,' offered Dalton. 'The airline carrying the gold.' For a moment, the guv'nor looked blank, then slowly, like the glory of the rising sun, a smile of near-affection broke across his craggy face.

'That's what I call using your noddle. Good lad.'

Lists of valuable cargoes were circulated through secure Heathrow Met channels, for information and action as required. On any given date, you could check who was carrying what, where to, point and time of delivery and the insurable value of the consignment. They already knew the date and the cargo. The rest was easy. With that little item up Tindall's sleeve, the CI could hardly say no to Tindall's contingency plan. It had to go through the usual channels first, of course; but a potential hit worth anything between one and five million in gold had to be looked at seriously.

'Find out,' ordered Tindall, already on his way to the door. 'I'll be with the chief. Get it to me there, OK?' Dalton was already dialling the extension number of the collator's office. Blow the brass – *he* wanted to know. It was his idea in the first place, wasn't it?'

'You've given me a fair case, Alex,' said the Chief. His shrewd eyes studied the officer before him, assessing not only the proposition, but the man himself. A speculative venture, if successful, could bring commendation, promotion, probably publicity as well. An ambitious officer might well consider this the quick way to better things; but Tindall was known as a first-class Jack, dedicated to catching villains, not a deliberate seeker after promotion. If he asked for an extensive back-up, it was because it was essential.

'But *where* is this hit to take place? You can't hope to cover every major airline in the Cargo Village, man!'

Tindall looked at the covey of phones on the big oak desk, and prayed, silently. Not so much to God, as to Dalton. A moment's panic fluttered through his mind; supposing nothing really valuable was coming through Heathrow on that day? Jesus, he'd look a right idiot! The phone rang.

The Chief Inspector answered it, said next to nothing, listened and replaced the receiver. His face showed no emotion. One finger gently stroked the iron-grey clipped moustache. Then he spoke.

'You've got it wrong, I'm afraid, Alex.' The Inspector stiffened, ready to take a tongue-lashing; it'd smelt right, he'd felt it in his bones. But he'd been conned. His chin lifted, as the Chief went on: 'The actual delivery date is the 9th – this Sunday. Air India.' He looked at Tindall, calmly. 'Two and a half million in gold bars.' Tindall relaxed, almost smiled, thought better of it and simply acknowledged the good news with a cool nod.

'Yes, sir,' he said. 'Makes sense to make the hit a day later.'

'Then you'd better cover it. Keep me informed.' He stood up, and so did Tindall.

'Good luck,' he said. Tindall would need it.

The call came through just before they left Tindall's office for the stake-out. Dalton took it; he was on edge, eager to get the surveillance organised. Any calls not connected with the job in hand were an unwanted intrusion into precious time.

'Yes?' he demanded briskly.

'Give me Tindall,' said the voice, dry and rasping, polished but colonial.

'He's busy. Is it urgent?'

'Get him!' It was a cry of rage, of pain, of desperation; it got through to Dalton and he didn't argue any more, simply held out the phone for the guv'nor to take.

'Tindall here,' said the Inspector flatly.

'You bastard,' whispered Rogers. He didn't need to name

himself. Tindall would need no explanations. 'You sadistic bloody butcher!'

Tindall knew the voice, recognised the sound of pain, and guessed at its cause. Someone had found the leak and plugged it. Hard luck on Rogers, but it backed up Tindall's hunch that something was going to break. They'd killed Gus Fulmer, they'd hurt Doc Rogers to shut him up; the mob behind the violence weren't playing games, but neither was he. There was a chance that Rogers could be needled into getting his own back against the heavies who'd marked him.

'I didn't tell anyone, sport,' said Tindall. 'But give me a name and I'll even the score.' There was no reply. 'One name, now,' insisted Tindall, 'and a statement later.' His voice dropped a tone, smooth and reassuring. 'They won't hurt you again. That's a guarantee.'

'The boy,' whispered Rogers. 'They marked the boy!'

Tindall felt cold; his grip on the handset tightened, as the choked voice stumbled on. 'You saw him, Tindall ... you know what he was like ...'

'For the boy's sake, Rogers – *tell me*!'

'No!' The despair became a croak of anger. 'Next time, God knows what they'll do!' The voice slurred at the thought, then came back in accusation, sour with hate. 'You should see him, Tindall. You should see him now. You'd enjoy what they did. You're the same bloody kind!'

'How did they mark him, Rogers?' No answer. Tindall's voice cracked like a whip, making even Dalton flinch. 'Answer me!'

The voice in the telephone grew calm, cold and medical, inhuman. 'They broke his fingers. Then they marked his face ... He'll be scarred for life.'

'Five of diamonds,' said Tindall, to himself. But Rogers heard, and understood.

'You *knew*,' he whispered. 'You knew they'd do it. Only you thought it'd be *me*!' Suddenly he started to scream, rage and anguish making the stream of invective grotesque and incomprehensible. There was nothing more to say. Tindall put down the phone, and for a moment didn't seem to see Dalton or the scruffy room around him. Then he focused on to what must be done. His voice was dangerously quiet.

'Let's catch these bastards at it,' he said. 'I want them.'

What Dalton called the logistics of the ambush operation were almost complete, but Tindall was far from happy. By having to go to top brass for the OK for an elaborate back-up and surveillance job, he had put himself into a situation where he'd have to go by the book. Drawing police issue shooters from the armoury, through to communications procedures, he'd be tied to regulations; and that could make life difficult when it came to the crunch. It had also meant having to inform Air India and BAA security; Tindall would have been far happier setting the trap with only his men knowing what was what. Too many cooks meant too many ears and eyes and whispers. It only needed one insider to be in on the robbery, and the game'd be up.

He had pleaded his case, but without much hope. This was where internal politics came in, and a fine balls-up they could make of things; Tindall knew that only too well from bitter past experience of stake-outs where everyone had grabbed for the glory and the villains got away. This job wasn't easy. To be effective and not blow the surveillance cover, it had to be discreet; normal traffic patterns had to be maintained, with no hint of the unmarked cars waiting to form the cork in the bottle, should the visiting villains manage to break out after pulling off the job. The usual gimmicks were used to conceal the waiting officers: road works, a telephone repair vehicle and crew, a furniture pantechnicon apparently waiting for a consignment from abroad, parked in the loading bay; inside, a dozen men gently sweltered, playing cards in stifling silence and waiting for their call to action. No one showed; the chances were that the villains would send in a scout driving by along the main South Side road, to spot anything unusual that would signal trouble. If that happened, and the ambush was a giveaway, there'd be no robbery. A wasted back-up and standby operation with no robbery would mean someone was for the

CI's carpet, and a right old roasting; that scapegoat already had a name: Detective Inspector Alex Tindall, CID.

One by one, at regular intervals, the various units reported to Tindall's HQ. He wasn't bothered. The bullion shipment had only just arrived, airside; next it must be cleared and secured in the main strongroom. Villains weren't likely to try a hit in broad daylight; the dusk till dawn hours, Sunday into Monday morning, were the most likely. The surveillance cover could be extended if necessary; but Tindall knew in his bones that if the bullion hadn't been hit by dawn on Monday, he might as well give up. Dalton watched his guv'nor sit hunched and withdrawn, to all intents and purposes totally indifferent to the crisp, formal calls from the outlying units.

Lomas had come to the conclusion long ago that being engaged to a girl like Lynn was dead frustrating; on the other hand he reckoned she was worth it, all things considered. He'd been around, known plenty of birds, and tumbled his fair share; the uniform had seemed to help, it gave a sense of trust, perhaps.

Lomas had always liked his bit of fun, but it was different since he'd first met Lynn. She was a nurse, just qualified, with a slender, graceful body and strong legs; her sweet, thoughtful face had an ever-ready smile, a mouth that welcomed and then teased you; but she had definite rules and stuck to them. She looked great, and knew what it was all about, but she was nobody's pushover. She wanted Lomas, but she wanted marriage too; as far as she was concerned the two went together. Lomas wasn't sure why, but he found himself agreeing.

Last night, with wheels of his own for the first time in months, Lomas had brought Lynn to the very edge of taking him, but at the last moment she'd gone cold, and sternly fought him off.

'Not here, Roy. Not in the back of a tatty van. Please.' It was Goldhawk's vehicle, and nearly new, but he understood how she felt. He'd given in, and she'd found her own way of making it up to him, but it wasn't the same. Tender but unhappy, they'd driven to her home; she'd made a little joke before kissing him goodnight inside the van, her hand gently reminding him of their earlier pleasure.

'Probably just as well, love,' she murmured with a little smile. 'It would've lasted all night. I'd've looked a wreck in the morning . . . '

She was on early that Sunday and then again the same evening, as a favour to one of her mates. Now, with the prospect of an empty day ahead, Lomas was driving over to the pub, half-hoping to meet Jimmy Dalton and patch up the peace between them. The idea of snouting, even for an old mate, wasn't on, but Lomas wanted some advice. Yesterday, he'd seen a face at Goldhawk, the sort of face he felt he should know. A Mr Samuels, Nik had said. New customer, flash car, a black Mercedes; can't be bad. Lomas was no great Sherlock, but he knew villains, he had that much of a nose. But he wasn't a copper any more. Whoever Mackay did business with was his own concern. On the other hand, Samuels, or whoever he really was, could be setting up some con-game, using Mackay without him knowing. Either way, Lomas didn't like it. While he was outside, brushing out the van after the morning's last delivery, Nik had told him about the raid and Lomas had offered to help. Nik had said thanks, and warned him to steer clear of Mackay, the guy was in a mean mood. Lomas had stayed outside and made a nice clean job of the van, ready for his date with Lynn that night. Seeing the big man arrive had set his mind ticking over. Villains? A raid? What was going on?

It was difficult not to get involved. As a joke, being turned over by the local rozzers wasn't even funny. A nastier thought now drifted through his mind, and drawing up outside the pub Lomas sat for a moment and considered it; a plant that had gone wrong. There were plenty of shady operators, rivals just on the right side of the law who wouldn't mind fixing Goldhawk. Lomas knew that kind of game. People had been put out of business with planted drugs, or stolen property on their premises. But the place had been clean, so Nik said. Mackay was in the clear. Or was he?

Lomas had the trained mind of a copper, besides being suspicious by nature. He looked for all the crooked angles, and had to admit that Mackay could have a few extra wrinkles up his sleeve, too. A business like Goldhawk could easily be in trouble even though it looked sweet; when things got really bad, there was always one way out, strictly against the law but temptingly simple. Raise your insurance cover and realise your assets, as the lads in the Fraud Squad used to say. In other words, you could look at the raid and the visiting villain from a very different point of view: Mackay was setting himself up for the big crash. And he was getting a pro in, to help.

The pub was only half-full, and Jimmy Dalton wasn't there. Lomas had a quick half, and moved on. He decided that Mackay had a right to the benefit of the doubt; he'd given Lomas a fair crack of the whip, and deserved at least that much consideration in return. With all the clearing up to do after the warehouse had been turned over, it was more than likely that Mackay had gone in to Goldhawk even though it was Sunday; it would be just like him to get stuck in, jacket off, and put the place to rights himself. It would take Lomas less than fifteen minutes to get there, find Mackay and say his piece. He turned on to the Great West Road and put his foot down. It was almost like the old days.

Mackay wasn't in the Goldhawk office, but John Swinford was. He looked up in alarm as Lomas breezed into the warehouse, and the driver could have sworn that he was sweating.

'Chief anywhere around, John?'

'It's Sunday, Roy,' Swinford tried to raise a smile. He looked even more nervous. 'What're you doing here?'

'Loose end, you know how it is,' Lomas grinned. 'The girl-friend's working.' He looked around; the tidying up was virtually done. 'Where can I find him, d'y' reckon?'

'Who?'

'Mike. Want a word with him about the big feller that was in here yesterday morning.'

Swinford frowned. 'Mr Samuels?'

'Drives a big black Merc. D'you know him?'

'New customer. Why?'

'Dunno. My copper's nose, maybe.' Swinford tensed and

Lomas noticed. Swinford didn't know, Mike hadn't told him, he realised. It was too late now. 'That was my last job,' he explained. 'On the Pandas.'

'I didn't know.'

'Past history. I'm a civilian now,' he said. 'D'you mind not telling the other lads?'

'Of course not,' muttered Swinford. 'But Mr Samuels –'

'Him and this place being turned over. Don't it seem fishy to you, John?'

'It's been bloody hard work putting it to rights, I know that.'

'Yeah, well – I fancy chatting to Mike, give him a few wrinkles, you know. Any ideas where he is?'

'Joan's,' said Swinford. It was the first thought that came into his head. He needed time, time to think, to contact Berghoff or Fenn, to warn them. Berghoff had carried Mackay's unconscious body out to the big black saloon and driven off after ordering Swinford to stay and finish work as per normal. As far as he and Nik were concerned, Mackay had gone to a lunch appointment and never returned. That was yesterday. But right now, Lomas was in the way, and had to be removed, preferably without trouble or violence.

'Here,' Swinford said, scribbling the address on to a scrap of paper. 'He said he'd be seeing the kids.'

'Sure he won't mind me barging in?'

'You know Mike and business,' answered Swinford. 'If it's urgent, he'll listen.' He watched Lomas leave, then hurried to the phone. He stood for a moment, hesitating; lifted the receiver, started to dial the number he'd been given, then stopped halfway and put the phone down again. His head was pounding, and he felt almost physically sick, but he knew there was no other way. It was all happening too fast, getting out of control, and he must have it out with Fenn or Berghoff, face to face. Not just to tell them about Lomas; most of all, Swinford had to know if Mike was still alive.

As soon as Lomas pulled up ouside the house, he sensed that something was wrong. It was too quiet, no sign of kids anywhere, yet a big yellow Cortina was parked in the drive. Mackay's own motor must be off the road for some reason, and this salesman's special was a weekend replacement. He walked up to the front door, and rang the bell. No response. He rang again and waited, restlessly. The car was there, someone must be in. A thought snickered through his mind, and he stepped outside the porch to look up at the front bedroom window. The curtains were drawn. He smiled and hesitated. With the kids out playing with their pals, maybe Mike was having a quick Sunday morning snuggle. Lomas had just decided that his rabbiting could wait, when the front door opened.

'Yes?'

He turned back to see a woman standing in the partly open doorway; this had to be Joan. Her hand fumbled to button the top of her house-coat, but the peep of her thigh hinted that whatever she had on underneath was skimpy, if there at all. Bright, feverish eyes stared at Lomas from a face that was pretty even without make-up; she was jumpy, but not particularly bothered.

'I'm Roy, from Goldhawk. Any chance of a word with Mike?'

'He's not here,' she said, and Lomas knew she wasn't lying. She saw his surprise and a glint of amusement showed in her bold, dark eyes. She let the door open slightly wider, enough for Lomas to see the fur-collared car coat and brief-case at the foot of the stairs; not Mackay's style. 'Honestly, he isn't,' Joan said.

'Sure, thanks.' Lomas turned to go, but looked back as she called to him, mischievously, looking out through the now almost-closed front door.

'No bother,' she said. 'Anytime.' He caught a brief glimpse of her smile, gleaming out of the shadows of the hall, and then the door clicked shut. He walked down to the Goldhawk van, and glanced back at the house. The bedroom curtain dropped back into place; he never saw who'd been watching him go.

Lomas started the engine, and frowned. It wasn't Joan Mackay's Sunday morning fun and games that worried him, that was her business and good luck to her. Suddenly Lomas was certain that Swinford had lied to him. Deliberately. For a reason. He'd known all along where Mackay really was, he wasn't letting on, and the whole weekend began to smell rotten. Civvy or not, Lomas wanted to know why. Swinford had better have some answers.

The Goldhawk offices were locked and deserted, but Lomas had a key to the warehouse. He moved quickly through the storage area into the offices, but Swinford was gone. He'd half suspected that'd be the case. Swinford, and what was happening at Goldhawk, worried him a lot. It had something to do with the warehouse, Mr Samuels, and the crate marked with the boldly stencilled five of diamonds, a combination that left Lomas feeling definitely leery. He looked the crate over, and wondered. It had been repacked and nailed down, but not too tightly; that was queer for a start. But snooping around customers' goods wasn't on, not without Mackay's express OK. He was a Goldhawk driver now, not the fuzz, not even a nightwatchman. If he fancied playing cops and robbers, and he was wrong, he could be in dead trouble, even lose the job, and he didn't want that to happen. But if he left it, and the boss was being taken for a pigeon, that was almost as bad. He was stuck, and on his own. No sergeant to turn to, no HQ to call for instructions; no uniform, no back-up, just Lomas on his tod, a civvy. He paced the concrete floor, slowly, restless, mind tumbling; coming back to the crate, he drummed his fingers against it, adding up the pros and cons of breaking open the lid and what he might – or might not – find inside. He sighed, trying to get a clear picture of the big, easy-moving visitor. Mr Samuels. He was the key, Lomas sensed it. If only he could be sure; a mug shot from Criminal Records would clinch it, but he couldn't tap that source any more. Jimmy Dalton would help, but he wasn't around. It looked like a dead end. Lomas leaned back against the crate, eyes closed, face tilted up towards the distant, dusty ceiling. It was then he remembered Mackay's new toy: the video.

He looked to where he knew the camera lens should be, concealed on the highest rack, amongst old, disused boxes. He had to peer, the shadows made the hiding-place difficult to penetrate, and for a second his heart sank; the boxes had been rearranged. Then he caught the glint of the tiny glass eye; it was pointing full at where he stood. Whoever had unpacked, repacked, or fiddled with the BS Marine crate should be on record. Lomas hurried back through the offices into Mackay's own room. He knew he was being watched himself by the second lens that the boss had planted, but that didn't matter. He opened the drawer that contained the video recorder master control; it was working all right, the controls set and operated by the time switch. He found the instructions, painstakingly read and reread how to rewind for replay, and to watch out for accidentally wiping the precious tape clean. He knew that Saturday morning must be on the early section of the tape, and switched it on to fast rewind. It took him what seemed ages to find the spot he wanted – and then, just when he'd got it wrong for the ninth or tenth time, he stumbled on the real cough. The crate was there, open. Swinford, too, and Mr Samuels. Just as they were putting on the lid, Mackay came in. He looked cheerful. Swinford looked panicky, especially when Mackay poked inside the crate. Then Samuels moved very fast, and Mackay was down. Lomas replayed that twice, then stopped the tape. He still didn't know the game, but now he hardly needed to; the moment of violence was enough. He dialled Heathrow Police Station, and asked for CID.

When Mackay first came round, it felt as though the left side of his head had been run over by a bus. He couldn't move his hand; it was caught in some way, tied to something; so was his right wrist, and both ankles. He realised he was lying on his back, on a bed, a feminine, frothy bed, with black imitation satin sheets and pillowcases. The wild, ridiculous thought came to him that this was a new Joan-nightmare; she had captured him and chained him to her orgy-pit, and now she was going to screw him to death, orgasm by orgasm. What a way to go! The old punch-line made him giggle, but the pain soon put a stop to that. He tried to wake, to end the nightmare, to drag himself back to sweet reality. A moment later and he knew it wasn't a dream; this *was* reality. A face hovered over him, and by an effort of concentration, he brought it into focus. It was Angela.

He closed his eyes, refusing to believe it. A soft voice crooned at him, and something cool was pressed against the agonising welt that ran across his face from jawbone to just above his torn left ear. He opened his eyes. Angela was still there, playing Florence Nightingale. The tight red sweater didn't suit the nursing image but her touch was nice.

'I dunno, lover,' she said pleasantly, 'you do get yourself lumbered, don't you?'

'How're you feeling, Mackay?' The crisp voice came from somewhere just out of view. Mackay lifted his aching head and saw a darkly handsome, Napoleonic figure standing by Angela. His hand seemed to be absent-mindedly fondling her buttocks, and she looked as if she liked it.

'Stop it, Jack,' she purred, 'you'll make him jealous.'

'Anything you say, baby,' chuckled Fenn. 'Save it for later, OK?' Mackay slumped back; the strain on his neck was too much. The impact of his head on the soft, fragrant pillow made him groan.

'Didn't mean to hit you so hard, kid,' said another voice, and this head obligingly came into view as Mackay rolled his eyes carefully to one side.

'Mr Samuels,' said Mackay.

'At your service,' said Sammy Berghoff. 'Take it easy, eh?'

'You must be joking,' said Mackay. 'What the hell am I doing here? Where am I, anyway?'

'A guest of the family, squire,' said Fenn, moving up to take Angela's place. He was smoking, but considerately brushed the exhalation away from Mackay's bruised face. 'Where, doesn't matter.'

'It does,' said Angela. 'My bed, that's where, lover,' she added, leaning round Fenn to speak directly to Mackay. 'Comfy, isn't it?'

'Bloody marvellous,' muttered Mackay. 'When do I get screwed?' The others laughed at that. They were a cheerful crowd.

'Any time you want it, squire,' chuckled Fenn. 'We owe you that much.'

'At least,' said Angela. 'I'll look after you, don't worry.'

'Angela's always ready to oblige,' agreed the big man.

'He knows,' said Angela, and looked to Mackay for confirmation. 'Don't you, lover?'

'What're you after?' asked Mackay, drowsily. The headache was getting worse; he closed his eyes, not caring what they wanted, so long as they'd take the hurting away and let him sleep. 'Ransom?' The thought tickled him in spite of the pain. 'Must be bloody idiots . . .' To his surprise, they laughed too; proper clowns, he should be so lucky, but what did they *want*? Then he remembered being at Goldhawk, being thumped by Samuels, and just before that, Swinford poised over the open crate. There'd been something wrong about that crate. It was some sort of fiddle, it had to be. He knew that much.

'Smuggling,' he muttered. 'John was helping you smuggle something . . .'

'You could say that, squire,' said Fenn, as Sammy laid a folded handkerchief across Mackay's nose and mouth. The fabric smelled of something medical, sickly sweet and pungent; within seconds, he was slipping away from pain and into darkness.

'Let him rest for a bit,' said Fenn. 'No point giving him a worse headache, eh?' Mackay never heard them. He was out cold.

He was that way, on and off, all through Saturday night and Sunday morning. They freed his feet long enough for him to sit up and eat breakfast, with Angela, full of giggles, feeding him. She even wanted to be there when Berghoff brought in the bed-pan, but Mackay drew the line there. Berghoff was amused.

'Angela's seen worse than that, my son,' he grinned, 'but if you're that bothered –' The big man jerked his head, and Angela bounced out, pouting.

She'd taken to wearing a gaudy, clinging, wrap-over kimono

decorated with a fire-eating dragon. Berghoff took away the bedpan. Angela came back and retied his ankles. She made a good job of it.

'I thought we were friends,' he said.

'Yeah, it was nice.'

'A bloody great put-on,' Mackay said bitterly. 'For Christ's sake, why?'

'Jack'll tell you soon enough, lover,' she said, and leaned close to his face to check that his wrists were secure. The kimono was loose, and he found himself looking at the softly shadowed swell of her naked breasts. Knowing it, she paused there longer than she needed. Berghoff came back and Angela straightened up, pulling the thin gown closer around her randy little body.

'Not now,' she said. 'Time for beddy-byes.'

'That isn't what your guv'nor said.'

'Tonight'll be nicer,' smiled Angela. 'The blokes'll be busy then, and we'll have the place to ourselves . . .' She touched his middle, meaningfully. 'See you,' she said, and Sammy put the lights out.

The bedroom was across the landing from Fenn's office. Sammy let the kimono-clad bottom strut ahead, and for a moment envied Jack. Angela looked back as she opened Fenn's door, saw Sammy's hot-eyed glance and laughed.

'Naughty,' she said. 'Just 'cos you've been doctored.' Sammy knew he could have her, and knew she wouldn't tell, but he wouldn't risk it, even so. It wasn't just Molly he was thinking about; here at the club, Angela had her own pet watchdog ready to take umbrage, and even Sammy wasn't stupid enough to get into a tangle with *that* one. The thought vanished as Sammy saw who was standing in front of Fenn's desk, and his face grew angry. It was Swinford.

'Look, my son,' growled the big man, 'I told you to stay put!'

'Easy, Sammy,' said Fenn, with a watery glance that said trouble was in the wind. 'Our friend has got bad news.'

Swinford stared at Angela and swallowed hard, unable to believe that this bed-eyed hooker had even been the drab, dreary secretary he'd helped to plant on Mike Mackay. She smiled at him as she lit two cigarettes, one for herself and one for Fenn. She stood by Fenn's chair, letting him fondle her, and that wicked little mouth taunted Swinford, laughing at his fear.

'Hello, John,' she said, 'wetting your knickers, are you?'

'It's Lomas,' he answered; his mouth was dry, but the expression on Angela's face, when he explained, made enduring her sly needling worth the while. 'He's an ex-copper and he's asking questions.'

'Reckons he knows your face, Sammy,' said Fenn, 'but can't put a name to it.'

'He wants to talk to Mackay about that raid, too,' said Swinford. 'I've put him off – but not for much longer.' White cheeked, he was trying desperately to convince the scowling faces all around him. 'For God's sake, call it off!' he said. 'It's too dangerous!'

'Get knotted,' Sammy retorted. 'We're in too far!' He turned to Fenn, sitting with hooded eyes behind the smokescreen of his cigarette. 'Let's fix him, Jack. Now. Today.'

Angela nodded. 'Roy's a driver. Drivers have accidents, don't they?'

'No.' Swinford's protest was a whispered moan. 'No more violence – please, nothing like that!'

'You fingered him, squire,' said Fenn coldly. 'What did you expect?'

'Bloody Delilah could pull that trick,' said Berghoff.

'It'd be a doddle,' agreed Angela, smiling at the thought.

'What you did to Furmer –' whimpered Swinford. 'And Mike – '

'Chummy here thinks we topped his pal,' said Fenn.

'He's having a kip,' said Sammy.

'In my bed,' added Angela, smiling wickedly. 'Fancy taking a turn there with him, lover?' Swinford wasn't interested; he leaned across the desk, bravely confronting Fenn.

'I want to see him.'

'So you shall, darling, but it'll be a dead give-away, won't it?'

'If you want me to play ball, Mike doesn't get hurt!' demanded Swinford.

The cigarette left Fenn's face and, for one brief moment, hovered over the gleaming ashtray, rolled and finally settled, poised and tilted – and then at the brisk tap of Fenn's fingertip released its ash into the dish below.

'Show him,' said Fenn.

Sammy hadn't been lying; Mackay was sleeping like a babe, for all that he was tied by wrists and ankles to the upright of the big brass bed. Swinford pointed to the ropes.

'We like having him here,' explained Fenn with a thin smile. 'Don't want him to go, do we? Not yet.'

'Got a job to do, hasn't he?' said Sammy. 'Like you, my son.'

'He won't help you,' whispered Swinford. 'You'll never make him!'

Sammy was just going to put Swinford right on that when Fenn cut in, coldly.

'That's our business, squire. You screw this deal up, and he goes first – understood?' Swinford stared at him, bleakly. He should've known all along; Fenn was a bookie by nature, always covering his bets, always making certain he'd come out on top. Getting Swinford in debt over his limit had only been the teaser; the threat of being done over had kept him hooked, but just in case the worm decided to turn, they'd pulled this stroke.

Mackay was the hostage to Swinford's loyalty. They'd put this slut into Goldhawk to keep Mike occupied and she had played him along with all the skills of a high-class whore. Delicious bait for a stupid sucker, and Mike had taken it. Now they were both caught in the trap. Somehow he had to protect Mike, but there was nothing he could do about Roy Lomas.

Someone entered the room, and Swinford turned; Fenn made the sarcastic introduction.

'Bloody Delilah, meet the pigeon.'

'Hello, Mr Swinford,' said Queenie. 'All right, dear?'

Swinford stared at her, stupefied. He knew Fenn never joked about violence; yet the thought that this burly harridan, the shrewd, painted club cashier could have wiped out Fulmer seemed impossible. Then he saw her eyes, and knew why Fenn and Berghoff handled her so warily. A hag with a temper – but never a killer, surely?

'Trouble, Jack?' said Queenie.

'The new driver at Goldhawk, darling,' Fenn replied, his watery eyes fixed on Swinford. 'He's ex-fuzz.'

'Might have an accident,' suggested Sammy.

'He's got nothing to do with the Force now,' begged Swinford. 'He left!'

'Once a copper, always a copper,' crooned Queenie, happily. Her eyes glittered with excitement. 'When, Jack?'

'Now.'

Queenie's painted smile arched and glistened over the perfect teeth; then she saw Angela, in the loose and skimpy kimono.

'You'll catch your bloody death,' she snapped. 'Put proper clothes on!'

'I'm all right!'

'Don't you spite your mother, my girl,' said Bloody Delilah, and patted Angela's left cheek, very gently, with her open palm. The girl drew back, and Swinford saw that for a split second she was frightened stiff. 'Do as you're told, yes?'

'I'll make sure she does, Queenie darling,' soothed Fenn, diplomatically. 'What about this flaming driver?'

'Where do I find him, dear?' Queenie asked Swinford gently. He met her eyes and he didn't argue. He told her the address of Roy's digs. 'He's going to know you sent him on a dummy run,' said Fenn, tapping Swinford's arm like a reproving uncle. 'He'll come after you, squire. Stands to reason, don't it?'

Swinford nodded, miserably.

'Finish in the warehouse, did you?' asked Sammy.

'Nearly,' whispered Swinford.

'He'll reckon on catching you there. Probably poke around in Sammy's crate.'

'You'll know if he's there, Ma,' said Angela brightly. 'The Goldhawk van'll be parked outside.'

'Just right,' smiled Queenie. 'It shouldn't take long.' She moved to the door, briskly. 'Get yourself put to rights, girl, before I get back.'

Fenn turned to Swinford with a nod of approval. 'I'm glad you co-operated, squire,' he said. 'Queenie can get very rough. Very rough indeed.'

'She's your mother?' Swinford murmured wonderingly, his eyes on Angela.

Angela nodded. 'Crazy old bag she is sometimes.' She smiled, the touch of bitterness dismissed. 'She's a good sort really, though. Thinks the world of me.' She laughed. 'Bloody Delilah. Fancy having a mother with a name like that, eh?' It was Fenn who explained, taking Swinford by the elbow and guiding him out on to the landing.

'Queenie's got a past, y'see, squire,' he said. 'Twenty years ago, she was a lady wrestler. Straight up. Bloody good she was, too. Would've been champion at her weight. Great performer . . .' He paused, looking over the balustrade into the stairwell, two flights down. 'Had a vicious streak though. Temper like a bloody wildcat, a tiger, I'm telling you.' He paused again, and smiled at Sammy, who nodded. 'Lost her rag against a real odd slut, a tearaway –'

Sammy supplied the name at the snap of Fenn's fingers.

'Queenie nearly killed her,' said Fenn. 'Used a necklock and bloody near choked her to death. Took five of 'em to drag her off. Banned for life after that.'

'Left her trademark though, didn't she, Jack?'

Fenn showed Swinford his hand, fingers crooked into a wicked claw. 'Five of diamonds.'

'Fulmer,' whispered Swinford, feeling weak at the memory. 'She did that to him?'

'And the knees,' said Sammy. 'She's a pro, my son. No question.'

'Don't worry about this driver of yours, squire,' rasped Fenn. 'He won't feel a thing. That's a promise.' Swinford said nothing; there was nothing to say.

'Go home, my son,' said Sammy, putting his big hand on Swinford's shoulder. 'Keep out of the way until you're needed, right?'

'The delivery,' acknowledged Swinford, dully.

'That's the ticket, squire,' smiled Fenn. 'After that it's business as usual.' The smile dropped. 'Just be there.'

As soon as Queenie's chunky figure strutted into the office, Fenn knew she'd done her stuff, and he was pleased. A job well done could keep her purring for weeks, even months, and she'd do anything to please her Jack. They'd had a hot thing going, years ago, when he'd tumbled her regularly; then she'd been young and wanted it. The fact that now her Angela was on call to 'uncle' Jack, with a lush little love-nest of her own across the landing from his office, worried her not one bit. Only Fenn knew how many times Queenie had been at his secret peephole, proudly watching Angela at the work she enjoyed so much and did so well. It was a strange bond, made all the stronger by that one wild night – Angela's first – when he'd taken both of them, mother and daughter, in the same bed, turn and turn about. Since then, they'd been together like a family, and God help anyone who tried to break it up.

'All fixed up, darling?' he asked.

'A doddle,' said Queenie. '*He* won't be going far tonight.'

Dalton was out, Tindall was out, and the CID geezer who took Lomas's call was particularly bloody-minded. Not that he wasn't being correct, just awkward; he wasn't going to offer any real help unless the caller told him what it was all about, and Lomas wasn't having any truck with anyone but his old mate. Even attempting to explain made the mind boggle. All the wary, plainclothes twit could say was that if Lomas had information leading to a crime, he should spill it now unless he wanted to be clobbered for conspiracy. Lomas – still anonymous – told him to stuff it.

Putting the phone down, he could see he had problems. Jimmy or his guv'nor, and preferably both, had to be shown the video tape; which meant that somehow, they had to be brought to Goldhawk. Right now, that wasn't on. Going across to Heathrow nick in person seemed the best answer, and to take the tape; leaving the only evidence behind was asking for trouble. Carefully, he rewound and removed the tape, then put in a spare. He hurried out to the van, pausing to lock up the warehouse and curse the steady drizzle that would make night driving such a bind. He walked to the van, unlocked it and got in.

Placing the boxed video cassette beside him on the passenger seat, Lomas put the ignition key in, and turned it. The starter motor whined in protest; there was either no spark or the juice wasn't getting through. Lomas peered through the rain-distorted windscreen, and cursed again. He didn't fancy poking around under the bonnet in this weather, but there was no other way. He released the bonnet catch and got out. Shrugging himself deep inside his reefer jacket, he raised the engine hood and fixed it open. Condensation on the distributor, OK; but the whole engine area was wet. Then it hit him. Someone had been poking around in there less than half an hour ago. He checked. The battery was in place. Then he saw the bomb.

He froze. Panic started to rise from deep down, but he checked it. The neat little package hadn't gone off yet; if he had any sense, he'd move right away, slowly, get to the nearest phone and call the bomb brigade. That was correct procedure. Then he realised that the device had no watch or timing mechanism, and that it couldn't have been connected to the ignition – or he'd have been spattered all over the tarmac by now. His shrewd mechanic's eyes followed the simple, undisguised wiring and suddenly realised his luck was in. A thermo-coupling switch; it needed heat to bring the breaker points into contact. While it was cold, it was safe. His glance fell on the distributor cap. Whoever had poked under the engine hood had let the rain in sufficiently to affect the points. But for that, he'd be on the way to Heathrow's main entrance, and the big bang. But why? He was close to something, those questions about Mackay had given somebody a fright. Not Swinford. He'd lied, and he'd run, but violence wasn't his game. It had to be Samuels. What was his tie-up with Goldhawk? Lomas kicked himself for playing copper. If he'd still been in uniform, he'd've been roasted by his sergeant for wasting his time. This was not his patch, and not his game, either. CID would listen to him now, but how was he to get there? Strip the bomb. Any other way would only waste precious time. It looked straightforward enough. He decided to give it a try.

Thoughtfully, he took the video tape and placed it safely in the dry, well away from the effect of any explosion if he made a mistake. Then, very carefully, he tackled the wiring. There was no chance of the damp, chilled motor getting warm unless it was turned over; that meant he could leave the thermo-coupling device alone. If he could just render the detonator useless, he'd be safe. It took some doing; wet fingers and only torchlight made a nightmare of disconnecting those wires. Thirty seconds was enough, but it felt a lifetime. With the bomb safely in the car, Lomas hurriedly dried the distributor head contacts and leads, then closed the bonnet and turned the engine over. It started, second try. As he moved off, the rain was getting heavier. It was going to be a bloody awful drive..

The Heathrow police station is on the northernmost point of the airport, outside the main entrance tunnel. Never exactly peaceful even on a Sunday, tonight seemed more hectic than usual, with Panda and patrol cars nipping out at a pace that suggested something big was brewing. Lomas parked the van and went inside. In one hand he held the video tape, for Tindall's eyes only. Under the other arm, in a small cardboard box, were the dismembered components of the booby trap.

The station desk and the usually crisply organised area behind it seemed more like a market first thing in the morning. The station sergeant was taking call after call. Everyone around him was on edge, snapping at each other, except for those lads who ploughed on by keeping their feelings to themselves. Lomas found himself feeling sorry for them, but that didn't do any good. Neither did the sprog who reluctantly offered to help, at the same time filling in the daybook with details of the last small crisis.

'Yes, sir?' he said to Lomas flatly.

'CID, please.'

The constable looked up. 'Nature of the complaint?'

'I need to speak to Jimmy Dalton,' explained Lomas, careful to be polite. If he handled it wrongly he'd get nowhere fast and only a handful of awkward questions to show for it. 'Detective Constable Dalton, that is.'

'Personal, is it?'

'I know him personally, yes.'

The peeler's eyes looked at him distastefully, and Lomas suddenly realised what he was thinking: he reckons I'm a bloody snout with something to sell! 'Information?' The word came out in a sarcastic drawl. Lomas felt his self-control beginning to slip, but managed to hold on – just.

'It's special. Urgent,' he insisted. He put the box down on the counter, and leaned on it. 'If he isn't in, Inspector Tindall will do.' It was a way of pulling rank; it didn't work.

'Will he, now?' the constable sneered. 'If it's that important, what about the CI – or the Superintendent?'

'They wouldn't understand,' said Lomas, getting angrier by the minute. 'Are you going to help or not?'

He'd said the wrong thing and he knew it; now the rozzer would play it by the book, and it could last all night.

'Name?' said the constable, stony and polite, pen poised over the daybook, waiting for the required information, and refusing to budge an inch without it.

'I want Constable Dalton in CID!' exclaimed Lomas. 'You're not bloody deaf, are you?' The young eyes stared back at him, blank and silently insolent. Lomas remembered his own lessons in handling aggression from the public and knew he'd get nowhere from now on. He tried a softer tack, but it was already too late.

'I asked for your name, sir,' said the constable. 'Now – I'll help you, if you help me.' He gave an impatient gesture as if to put his pen away. 'That is, if you have a genuine complaint?'

'Where's Tindall?' demanded Lomas so vehemently that the nearby sergeant noticed and answered, with a frown.

'Busy,' he said tersely. 'On the South Side.' He flicked a glance at the constable who indicated that this was a right one, an awkward customer, but he could handle him. The sergeant took in the situation and nodded brusquely. 'The constable will deal with it,' he said.

'Like hell,' said Lomas, and walked out, deliberately leaving the box behind.

'Berk,' grunted the constable, then grinned, smugly. 'He's left his box, Sarge,' he said. 'Shall I chase after him?'

The sergeant gave a tired smile. 'Don't bother, lad. Let him come back for it.'

'He'll have to talk to me then, won't he?' chuckled the sprog, then looked inside the box and saw the dismantled bomb. He went white, and almost choked. 'Sarge –' He drew back from the box, very carefully, and his voice went up a tone, close to panic. '*Sarge!*'

Bev Ackermann's missus always knew when he was due for a job of work; he'd take her to bed for an hour, just before it was due to happen.

'Never know when I'll have the chance again, do I love?' he'd say when she teased him, hurrying to get undressed. She never objected, never dreamt of putting him off; he'd been inside enough times already and he'd never change, no point in trying to make him. She was happy the way they were, they'd had a good run this time. Bev was more careful these days. He'd got more choosey. Not that he ever talked about his jobs, least of all in bed. No time to waste there.

'Best way of relaxing there is,' he'd say, and do it once more for luck. That was part of it, of course; like touching wood, leaving her bang to rights was Bev's lucky charm, his way of crossing his fingers, and a lot more fun than stroking a rabbit's foot. She'd lie there, rumpled and content, watching him dress; that was part of the ritual, the way footballers put their gear on in a certain order. He was heavier now but still good to look at, thick across his shoulders and a tight little ass, even at his age. He'd dress, brush his hair, then stand by the bed looking down at her. Then he'd pull the sheets right off and look at her properly, all over, and she'd let him.

'That's worth coming home for,' he'd say, and leave her like that. She never moved, even if she was cold, not until the front door banged shut after him. She'd just lie there, thinking about that lusting stare of his, and praying that it'd go as well this time as the last, that he'd be back and no rozzers breaking in the bedroom door saying, 'Get your trousers on, Mr Ackermann, you're wanted down the nick for questioning.'

This time it was the same ritual, the same hard loving, but Bev kept having little laughing fits. He wouldn't tell her why, just shut her up with a long tasty kiss every time she asked. But by the time he was ready to go, he couldn't stop himself saying something. He looked down at her sprawling, naked body, and grinned.

'That's worth coming home for,' he said, same as usual, then added cheekily, 'keep it warm for us, eh?' For once he covered her up, breaking the pattern, and she looked at him, wondering. 'Only a short turn tonight, love,' he explained. 'Nothing heavy. Just a few phone calls.' He was at the door and looking at her like a kid. 'See you later, sweetheart,' he said, and went out whistling.

Tommy Long looked at the clock, then back at the glowing, green baize table; three reds and all the colours still to go, and just twenty minutes on the ticker. One good break should do it.

'Straight run,' he announced to the shadowed figures gathered round. 'Any takers?' He was well known for his cue-work under pressure. On form, he was brilliant, Joe Davis couldn't have touched him; it was like his cue had been dipped in honey.

'A quid says you can't,' said a husky Welsh voice; two more brought the stake to a fiver, and Tommy matched it with a note. He chalked his cue tip, gently, rhythmically, economically, his eyes on the minute hand of the quietly ticking clock. 'Sixteen minutes, all or nothing,' he said, and bent over the table, hand spread into a firm yet resilient bridge, eyes staring down the shaft of wood, body tensed and poised, ready for the strike. He did it in thirteen minutes flat, picked up his winnings, and spent most of it paying for the final round, all shorts, nothing on the cheap for Tommy.

'In my mouth, round my gums, look out bollocks, here it comes,' he said, downing the tot of dark rum in one gulp. The others took their time, they weren't going anywhere, and they didn't ask Tommy's business either. If it went all right, he'd be back at the snooker table, sharp as ever; if not, they'd have a whip round to pay for a welcome home booze-up, when he'd done his stir. They knew his trade, and they weren't bothered. He was a good sort, and a bloody marvel at the table. On tonight's form, he couldn't lose. Only the barman was nosey.

'Got something hot waiting for you, chief?' he said. He didn't expect an answer; it was just a joke; Tommy kept his love-life strictly to himself anyway, but tonight he was on the up and up, and threw back his answer as he left.

'Going for a midnight spin, aren't I?' he said. 'A bloody picnic. See you!'

Alan found the last set of wheels he wanted in the rear car park of the Allenby Hotel. Nothing too flashy or too new; something with a bit of room and enough poke under the bonnet to get him out of trouble if he needed it. He'd had a choice, but the first one, an 'R' registration Princess, was low on gas. He'd ended up taking the big Vauxhall; it turned over quietly, first time, and he eased it out on to the dark back street without turning its lights on until he was well clear. Just over twenty-five thousand on the clock; it ran OK, someone had been taking good care of it, regular servicing, that's how it should be. Now all Alan had to do was find the change-over point, and leave the hot car ready for the last stage of the getaway. It seemed funny not having to supply the wheels for the hit itself, but when Sammy had explained, Alan took the point with one of those thin bony smiles he used to show his indifferent approval. Carefully, he kept to the speed limits and obeyed the signs; there'd been one job that he'd nearly ruined by picking up the wheels too late, then getting warned for speeding. Luckily, he had the kind of face that once seen was almost immediately forgotten, impossible to recall or describe, the Identikit nightmare. Alan had baulked at Sammy's condition that he would need a tool and take part in the actual grab. Playing the heavy wasn't Alan's skill, but when he was told his weapon would be an aerosol of ammonia, and yes, he would be driving once the goods had been lifted and stashed away, his ghostly smile returned, and he was happy. Sammy knew what he was doing. The way the big man painted it, this fit-up was going to be a right charmer, so simple it made Alan feel more like a boy scout than a wheels merchant. He smiled at the memory of bob-a-job; this one would set Brown Owl's ears buzzing. Five grand; you could buy more than a few Girl Guides with that.

Fenn was having a brandy with Angela and Queenie when the phone rang. It was Sammy, and he was cheerful, calling from a Stanwell coinbox.

'Just seen Bev,' the big man said. 'Having the time of his life, he is.'

Fenn smiled at Queenie and she winked back.

'Bev's got the fuzz hopping all over the place,' he said, then spoke into the phone. 'Tommy and the lads are on their way now, Sammy.'

'Great. Like a bloody picnic for them, isn't it?' It was a good description; when the lads had been told what they had to do, they'd hardly believe it. It had appealed to Bev to do his bit with the 999 calls, and the most they could hit him with would be malicious phone calls – if they ever caught him at it. A Sunday night joy-ride, Tommy had called it. If it was going to be that cushy, why not take some birds and booze along as well, weasely George Moffat had suggested. They'd had a good laugh at that, especially when Fenn had promised that if they were all good boys, he'd give them the fun they wanted on the club – after the picnic was over. Wednesday was going to be Angela's birthday, and everyone bringing her a pressie would get a lovely 'thank you' in return. They'd howled at that one. Queenie wasn't so pleased; it was all in fun, she knew, but put an idea like that into Angie's randy little head and she'd do it, just for a giggle. Her mum had no time to moan about it right now, though; Sammy was filling in the details of what was to happen next.

'Tindall's fallen for it, Jack,' he said. 'There's half-a-dozen of 'em at least, all round the Air India warehouse. *And* it's pissing down,' he added.

'Lovely,' chuckled Fenn. 'He'll be even more miserable by the morning, stupid sod.'

When trouble came, it was the last thing that Tindall expected. The area around the main block of cargo warehouses, and Air India in particular, was if anything less busy than normal; the rain didn't help, and the stake-out was beginning to drag. The road works and telephone cover had outlived their credibility, and the various units were now spaced out in the sort of vans and trucks that were always to be seen dotted around the parking area at all hours of the day or night. Dalton spotted it first.

'Control's busy tonight, guv'nor,' he said. Radio contact between the police communications centre and the various mobiles cruising or actually tackling reported incidents was a constant background to routine police work. The ear soon got tuned to one particular call sign and tended to blot out any unnecessary chat affecting other vehicles or areas not covered by the listening unit. But waiting made keener listening inevitable, and Dalton was beginning to notice the pile-up of calls, the hint of edginess at Control, the sullen response of the mobiles receiving, and the uncommon bluntness of the 'proceed and investigate' instructions.

Tindall listened to the continuous crackle of voices and he too was uneasy.

'Too busy,' he said. 'Get them for me, lad.'

He had a muttered conversation with an impatient Duty Officer who resented having to give Tindall a run-down. Rushed off his feet by a spate of minor calls, he was already having to pull in units from neighbouring areas and that left nobody very happy. Reported break-ins, traffic snarl-ups, more than a dozen after-hours pub punch-ups, suspicious characters loitering, entry alarms set off with no sign of intruders: standard complaints, but never so many on a normal Sunday, and all at once. Tindall spotted something else.

'None of it's near here. Have you noticed?'

'Funny that,' Dalton replied.

'Not a joke. Deliberate. Someone's trying to tie our lads into a bloody reef knot.'

'Stretching us, y'mean?

'Taking away our back-up if there's a chase. Most of those 999 calls, they're too pat. And too close to each other, half the time.'

'The Southall side,' agreed Dalton. 'And Colnbrook – that snarl-up on the by-pass . . .'

'Someone,' said Tindall grimly, 'is trying to bugger us about.'

He wasn't the only one who smelled a rat. His call sign came on, and he was put through to the CI's office. People in high places were beginning to take notice, and now Tindall had to justify himself again. Seeming not to overhear, Dalton listened and admired in silence. So much confusion, but Tindall shewdly turned it to his own benefit, glib and to the point; someone was going to a hell of a lot of trouble to pull nearly all mobiles away from Cargo Village. Well, let them. Tindall was staying put.

The dark-green liveried security truck trundled to a halt, its beefy engine revving as reverse gear was engaged. The driver, well-used to this run, backed the rear end of the massive vehicle in a tight, smooth turn so that its heavy rear-opening door was almost touching the steel shutters of the Eagle Airways warehouse. Two short blasts on the truck's horn, followed by one longer signal was the code for the roller door to be raised. The driver, holding down brake and clutch ready to ease the vehicle backwards, waited patiently. The windscreen wipers whined their endlessly repeated arcs across the glass, never quite clearing away the steadily falling rain. The driver looked across at his mate, who was yawning as he rubbed his eyes beneath the peak of his helmet.

'Bloody rain,' he said. 'Wears you out, don't it?' His mate nodded, and blinked his strained eyes clear, then looked at the rain-dappled wing mirror through the side window. The roller door was just beginning to rise, glowing red in the rear brake lights of the truck. Once the doorway was fully open, they could reverse into the loading bay, under cover, and with the steel shutter brought down and secured, get out and stretch their legs. Until then, the truck crew stayed put, that was the routine. Not that they were actually carrying anything vauable; this was a pick-up job and the portable strongroom at the back was empty, except for the two other members of the team. They would sit tight too, until the truck was still, the security shutter down, and the signal given by the team gaffer.

The warehouse roller door slammed shut with a jarring metallic crash, only partly muffled for the security guards by their strongbox on wheels. As long as the team stuck rigidly to their standard procedures, the truck was virtually impregnable; no one could get in or out while the emergency central locking system was in effect, short of villains using a plasma torch to cut their way through the sheet steel of the sides. The truck *could* be stopped, *could* be opened; nothing was impossible to well-organised villains these days. But it would take time, and the sort of high-class equipment normally handled by an Army commando team, to make a job of it. With the warehouse shutter down, the driver looked out at the foreman ganger and got a cheery wave of welcome from the hand that held a mug of tea. It was a face he knew, identifiable even through the rain-spattered wire-meshed windows, and the harsh shadows of the warehouse lighting. That mug of promised tea was a well-known signal, too; not on the procedure sheet but all the more welcome for that. The co-driver reported in on the radio-link, timed the call, signed off and gave the nod to his mate. At the turn of a switch, all door locks were released and at last the security squad could get out for a breather, before the routine transfer of valuables began, from the airline strongroom into the safety of the armoured truck. The driver was the last to go, after switching off the ignition. The engines shuddered into silence, and in that moment all hell let loose.

The attackers seemed to come from nowhere, and they moved fast. The driver's feet had hardly touched the ground before a blast of ammonia squirted into his face, burning and blinding his eyes. He screamed. A pickaxe handle smashed across his chest and throat, slamming him back against the side of the truck, and he was finished. The co-driver was quicker and managed to dodge the first blow. Then he turned to try to activate the truck's emergency alarm circuits, and the butt of Sammy Berghoff's shooter thudded across the side of his neck and he went down like a rabbit. The two guards from the rear compartment were picked off just as cleanly. One was out cold, with a fractured skull where the head of the lashing pickaxe handle had caught him on the temple, unprotected by his helmet; the other lay moaning on the concrete by the truck, clawing his blind, streaming eyes and twisting from the agony of the blow which had smashed across his spine. It was over in seconds, and Sammy was pleased, but that wasn't the end of it.

'Alan,' said the big man, and the scrawny wheels merchant didn't need telling twice. He clambered into the cab of the truck and checked over the radio link controls, then gave a wink and a thumbs-up sign. It was just as they'd been told, a doddle. From now on, Alan would report in as per standard security procedure; he knew the form. When the call came from security radio control, he answered by the book and grinned as he reported the current status of the job; he didn't even have to lie.

'Loading now,' he said, timed the report, and signed off.

Sammy's team had stripped the uniforms from the security guards, then bound and gagged them, even though at least two of them were looking very sick. No sympathy, no risks; this was a job, not a church bazaar. The foreman ganger, having been forced to play his part with the twin barrels of a sawn-off twelve-bore poking into his kidneys, was trussed and gagged, and stowed away next to his equally helpless mates. They could only watch as the team moved swiftly and silently through the next stage of their plan; the irony was, once they'd put on the security guards' gear, Sammy and his boys did precisely what should be done; they loaded the truck. Only once did they pause, when Sammy was shown an unexpected find; several boxes of currency. He looked, saw that it was all new notes, consecutively numbered, and shook his head. Too hot. What they'd come for was the cream, easy to lift, and safe: five small, ribbed aluminium caskets each one holding a fortune in diamonds, safe ice. Sammy checked the contents, letting the others have a peep to prove the bother had been worthwhile. They grinned, briefly, through the eyelets and mouth gaps of the masks they still wore. The masks would come off only when they drove away; until then, the faces behind them remained anonymous.

The loading was soon done, and the gang took their places in the truck. Sammy sat in the co-driver's seat, and signed the consignment chitty: Adolf Hitler. That got a chuckle from Alan, togged up in the security driver's gear, and ready to roll. Only George Moffat hadn't changed into uniform; he wouldn't be travelling with the truck, his job was to work the warehouse doors and tidy up before slipping out to make his own way into the dying night drizzle. Everything, including the security truck's exit, had to look normal. If one of the guards had worked the warehouse door, and been spotted by a know-all, it could put the kibosh on the whole job. Jack Fenn and Sammy had covered all the wrinkles on this one; even to having the truck wait until security control requested its departure coding and confirmation that all was well. The call came, was answered, timed and signed off. The warehouse shutters opened, and the truck drove away, with Sammy giving George Moffat a thumbs-up as they left. Two warehouse blocks away, Tindall was sitting in the rain, watching Air India and a pile of unwanted gold. Sooner or later, his troup of pansies would go into action, looking for a dark-green security truck last seen leaving Eagle Airways. He'd find it too, but not where he expected. Before that, Sammy had a delivery to make, strictly local.

It was nearly dawn and Tindall wasn't talking to anybody when the call came through from one of the cars on road block standby. A van and a car had been seen proceeding east from the Stanwell Road roundabout; waiting its turn to join the thin flow of traffic heading towards Heathrow, the car had paused just long enough for a keen-eyed lad with a good memory to spot and recognise Tommy Long. The registration of the car had already been flashed through to Records for details of owner, where stolen, and when and if reported. No answer to that query yet, but the van and the car were headed in the right direction, right into Tindall's lap. Dalton brightened up, but the guv'nor seemed hard to please.

'It's too pat,' he said. But he had to agree it was a tasty time to pull a job; after the mauling chaos of the 999 calls, nobody on mobiles was feeling very bright. The coldest hour of night usually found security staff at the airline sheds brewing up, or even if they were on routine patrol, only too keen to cut corners and get back to the cosy warmth of their cabins. It was a time when everybody on night shift was at low ebb; a hit now would really catch them where it hurt.

It was that way with the stake-out team, too; but this early warning brought them smartly back to life. If it *were* Tommy Long, and if the car *were* stolen, then it was odds-on favourites to be the hit team moving in. Tindall's plan was for his lads to wait until the heavy mob parked their wheels handy to the air cargo shed and entered the premises; then the squad could move in and take them in the act – with luck, before they could do much damage. Dalton looked sharp now, as he waited; Tindall seemed more miserable than ever. Another report crackled up; the suspect car and van were turning off the main thoroughfare on to the interior south-side road, cruising at a steady speed towards the block of cargo sheds under surveillance.

Then, with only minutes to go before the action started, things began to crumble.

First, Records came back with details of the suspect car: owner Thomas Long, licence clean and up to date, not reported stolen.

'His own car?' said Dalton in quiet amazement. 'He must be crackers!'

'He's up to something,' responded Tindall, gloomily. 'It doesn't smell right.' There was no more time for speculation; the car and the van appeared, and the comedy started. From every window of each vehicle, long woollen scarves banded red and white in Arsenal colours appeared. The passengers inside the vehicles were chanting and shouting, high as kites.

'Up the Gunners! Ar-sen-al, Ar-sen-al, Ar-sen-al!' Football supporters, on the razzle. But one of them was Tommy Long, a known villain, and this was Heathrow, not Highbury. Dalton stared at Tindall.

'What do we do now, guv'nor?'

The van and car were clowning round and round the cargo shed car park in a slow, ribald precession, horns blaring, the yobbos inside shouting their heads off. Tindall knew what was on. They knew his lads were there, undercover, waiting, they'd known all along. Now they'd come to send the fuzz up, have a giggle to show that the whole bullion caper had been a put-on, a gas to make the rozzers look right idiots.

'Pull them in,' said said Tindall, and started to get out of the car.

'What charge, guv'nor?' asked Dalton. 'Possession – they must have gear with them!' he answered himself, hopefully.

'You'll be lucky if they're carrying a bloody can-opener,' said Tindall. He was right.

Out of the night, from half-hidden corners all around the block of cargo sheds, a clutch of unmarked cars screeched in to form a circle round the jolly offenders. The same order brought the whole cork and bottle road block into operation.

By the time Tindall had strolled over to the scarf-decorated car and van, the occupants of both were standing, legs spread, hands on the vehicles, being thoroughly searched. Several giggled, complaining they were being tickled; one asked if he could have a WPC run her hands over him; a sharp elbow in his kidneys soon shut him up. The mood changed. The so-called football suporters were all clean, so were the vehicles. Nothing; not a tool, shooter, pickaxe, mask or woolly balaclava hood to be found. Tommy Long was cheeky with it, and demanded to know what he'd done.

'Persecution, that's what it is,' he said. 'Got something against the Gunners, have you?' His sly sharpshooter eyes were laughing as they met and challenged Tindall's dour glare. The Inspector realised bitterly that the whole night's work – the whispers of a bullion fit-up, the flood of hoax police emergency calls, and now even the robbers themselves – the whole thing was a put-on, leaving a trail of chaos behind and Tindall with egg all over his face. But it hadn't been done for fun, he was sure of that. There had to be a reason, and he'd screw the lot of them to find out what. His eyes were like flint, stony-cold, and his voice jerked Dalton into action.

'Book them,' Tindall rasped. 'Anything and everything that fits.' He looked at Tommy, who didn't flinch, but he wasn't smiling either. 'Take them to West Drayton. I'll give them bloody Arsenal.'

The arrival of the security truck at Goldhawk was like playing a party game, or an amateur dramatics panto; scripted, but acted out for real. The truck drew to a halt, signalled brusquely on its horn, and Swinford pulled open the warehouse door. Berghoff, dressed as the security gaffer, went through the solemn ritual of delivery, with his mates taking up standard defensive positions as the five sleek boxes were carefully handed over. Delivery complete, the lads climbed back inside, while Sammy escorted Swinford into the warehouse. The crate was already open and Sammy carefully slotted the five boxes into their waiting compartments, then insisted on getting a signature for the joke consignment. Swinford was sweating, desperate to close and nail up the crate, and Sammy enjoyed making him hop. At last the routine was completed, unhurried and formal. Even before Berghoff had reached the truck, Swinford was putting the lid on to the crate. Sammy had to call back, sharply, 'Mr Swinford, sir. Close the bloody door.' Sammy watched him do it, got back into the truck and nodded for Alan to move off.

'Time for control to give us a call,' the scrawny-faced driver said calmly. Fenn's man, a sleeper planted months ago inside the security firm for just such a job, had only been able to pass on the call and code routine for the Eagle Airways delivery; from now on, having broken the known delivery pattern, they were on their own. Ahead, they could see the build-up of the police road block, cordoning off the area. With luck, they might pass through before the wires started buzzing.

'We'll get through that lot first,' said Sammy. 'Then we'll plck up our clean wheels and go home.'

When Mackay woke up, he knew he wasn't at home. His head still throbbed and it took him more than a minute just to focus on the ceiling; he became aware that someone was unbuttoning his shirt and tongueing his naked ribs. He lifted his head to see and groaned as the throb increased to a stab of heavy pain. He sank back and the weight pressing against his thighs wriggled up his body, bringing Angela's rumpled hair into view. She smiled, wickedly.

'About time you joined in, lover,' she said. 'It's no fun on my own.'

'Where is everybody?' he murmured. Talking aloud seemed certain to bring back the bells ringing in his head.

'Busy,' said Angela, looking down at him. 'I said I'd be back, didn't I?'

'Angela – do us a favour –'

'I'm going to,' she purred, and kissed him slowly and lecherously. The chemistry worked, but not for long. Mackay had other things on his mind apart from being raped.

'Not fair,' he gasped, pulling away from her mouth. 'I need hands.'

'You'd be surprised,' she giggled. 'Lie back and enjoy it, as the bishop said.' She rubbed herself against his bare chest. Mackay realised that most of Angela was naked, too; the kimono was hardly around her at all. The throb in his head was fighting a losing battle with lower ache.

'You don't need hands,' she crooned. 'You've got all the tools you need . . .' She started uncovering him and he gave a yelp of pain. 'Does it hurt?' she laughed, lifting her head and looking along his helpless body; his head was twisted to one side, buried in the black satin of the pillow. 'Shall I kiss it better?'

'Cramp,' he gritted, straining his leg. It was a lie, but he had to call a truce somehow. He knew Angela only too well. Now she was roused, she wouldn't pause until they both went pop, and once wouldn't be enough, either. He winced at the invented agony again, and she took pity on him. Pulling back from his half-naked stomach, she knelt farther down the bed, and finding the calf muscle, started to knead it with her strong, probing fingers.

'Better?' she asked, her flushed face concerned and serious.

He nodded, and let his head fall back in mock-relief. 'It's my ankles,' he said. 'No circulation. These ropes are killing me . . .' She laughed as she cottoned on to his little game, and turning to face him, ran her skin-tingling hands up the full length of his legs, loins and body; he bucked, involuntarily, and she hung over him, her smoke-grey eyes wickedly reproving.

'Naughty,' she said. The kimono was completely open now, and Angela knelt upright, peeling it off altogether. 'Taking advantage of your little angel . . .' She giggled as his eyes ate up her flesh. 'Have to teach you a lesson, shan't I?' She never had the chance.

'Get your clothes back on, you little tart!' spat a low, throaty voice. Bloody Delilah's eyes, dark with hate, shifted from Angela to focus on Mackay. 'I'll deal with *him.*'

While Angela hurriedly covered her body, Queenie moved in, the hate in her painted, hooded eyes glinting into pleasure at the prospect ahead.

She stood by the sin-black bed, her shadow hulking across Mackay, her sinewy fingers cupped lightly but menacingly around his chin and jaw. Gentle though her gesture was, the pressure was excruciating; he could hardly swallow, let alone speak or cry out.

'I know the things you've been doing to my girl,' she said. 'She told me. Filthy things. Disgusting. It was you that made her like it, corrupting her, you animal, you pig!'

'*Your* girl?' croaked Mackay, just before Queenie's hand shut his face for him. He knew that pleading or protest would be useless; this female gorilla was halfway round the twist. He'd seen that look before; a kid with a knife who'd slowly, sadistically, screwed himself up to a climax of drooling hate; the knife-thrust had been the final reflex, the instinctive explosion of pleasure. Queenie was going the same way, stoking her venom, until it reached bursting point. She was taking her time, she could afford to; Mackay wasn't going anywhere, tied and spread-eagled, still half-undone, the way that Queenie's randy angel had left him.

'My kid, that's right. And you've been messing her about.' Pain shot through him as her hand shifted the angle of his lower jaw, and his eyes flicked at her, rolling in a silent, agonised appeal. She laughed. 'I could do things to you. Like dislocate your jaw.' Another touch of pressure and a scream choked Mackay's throat. 'That'd stop you kissing her,' said Queenie. She leaned closer, hissing at Mackay's bulging eyes. 'I could do things to you, you'd never touch my baby-love ever again. Not any girl. Not even a poof would have you, dear . . .' The grip of immensely powerful fingers tightened like a vice. Mackay was sweating, cold, when Fenn's voice cut across the room.

'Leave him, Queenie, there's a darling.' It wasn't quite a command, he knew better. 'We need the poor bastard for later.' He met Queenie's eyes, and after a moment she seemed to withdraw. The hand eased its pressure slightly, but didn't move away.

'I want to fix him, for what he did to Angel.'

'Oh, honestly, Ma,' complained Angela, standing behind Fenn's shoulder. 'You could at least wait.' She had seen the warning signs the moment Queenie had walked in. The truth was, Ma got jealous of the games that Angela could play, the tricks her body got up to, the grunts and cries of delight she could pull out of the blokes. Like mother, like daughter, only Angela's technique was pleasure, Queenie's violence and pain.

'You can have him, all in good time,' said Fenn. 'Besides, the poor sod doesn't know yet. Don't you think we ought to tell him?'

This evidently appealed to Queenie; she laughed and drew her hand away. 'Why not?' she said.

'What bloody game are you trying to pull?'

'Now be polite to your betters, squire,' said Fenn, taking Queenie's place and sitting on the bed alongside Mackay's prostrate body. He looked down at Mackay's half-naked groin and shook his head, good-humouredly tut-tutting. 'It won't do, Angel,' he said, casually putting zip and waistband to rights. 'It's not kosher, darling. Sheer torture if you don't let a gentleman handle his own affairs.' He smiled into Mackay's face. 'She means well, squire. It's just that she comes on quicker than a soft-boiled egg.' He grined at Angela. 'Don't you, sweetie?'

'Quicker, for you,' smiled Angela, and pulled the kimono tighter across her pert little nipples.

'I don't mean her,' insisted Mackay. 'What's in it for me?'

'Not a lot, squire,' said Fenn. 'Did you know your firm was going down the drain?' Mackay grunted; he couldn't see what Fenn was getting at. 'That's why there's going to be a robbery there – tonight, after everyone's gone home. Clumsy, mind. The old game. Take what's in the safe, stage a burglary, then a spot of arson to burn up the evidence and raise the ready through insurance. Beats paying income tax any day.'

'Goldhawk's straight!' croaked Mackay. 'In profit, no trouble!'

'Have you looked at the books lately, squire?' asked Fenn, cheerfully. 'It's all there.' He nodded across at Queenie. 'Knows how to fiddle, does Queenie. A real pro.'

'Me too, remember,' complained Angela. 'I helped as well.' She grinned as Mackay looked at her. 'Apart from the fun, I mean.'

'Trebled your insurance cover, didn't she?' explained Fenn. 'You signed it, but you won't remember doing it. Forge anything, can our little angel. Your moniker wasn't very hard.'

'Easy,' said Queenie's little girl.

'You need me to pick up the insurance money,' said Mackay. 'Forget it.'

'You don't listen, do you, squire? It's a deal that'll go wrong. You'll be found out, but you won't complain. You'll be a victim of circumstance, as they say. Wiped out, handling the jelly. A stone-dead amateur.'

'But why? What have I ever done to you?' His wild eyes flicked across to Angela again. 'Not because of *her*, for Christ's sake?'

'Wait until your mate arrives.' Fenn saw the shock on Mackay's drawn face, and chuckled. 'That's right, squire. Swinford. Your manager. Our fingerman.'

Lomas had driven swiftly away from the North Side, intending to take the Colnbrook by-pass to the west and turn left down towards Staines; there he'd turn left again on to the Southern Perimeter Road towards the main cargo area, and seek out Dalton; it shouldn't be difficult. He soon found it was going to be nearly impossible. Traffic was backing up for nearly a mile before he'd even reached the Colnbrook roundabout. Nose to bumper in the rain had produced several shunts, which only made things worse; irritated drivers huddled in their rain-flecked headlights, exchanging licence details and swearing miserably. Lomas could do nothing; even in the outside lane, it was a rotten mess, and he was stuck with it. All he could hope was that whatever Swinford and the big man were up to, it wasn't happening yet. But with the way today had turned out so far, he didn't reckon that much on his luck. Plain bloody awful wasn't in it.

It took all night for Lomas to get away from the chaos of the Colnbrook interchange. What with the rain, a broken-down articulated lorry, a series of shunts, and a truckload of oranges that had caught fire after a collision with a fish and chip van, what had started as a simple traffic jam had become a minor nightmare. Forcing a way through for fire-engines and ambulances had only aggravated the situation, but by dawn the worst was over. Lomas drove slowly past the burnt-out skeleton of the fruit lorry; on the ground close by was a solitary, perfect orange, undamaged by the collision or the fire. Minutes later he was speeding as fast as he could towards the roundabout that would bring him to Heathrow's south side and the cargo complex where Tindall was supposed to be. The Goldhawk van had barely turned on to the south side carriageway when Lomas again hit trouble; a road block, preventing any vehicles from entering or leaving the Cargo Village. Lomas could only sit and curse as he waited to be questioned. He was so near, he could look across the grass verge and see the agents' building easily from where he was now parked. Tindall would be only another couple of hundred yards beyond. For a moment, Lomas toyed with the idea of leaving the van and making his way on foot, but a glance at the number of police mobiles covering the area made him realise he'd only end up with more trouble. He wondered why all the fuss. It looked like a set exercise, maybe anti-terrorist. Was this what Jimmy and his guv'nor were tied up with? Then, glancing across at Building 521, so near and yet so far, he looked again. A dark-green security van appeared to be leaving the Goldhawk loading bay. That second glance brought into play all the recognition training that Lomas had been given; vehicle description, number plate, direction, speed, all registered in his mind automatically. It looked a routine call, and no alarm bells rang inside his head. Knowing that he'd left Goldhawk locked up, he dismissed the idea that it had called there; the movement of a figure outside the adjacent air freight agent's warehouse decided Lomas that the call wasn't at Goldhawk at all, but close by. Liveried security vehicles made deliveries in and around the Cargo Village at all hours of the day or night; they were part of the landscape, like the milkman or postman in the city. Lomas, preparing to be questioned by the constable now advancing towards him, pushed the security van out of his mind.

He wasn't to know that barely three hundred yards away, one of the Eagle Airways night staff had managed to free himself and raise the alarm. The sergeant controlling the road block on vehicles leaving the complex wasn't to know, either. Seeing the security van waiting in the queue, he waved it forward, giving it priority. A glance at the identity card through the rain-dulled windows of the truck, and he was satisfied. Sammy, the shooter tucked under his knees but ready for use if needed, gave the rozzer a little wave and smile of thanks. Alan stared ahead, and as he weaved his way past the clutter of police vehicles, let out a low whistle of relief.

'Stupid bloody fuzz,' he said and, hitting the main road, put his foot down. They were clear.

Tommy Long and his football stooges had been carted off to West Drayton nick, and Tindall had dismissed the stake-out squad when the message came through about the diamond heist at Eagle Airways. Now the whole frustrating jigsaw fell into place, and Tindall could name it. The hoax calls, the Air India put-on, none of it was a simple leg-pull; they were all a part of a finely organised diversion plan. Even the chaos that had snarled up most of the available traffic mobiles had proved to be a fix. The key lorry in the log jam was stuck there without a driver; he was found bound and gagged behind a hedge at Iver Heath, ten miles away, with a story of being hi-jacked that now made sense.

Tindall left his chief to fill in the scrappy details as they came in; he was on the spot, he had the manpower, and they were dying to make up for having been conned. He also had a lead, the dark green security van; it couldn't get far, it was too easy to spot. It was found almost as soon as Tindall's 'all mobiles' request went out via Control. It had been dumped three miles east of Heathrow, abandoned and empty, except for a set of security guard uniforms. The only item reported missing from the Eagle Airways vault – five small metal caskets of diamonds, current market value, seven million pounds – had vanished. The lead had suddenly become a stone-cold dead end. This, for Tindall, was going to be a long job, but he had a few tasty ideas already.

'We've got Tommy Long,' he reminded Dalton. 'And there has to be a tie-in with Sammy Berghoff. Start looking.'

'Yes, guv,' answered Dalton, wondering where to start. Tindall left him to it, and went back inside Eagle Airways to ask more questions. It was the worst possible moment for a reunion of old pals, and when he saw Roy Lomas being escorted over to him, Dalton groaned inwardly. He hadn't slept a wink all night, he was dog-tired and with a load of grind ahead of him; Roy would have to understand and take off. Oppo or not, this was business.

Lomas had had too much bother getting this far to be put off easily. The minute he'd driven past the freight agent's building towards the airline warehouses, he'd been stopped again. He'd got angry when his polite request to see Dalton had been turned down flat, and the sergeant in charge had got very shirty in return. But once the penny had dropped, the picture changed. The sergeant did the talking, and that saved a lot of explanations.

'Witness here reckons he saw a security van like the one we're looking for,' he said.

'It's been found,' said Dalton, 'but where was this, Roy?'

'Near where I work,' said Lomas. 'Half an hour ago.' Dalton's eyes grew wider at this, and after thanking the sergeant and sending him on his way, he took Lomas straight to Tindall. Tindall listened to the whole of Lomas's briskly told story. He looked at the video tape that Lomas thrust at him, and frowned.

'A big man,' he murmured. 'Smart dresser, big hands, moves a bit awkward . . .'

'Could be,' said Lomas. 'I'd know his face again.'

'Berghoff?' wondered Dalton.

Tindall nodded. He was already moving to the car, putting the facts together as he went, pulling Lomas with him.

'What you saw was the heavy mob getting their cover ready. They pulled this Eagle Airways job right under our noses, but they knew they wouldn't get far. So they dropped the stuff at your firm, then went on their way like a live red herring. We follow, walk right past the ice stashed away at Goldhawk, and later on today it'll go out as a normal routine delivery.' He bundled Lomas into the back of the car, with Dalton driving. 'Smart bastards, aren't they?' he said, but he was pleased.

He was wrong on one count though. The BS Marine crate had already gone.

Nik had been the first one in that morning, he told them, but he'd found Swinford already waiting and very twitchy. He'd practically ordered Nik to help him load the crate into the second company van, then insisted that as Lomas wasn't around, he'd make the delivery himself.

'He said you wouldn't be in at all today,' the puzzled clerk told Lomas. 'Reckoned you were sick.'

'Yeah,' said Roy, and pulled a wry face. 'Sick to bloody death.'

'He must've known –' Dalton started to say, but Tindall cut him short.

'Did Swinford say where he was taking the crate?' he asked, tersely.

'No – but I've got the paperwork,' replied the ever-efficient Nik. 'The address will be on their letter-heading.' It was there all right, and Tindall smiled, grimly, as he saw the letterhead design: five of diamonds. 'Someone's got a funny sense of humour, James,' he said. It took Dalton a minute to work that one out.

'Gus Fulmer,' he replied. Tindall nodded. It was still untidy, but things were falling nicely into place. They now knew the method, motive, goods stolen, and where they'd been taken, with any luck. They also knew some names and faces; while Tindall and Dalton had been questioning Nik Andreadis, Lomas had prepared the video tape. Tindall took one look at the replay and gave that small, rare smile.

'Berghoff,' he confirmed. He glanced at the address that Nik had shown him; it had to be a fake. Then he thought again. Why should it be? This cover job was so perfect, its double twist had worked so well, that even if the robbery had failed, no-one would have connected the consignment from Hamburg with a diamond heist at Heathrow. Bluff, double and then triple-bluff; bells started ringing inside his head. He'd recognised the address, and knew he'd got it right. 'The Diplomat Club,' he said.

'Swinford goes there,' said Nik.

'Us too,' said Tindall, 'but mob-handed.' He turned to Dalton. 'Jimmy – get me patched through to the CI's office, double-quick.'

It had to be diamonds, decided Swinford; nothing else that small could be worth so much trouble. An old man, first maimed, then killed; Mike kidnapped, God only knew what would happen to him; Lomas taken out, no knowing where or how; and Swinford himself in desperate trouble, way above his head, and drowning. He'd not only fingered the consignment for Fenn, he'd handled and even packed it. He'd been there when

Mike was jumped, and he'd pointed the finger at Lomas; now he was actually delivering stolen goods to a bunch of murdering villians, not even questioning what they'd already done. If they said jump, he'd jump; but after this one trick, all he wanted was to pick up the bonus Fenn had promised, and get out, buy a new life, somewhere, anywhere, it didn't matter, only not here. He wasn't just scared to death for himself, he'd even thought of breaking clear, taking the ice with him, letting Fenn stew. Fenn had seen it in his mind, and laughed. 'No tricks,' he'd said. 'Try anything stupid and I'll get to you if it's the last thing I ever do.' He'd pointed to Mike, tied, helpless and unconscious. 'And I'll start with him.'

It was the one threat that really held Swinford in Fenn's power. While he obeyed, Mike lived. But the reckoning had to come. Every move he made plunged him deeper into conspiracy, but all the time he knew he was the outsider, the pigeon, the mug outside the family. He knew too much, and that could be either his guarantee of safety, or his death warrant. For now, his mind refused to think ahead. The sickness he felt, the tremor when his hands left the steering wheel, was fear; it was taking all the concentration he possessed just to drive the van, let alone think of a crafty way out. There was always the video tape. But with Mike out of the way, who would ever think of running it and adding two and two together? Perhaps, once he was out of it a free man, away from Fenn, the tip-off could be made. Then he remembered the marking on the crate; five neat diamond pips, so different to those hideous weals on Fulmer's bloody face, but just as meaningful. The weakness in him rose again; eyes straining on the road ahead, he didn't notice the Panda car across the busy street, or its driver, eyes on the Goldhawk van, speaking earnestly into his personal radio link with Control. If he'd been Alan, Tommy Long, or even Bev Ackermann, he'd've spotted the fuzz a street or more away, and done the necessary, changed his route, doubled back, even if possible switched cars. But he didn't have their eyes, their motives, their experience. He was a pigeon; they were pros. He didn't stand a chance.

He'd been given clear instructions, how to find the club, what to do when he got there, and if there was any sign of trouble, get lost. He almost missed the pillared entrance first time down the road, then at the last minute, tooted three times as he drove straight past. Now there'd be someone looking to see if he'd been tailed; automatically, Swinford looked in his driving mirror and saw that the whole length of the quiet avenue behind him was empty, apart from one or two parked cars that had been there all the time. He drove on, turned left, round the block, back into the main road, then back down the secluded avenue; more slowly this time, as though he was lost, innocently trying to find his way. If everything was clear, Berghoff would be standing in the open gateway. He was, and signalled for the van to turn in. Swinford did so, then paused, waiting for instructions. Berghoff came to the driver's window, and looked in.

'Good boy,' he said. 'Round the side. There's a garage there. Drive right in, OK?'

Slowly, in first gear, Swinford moved on. The garage was big and dark, a coachhouse once, he guessed. He stopped the van, turned off the engine and got out. He'd barely unlocked the loading door when Sammy arrived. Picking up a tyre lever, the big man ripped open the lid of the crate and quickly removed the five gleaming caskets from their hiding places in the packing around the useless compressors. Swinford watched him, making no attempt to help. Berghoff glanced at him, and gave a quiet order.

'Make yourself useful, my son,' he said, replacing the lid and tapping it firmly back in place. 'Start closing those doors.' He indicated the two heavy coachhouse doors, not long painted in rich, wine-red gloss. By the time Swinford had swung the second massive frame to, Berghoff was ready to lead the way into the house. Swinford looked at him, uncertain about the van.

'I ought to go back,' he said. 'Business as usual?'

'Jack wants to see you first, my son,' said Berghoff, and led the way round the back.

In the penthouse office, the big man laid out the five metal boxes in a neat row on Fenn's desk. Queenie was there, and Angela, dressed in an emerald-green, skin-tight jumpsuit. She looked delicious and knew it, but Swinford never even noticed. Fenn leaned forward and one by one, opened the boxes; one hand deftly flipped open the velvet wrapping, and there were the stones. The family gloated in quiet excitement, then the sheer size of what they'd got brought them to the boil. Angela picked up two large-cut ovals and placed them over the nipples thrusting through her jump-suit.

'Can I have these, Jack?' she giggled, rubbing them against herself in small, erotic circles.

'Your own are better, darling,' said Fenn. 'Take the money. It'll do you more good.'

'Not bad, dear,' murmured Queenie, not really interested in the ice. Sammy knew the signs, the glances back to the landing and the room beyond; he knew what she wanted, more than all the loot: to get her hands on the geezer locked away there, Mr Mackay.

'Not bad?' mocked Fenn, then glanced across at Swinford, hanging back and nervous, the visiting fireman. 'Know how much we've got here, squire'? he boasted. 'Take fifty per cent away for trading off, it still leaves us with a cool three million.' The shark smile showed, briefly. 'Worth it?'

'You bet!' laughed Angela, but Swinford said nothing. Queenie was getting sullen and worked up.

'What about tonight?' she said. 'I want to get started.'

'Fair enough, Queenie,' agreed Fenn. 'Do the necessary.'

She grabbed Swinford before he even realised what was happening. She had him in a half-nelson, and her painted eyes were dancing, as whispering into his ear from just behind him, she drew him towards the door.

'The bedroom,' she murmured. 'Not here. You can choose who goes first, you or your friend . . .'

Swinford struggled in panic, but he was helpless. He started to cry out, but suddenly her massive forearm was across his throat, and he was choking. Fenn looked concerned.

'Queenie, darling, let him say goodbye nicely,' he said.

'My share!' Swinford blurted out, gasping for breath. 'Airline ticket – cash – my share!'

'We've had a change of plan, squire,' said Fenn, pleasantly. 'You've done your little bit, granted. But you know too much.' He paused, shrewd-eyed. 'It isn't as if you're one of our sort, squire. We could trust you, if you were. But you're not worth the risk. Sorry.'

'What are you going to do?' he cried in terror, his voice almost shrieking with hysteria and fear. 'I've done everything you asked – everything!'

'You're going to find your pal Mackay faking a robbery and fire at Goldhawk,' said Fenn. 'You'll try and stop him. A bit of a rumble, you know. But then the charge your old pal put on the safe will blow, bang, and since he's only an amateur, it'll do neither of you any good. There'll be a fire, the building will go, and you and him – *shame*...'

'But *why*?' whispered Swinford, remembering his only hope of turning the tables on this gang of psychopaths. 'What good will that do –?'

'I like things tidy, squire,' said Fenn, coldly. 'A total wipe out like that saves me a lot of headache.' He grinned spitefully. 'But don't fret. The big bang and the fire won't hurt. Bloody Delilah will have fixed you good and proper before then.' Queenie's arm tightened, preventing any protest as Fenn finally explained. 'Planting dead meat is best,' he said. 'It doesn't answer back.'

Swinford found himself lifted and turned bodily to face the exit. Angela skipped forward, but before she opened the door, she had a favour to ask.

'Jack,' she pleaded, prettily. 'Can I say goodbye to lover boy?' Her grey eyes swung to Queenie, who wasn't pleased.

'With pleasure,' said Fenn, moving from the desk to join the farewell party. He chuckled, and his hand fondled Angela's emerald green thigh, squeezing it meaningfully. 'On second thoughts, just goodbye,' he said. 'We haven't got time for what you fancy doing.' Angela pouted, but cheekily.

'You'll have to make it up to me,' she said. 'Afterwards.'

'It's a deal,' said Fenn, and walked across the landing to the bedroom.

Mackay was awake, and saw John, helpless in Queenie's grip. With a grunt, she tossed her prisoner from her, to fall across Mackay's aching legs. Swinford cringed there, almost in tears; not from fear now, but from sheer self-pity and disgust.

'Mike, I'm sorry,' he managed to whimper. 'It's my fault. I'm sorry.' Angela wriggled past Queenie and leaning over Mackay, gave him a luscious, tonguing kiss. It didn't move him. He'd seen Bloody Delilah standing there, pleasure and excitement growing in her eyes, and he knew that this time nobody was going to stop her. Angela flounced across to Fenn, and taking his arm, rubbed it against her breasts and asked him one last favour.

'A fair fight, Jack,' she murmured. 'One we can enjoy. through the mirror . . .' Fenn looked at her, surprised, then chuckled; the randy little lovebird *knew*. 'Undo his hands,' suggested Angela. 'While Ma's handling the other one, lover boy can try and undo his ankles. Then he can take her on fair and square. It's up to him, then isn't it?'

Fenn smirked. He looked at the hope in Mackay's face, and pitied the poor sod; he really believed that Queenie's angel had a soft spot for him, and was giving him a chance. The truth was, Angel wanted to watch, unseen from the comfort of the other room, and probably wanted screwing while it happened.

Suddenly the idea appealed to Fenn. Sammy didn't have to be there. He looked at Queenie; it was her turn to provide the entertainment for a change. She got the point. It pleased her, the prospect of having an audience.

'Suits me,' she said, taking off her cardigan. 'Now get out, while I enjoy myself.' They went, and Queenie locked the door after them, giving Swinford his orders as she did so.

'Untie his wrists,' she said. 'And say your prayers. Bloody Delilah's going to eat you for her supper.'

The Goldhawk van being driven by Swinford hadn't been difficult to spot; its bold yellow paintwork and winged insignia stood out just as it was meant to do. With the van's likely route established, it only meant instructing mobiles cruising on regular patrol in the area to keep a look-out; all along the network of roads and streets reports crackled in to Control, then on to Tindall: suspect vehicle proceeding as advised. Persuading the DI by way of the chief inspector had been less difficult this time; but although the manpower was sanctioned without too many questions, the issue of firearms had been granted only with reluctance. This was no longer an ambush designed to surprise armed raiders in an act of violence. Tindall had argued, forcibly, that the robbery team complete with weapons, could be shacked up and waiting, ready for trouble. Armed and dangerous men, who'd killed before. A pause, and then relief: request granted. Even so, halfway there and with the back-up force yet to be bussed into the familiar dark blue vans, Tindall had had a real fright. The Goldhawk van had turned into the broad avenue where the Diplomat Club was placed behind high brick walls and thick green shrubbery – and it had driven straight past.

'Not another bloody dummy!' Dalton exclaimed with dismay, glancing at the guv'nor, sad-eyed and glum as ever.

'Cross your fingers, lad,' his inspector replied patiently. 'He's been told to be cautious, that's all.'

By the time Tindall had reached the jump-off point for the raid, his hunch was confirmed and as soon as he gave the order, the net now hastily thrown around the Diplomat Club could be drawn, tight and secure. Police vehicles sealed off every possible road, street and avenue, including alleyways and pedestrian walkways between the big Edwardian houses. Diversion signs informed the public that this was a simple, traffic-flow experiment. A few gossips at the local shops swore it was because the Queen, or the Prime Minister, or simply the Mayoress was driving through on the way to Windsor. It gave a bit of excitement to a dismal Monday morning.

Calmly, Tindall checked his .38 regulation issue, silently hoping he wouldn't have to use it but glad it was to hand. He remembered Fenn from many years ago; canny, dead careful to keep his own hands clean, but ready to use the roughest kind of heavy if a job called for it. He may have put up a clean business as legal front, but he was still a rat; and Tindall knew that a rat, when cornered, could be deadly, especially when ice worth seven million was at stake.

'All present and correct, guv'nor,' said Dalton, bringing the welcome news that the two vanloads of uniformed police had arrived, plus handlers and their dogs; he had to admit that there were times when CID couldn't do it all by themselves.

'Better make a move then, hadn't we,' said Tindall, putting his shooter away tidily. 'Drive straight in, no nonsense. We take the front, one vanload goes right round to the back. Dogs tackle the outbuildings and grounds.' He'd said it all before, but it was his way of reassuring himself it was all in working order. Dalton nodded. 'Just give us the word.'

Queenie was disappointed in Swinford; he was young enough and healthy enough and scared enough to fight for his life against Bloody Delilah, but he wouldn't even try. He simply dodged and scurried where he could around the bedroom, with its slinky decor providing a bizarre backdrop for Queenie's anything but feminine intent. The room wasn't large, and Swinford was soon cornered, but his desperate retreat wasn't solely because of fear. He had untied McKay's wrists slowly, for as he did so he'd seen the state that Mike was in; those cramped fingers, already numbed from lack of circulation, wouldn't find it easy untying the remaining cords around his ankles. The answer was to play for time. Swinford knew that the moment he tried to match Queenie's skill and strength, he was as good as finished. So, like a hunted animal, he retreated. Even so, he had to stay alert; Queenie, for all her bulk and muscle, could move like a tiger, lightning-fast, when you least expected. At last, trapped in the corner by the dressing-table, Swinford had to make his stand, and Queenie laughed.

'Nowhere else to go now, dear,' she said, and pounced. Swinford picked up the only sizable weapon he could find, the dressing-table chair, and swung it against Queenie's charging head and shoulders. It broke, and she still came on, like a dreadnaught through a shower of rain. He backed away, but came up short against the ornate dressing-table; her hand grabbed his waist, and with a savage whip-throw, hurled him against the French-style lemon and white wardrobe, smashing the breath out of him in a scream of pain as the sinews of his arm were stretched beyond endurance. Swiftly, she followed through, and before he had slid to the floor, she delivered a forearm smash against his chest; then, as he tried to twist away, she pounded him again across his already damaged arm, and again he screamed. This time the surge of agony erupting from his lungs was choked into silence almost before it came. She had spun him round, limp and unresisting, and almost in the same movement formed a killing necklock on him; one forearm across his windpipe, the other across the nape of his neck, the two acting together like a deadly vice. Her face was pressed against his ear, and as the life and breath were slowly squeezed out of him, Swinford could hear the rapid, double-breathing hiss-hiss-hiss of her pleasure as she brought the killing to its climax; he never knew what happened next. He hit the floor, released from Queenie's arms as the big ceramic bedside lamp-holder smashed to pieces across the back of her skull. She turned, shaking her head against the surprise and shock of the impact, and saw Mackay standing there, stunned and disbelieving that she could so survive his blow.

'Cheeky bastard,' she said, and suddenly he was fighting for his life.

Numb though his wrists and ankles were, he was stronger, more athletic than John Swinford; Joan and Angela could both have vouched for the lean power of his body. He was close to a hundred and seventy pounds of vigorous muscle and bone, and in most tight corners he could handle himself OK. But it wasn't enough; it never could be, against a specialist in violence like Bloody Delilah. He set himself into a fighter's stance, fists ready to throw punches, head down and weaving, shoulder protecting his chin. Queenie thought it was a hoot, and laughed.

'Queensberry ponce!' she said, and slowly moved towards him, arms wide and grimly welcoming. Mackay's first instinct told him not to punch a woman; in any case, if you're going to hit her – where? She was built like a barrel, her bosom like a cliff-face overhang, but for all that, she *was* a female. She was also a killer, Mackay recalled in time to dodge her lunging hands. The female breast, he remembered from past experience, is a very sensitive, and delicate area. He hit her there, very hard, and found himself yelping from the pain that fizzled through his aching wrist. The blow had been like striking a slab of frozen meat; teak-hard, solid muscle, without even a suggestion of softness and resilience. Instinctively, he struck again, this time aiming lower, at the solar plexus. It was wild, but a good blow; wrist straight, knuckles making the impact count – a punch that would knock the puff out of almost any bloke. Queenie's gut muscles were like iron, and the punch was useless. More than that, in his amazement at her almost total lack of reaction, Mackay was on his heels, guard down, and gaping. Now it was Queenie's turn. She grabbed his forearm with both hands, one at his wrist and the other at his elbow, and swung him. Suddenly he found himself hurled across the room, almost flying, stumbling and falling backwards to end up flattened and shaken, with a rib-aching thud against the wall. Gasping, he obeyed his reflexes, and pulling himself together, went for her again. She was waiting for him, mouth arched and glistening, eyes bright with murder.

'That's it, dear,' she smiled, 'enjoy yourself.' She stopped his first wild swing with a short arm block, then as he countered with his left, timed her grab perfectly and hurled him by his arm across the room again. This time he hit the chest of drawers, head and shoulder taking the impact of the wood, and getting to his feet was like climbing Mount Everest. Surprisingly, Queenie helped him – but only to bring the fiasco to a suitably pleasing end. As though he was no heavier than a plastic bag of potatoes, Mackay found himself pitched across the room to land face down and breathless on the rumpled black satin of the bed. Before he could move, Bloody Delilah was kneeling over him, straddling the small of his back, and her arms were not only gripping him in that deadly necklock, she was pulling him up and back towards her, arching his spine to breaking point, until he was screaming wordlessly for mercy. She wasn't giving any, but she paused.

'No hurry, dear,' she whispered in his ear. 'I'm going to mark you first.' Then, holding him against her iron breast like Mother Kali, she set her tiger's fingernails against his face and slowly and deliberately tore the flesh in five agonising weals from ear to jaw. The roar of pain that ripped its way out of Mackay's throat was the last thing he remembered, as that killing forearm locked across his windpipe once again.

It was a big house, with a lot of rooms to cover, but Monday being a no-action day, they were for the most part empty and deserted, making the job of the search and question team almost easy. The few staff who were around had no cause to argue with the fuzz and said so; the one or two who tried to mix it only got belted for their pains, and gave no further trouble. But those were the scrag-ends; what Tindall wanted most of all was to nail Fenn and Berghoff in possession, either with the ice, or firearms, or both.

They found Sammy Berghoff first. He was sneaking through the back way, past the kitchens, when Dalton saw his hulking shadow slipping out along the passageway. He shouted, and Sammy started to run, but taking the risk that he wasn't going to use a shooter, Dalton hit him with a tackle from the rear that slammed Sammy down on to the hard, cool tiles. A second later, the big man was rolling from side to side, clutching his lower groin, and punctuating his groans of pain by calling Dalton every kind of bastard under the sun. Then Tindall strolled up, and stepping past him to pick up the cardboard box he'd been carrying, nudged the toe of his shoe sharply underneath the big man's crotch. There was one last howl of pain, and Berghoff shut up, seeing who it was who'd finally knackered him.

'Sorry, sport,' said Tindall casually, 'I forgot your privates are still sore.' Sammy said nothing, just gritted his teeth as Dalton helped him to his feet and put the cuffs on him. The box was marked 'Mixed Biscuits', but the caskets inside held something better. All the same, Tindall cursed softly and his face was sour. Dalton was surprised. Opened, the caskets revealed the glinting gemstones, a triumph for Tindall and a relief for the insurers.

'Not all there?' queried Dalton.

Tindall barely glanced at him. 'Of course it's all there.' He turned back to Berghoff.

'Sammy, old son, don't take all the blame. Give credit where it's due.'

The big man shook his head. Tindall stared at him, knowing how it would be, and that he was stymied. They would discover Fenn playing all innocent, with some mild occupation to occupy his mind, and not a sparkler within miles of him. The most the rat would get was a few odd years, and that only if they were lucky and could pin a handling charge on him. It was understood – Sammy would be doing the stir for both of them.

'I only hope he makes it worth your while,' Tindall said. 'Where is he?'

Sammy shrugged his burly shoulders. 'How should I know? Upstairs, I shouldn't wonder.' There was no need to rush to take Jack Fenn; he'd be there, lily-white and protesting, shocked at the villainy that was corrupting the respectability of his handsome club.

'What about Swinford and Mackay?' demanded Dalton, stepping aside to let a pair of uniforms take over the custody of the big man. Sammy gave a thin smile, and suddenly Tindall felt himself go cold.

'They'd better be alive,' he rasped, 'or you go down as accessory before, during and after, my son!' Sammy flinched at the whiplash in Tindall's voice.

'Where are they? Quick!'

Sammy wasn't keen on sharing Queenie's time as well as Fenn's. 'Upstairs,' he grunted. 'And you'd better bloody hurry.'

Mackay was still breathing, but only just. They smashed in the door barely soon enough to tear Queenie off his back before she finished him completely. It took six men just to hold Bloody Delilah down; it wasn't until Tindall borrowed one lad's truncheon and hit the screaming, struggling psycho hard behind the ear, that she finally shut up. Even then it needed one more blow to put her out completely.

'Ambulance, sharp,' commanded Tindall, and then he glanced over at Swinford, who was coming to, staring with gaunt, sickened eyes at Mackay, sprawled and seemingly lifeless on the bed.

'Oh Christ,' whispered the haggard man who'd once been Mackay's friend. 'What've I done . . .'

'More than enough,' said Tindall, and motioned a constable to take Swinford to the waiting van.

He was not aware that Dalton had received his introduction to the Five of Diamonds, and that he was holding his guts down with an effort.

It only remained to sort out Fenn. The door across the landing was locked, and seemed solid. Tindall thumped against it, three times, hard.

'Fenn,' he called briskly. 'You in there?'

'Who is it?' Fenn sounded strained and anxious.

'Alex Tindall. Open up.'

It was Angela's gasping, bubbling voice that answered him. 'Give us a minute, copper,' she shouted breathlessly. 'He's just coming.' Her voice faded on a cheeky giggle, and Dalton, staring into his guv'nor's suddenly stony face, almost choked.

'No minutes,' snapped Tindall, and he kicked in the door.

He stopped dead in disgust, not at the view of their naked, writhing bodies, but at the realisation of his fears. Fenn's occupation was, indeed, as innocent as could be imagined. This was not a man with diamonds on his mind.

Fenn rolled over, his grin close to a snarl. 'Get lost, pig.'

'Let's get out of here,' snapped Tindall.

But Dalton, his mind still obsessed by the Five of Diamonds, wondered why the pattern should be repeated, in a milder form, on Fenn's right shoulder, but not on his left.

'Hold on,' he said. 'Chief . . .'

He took three quick paces forward and seized Angela's right wrist. He twisted. She flashed her teeth at him and produced a string of obscenities, but slowly her fist opened.

Clutched in orgiastic spasm in her hot little predatory hand were the five largest diamonds.